UBIQUITOUS

UBIQUITOUS

GEORGIA GERMOND

Ubiquitous
© 2024 by Georgia Germond

ISBN: 978-8-9908958-0-5 (Paperback)
ISBN: 978-8-9908958-2-9 (Hardcover)

Library of Congress Control Number: applied

Printed in the United States of America
Little House of Music Publishing
Satellite Beach, Florida

CHAPTER 1

FRIDAY, MAY 1ST
EMIL MASHADUK
NASHVILLE, TENNESSEE

Emil Mashaduk, better known as "Duke" in Nashville, had long, greasy black hair and wore it in a ponytail with a black rubber band that used to be blue. His dark eyes looked scary and evil, making his beard and mustache husky and wild. From his appearance, one would assume he had been working in coal mines all day and a fish factory at night because he had a stench like a dead fish. Emil came across as not intelligent enough to work outside of a blue-collar position.

It was 5:00 p.m. on Friday. As Emil opened the door to his old efficiency apartment, the door once again hung up on the torn carpet. He hated coming to the apartment that was dimly lit and reeked of cigarettes from the nicotine that coated everything in the apartment. As he bent over, he took his hand with dirty fingernails performing his now never-ending duty of freeing the door while mumbling, "This is a damn hell hole." It had been the same every time he opened the door in his century-old apartment for the past four months. Even Cinnamon was lounging in the same place on the filthy bed, watching the worst television programs while drinking the cheapest beer she could buy and munching on cheap, oily potato chips.

Emil looked at Cinnamon with disgust and thought, I wish that filthy, moldy, sagging ceiling would fall on her. Cinnamon did not even acknowledge that her lover, Duke, had entered the room.

Emil said, "Hell, Cinnamon, this place is a pig pen; why can't you clean up during the day?"

Cinnamon, holding up her beer can to cheer him, said, "When I get home from work tonight, and you want a good fuck, you won't give a damn how this place looks. Besides, it has to look much better than any place you ever lived." Emil glared at Cinnamon with total disgust. She was wearing her normal bright red nail polish, half on and half off her fingers and toes, and that stupid looking dyed red hair. There was no doubt that by looking at her, she worked in the cheapest strip joint in Nashville, Tennessee.

At that moment, the phone rang. Maybe this was it; Emil's job was finished here; now, all he needed was the big money, all in cash, and he would journey into the golden life as far away from Tennessee as he could get. Cinnamon went for the phone as Emil lunged forward. "I'll answer it," Emil snapped as he clutched the phone.

Cinnamon listened to every word Emil said: "Yeah, yeah, I told you it is all finished. Yeah, I'll find it. I'll be there." Emil slammed down the phone with no goodbyes and no difference in the expression on his angry face.

Cinnamon knew better than to ask Duke about the phone call. It was none of her business, as was everything about Duke, not her business. She could handle the violence in sex, but a slap in the face for a harmless question was not her idea of fun.

Emil went to the small, dirty, apartment-sized refrigerator and grabbed his bottle of cold vodka to drink. He then sat down on the only chair in the room. Cinnamon said, "Guess it's time for me to get ready for work."

With his eyes glued on the television, Emil replied, "Yeah."

Emil drank the remaining vodka in the bottle when Cinnamon said, "I'll see you at two o'clock."

Emil again answered, "Yes," while thinking that by 2:00 a.m., he'd be long gone with sickening memories of the past few months in Nashville and being with Cinnamon. Emil looked at his watch. Only one more hour, and it would be over; Cinnamon, this dump, and the damn country music. Why did they have to choose Nashville? He hated the twangy country music, the people, and especially the tourists wearing all those ridiculous-looking outfits with matching boots.

Emil took a quick shower, put clean clothing on, and threw a couple of dirty items back in his bag. He then took a few minutes to wipe off any fingerprints he left throughout the room. Emil looked at his watch at least twenty times. One last glance at his watch, and it was time to go. He lived out of a suitcase, so leaving was quick and easy.

As he opened the door to leave, he felt as good as he did the first time he was ever with a woman; very masculine, proud, shoulder's back, and head raised just like he had finally won a first-place trophy for something he had worked hard on for so long.

As he left the apartment, the door got caught on the carpet again, but this time, he did not swear; he laughed out loud. Emil thought I need to take a piss; I think I'll do it on this damn carpet. He laughed until he finished, put everything back in place, and zipped up his pants. As he turned to leave, Emil said to himself, "It's a shame I don't have to take a shit!" As he bolted out the door, he left it wide open and hung on the carpet.

While walking to the car, he thought, All in there is Cinnamon's shit; who would want that crap anyway? She could not trace him because she had known him simply as Duke. He threw his bag in the back seat of the old Cadillac, which he had stolen from a junkyard, and made the necessary repairs to get her running. He started the engine and sped away.

As Emil drove down I-40 West toward Memphis, he changed radio stations at least ten times, thinking all the time that he'd happily settle for less money to get the hell out of there and hear some good music for a change. He finally saw the exit, drove down the ramp, turned left, drove another 2.2 miles, and then turned left again. He thought the big man was playing it safe as he looked in his rearview mirror and saw a thick cloud of road dust behind him. Emil looked at his watch, thinking, I'm almost there and right on time.

After traveling three miles down the country road, he finally saw the luxurious black Sikorsky helicopter with dark tented windows. Emil thought You have the best of everything the world offers when you're in the big league. He stopped the car as close to the chopper as possible, coming within three feet of the passenger door under the whisper-quiet propellers that were still rotating, waiting for Emil's arrival. He chuckled as he exited the car and said, "This damned old ugly pink '78 Cadillac was now history." Soon, he would have a white BMW with tinted windows, a Sirius XM radio, and a convertible. He

already knew nothing in the car was traceable, so he grabbed his bag and wiped down the car for any finger prints that may be left on the car and then jumped into the helicopter.

Four men were sitting, waiting for Emil in the helicopter. Each man had an AK-47 rifle by their side. Even though they were Muslim, they were dressed in expensive American suits, exquisite neckties, and thousand-dollar shoes. Emil then thought They would find my appearance appalling. They exchanged greetings as the helicopter took off.

The leader and messenger of the Al-Qaeda group, Jamal Amed Taymiya, handed Emil an envelope and said, "Good job, Emil, exceptionally good work. Now, this is only the beginning." The envelope contained thousands of dollars for Emil's expense money. The big money had already been deposited directly into a bank account in the Cayman Islands. Before leaving the Nashville hellhole, Emil called from his disposable cell phone to confirm the Cayman deposit. It was already there waiting for him to begin spending his well-earned money, and lots of money, millions of dollars.

In his most formal manner, Emil responded, "Thank you, Master Taymiya. Only the beginning? I thought my job for you was done?"

Jamal replied, "But, Emil, you've done so well; this next job is much bigger, and the money is double!" This next job, you will be the the master, overseeing that everything is done precisely, and you don't have to get your hands dirty."

Emil, always greedy for money, did not hesitate and said, "Where to next, Master Taymiya?"

Jamal said, "The Learjet is waiting in Memphis to take us to Los Angeles, where you will stay until all of your men have arrived and everyone learns their jobs. You will be staying in the penthouse at the Biltmore Hotel, where you will be 'The Master' in charge; everything is already set up for you there." Jamal continued, "Everything you'll need—instructions, supplies, and addresses—will be delivered to your suite at the Biltmore Hotel." Jamal then put his fingers to his mouth and said, "Perfecto," just like an Italian would do. All the men laughed out loud.

Emil said, "I'll go anywhere as long as I don't have to listen to damn country
and Western music anymore, and I can finally dress in style."

"Emil, in LA, you'll have your choice of music, the finest tailors, and many beautiful women. I am certain you will love this job."

All five men laughed out loud together as the chopper headed to the Memphis airport.

CHAPTER 2

FRIDAY, MAY 1ST
IZZY
YORK, PENNSYLVANIA

Izzy gave her belly a love pat as the warm water trickled down her body. Even in the shower, she smiled with joy. Finally, after twelve years of marriage, she would have the baby she longed for. As she dried off her body, a smile came to her face thinking of her flower gardens full of yellow Tiffany roses, blue Forget-Me-Nots, purple irises, pink carnations, white Shasta daisies, red Lady Washington geraniums, apricot pansies, and orange chrysanthemums. Then she laughed to herself as she was no longer bothered that the only flower she could ever grow was baby's breath. She always thought it was a bad omen. So many times in the past, she was disappointed for days when her pregnancy test was negative. Izzy was so excited, thinking of her last day, rushing to the office. Her maternity leave was only ten hours away. She thought, who needs a baby's breath plant when you are growing the real thing?

I love the spring in York, Pennsylvania, Izzy thought to herself. I'm curious if my baby will like to work in the gardens with flowers as much as I do.

Izzy dressed for her last day of work. Her face beamed with beauty, her long black hair shined, her big blue eyes gleamed, and she looked stunning in her new bright yellow maternity business suit. After she added her final touches of makeup and put on her jewelry, she looked at herself in the mirror. She thought to herself, Pregnant women are the most beautiful women. She gave her belly another pat and laughed. She said, "Off to work we go, baby girl." Izzy walked downstairs, picked up her briefcase, keys, and purse, and headed for the garage. She pushed the button on her car key, which beeped as it unlocked the door to her white Lexus. She entered the car, locked the doors, and opened the garage door. She thought to herself, I did it right again.

Her mother worried too much about Izzy's safety. Her mother heard about this safety tip for women when getting into a car on some talk show and insisted that Izzy lock herself in the car before she opened the garage door. Izzy thought to herself, Mothers, and Izzy then thought I'll soon be a mother and will do the same things. She backed out of the garage, hit the button to lock the garage door, and was on her way to work.

Driving down the driveway, she thought about her shopping spree with her friend Sandy the next day. They were going to look at every baby product that was ever made. She was so excited. Then she thought, I am glad I followed my doctor's advice.

Her doctor said she needed one more ultrasound, but she did not want to know if her baby was a girl or a boy. She thought that knowing her baby's sex would take away from the excitement. Her husband, Michael, would not hear of that, and her mother convinced her that if she knew the baby's sex, they would have so much fun decorating the nursery in the proper decor. Izzy finally gave in, and with Michael by her side, holding her hand, they found out their baby was a girl!

The nursery was going to be pink, every shade of pink. The walls were going to be whisper pink. Izzy picked snappy pink for the woodwork. Priscilla's pink ruffles were going on the crib with matching curtains and precious pink for the crib sheets and blanket.

Izzy arrived at work and pulled into her parking place in the parking lot under the building where she worked.

She looked at the clock on her desk and thought, where did this day go? It was already 3:00 p.m. Izzy thought that only two more hours and this office would never look the same. Other than pictures of my flower gardens on the wall, it will now display pictures of my precious daughter and the new family, Mother, Daddy, and Whitney Sue, sitting on my desk. She was filled with so much excitement and love in her heart. She gave Whitney Sue another love pat and chuckled once more at the notion of her baby's breath flowers always dying, which was a bad omen. She looked around; everything was for her best friend and Secretary Sandy to take over and hold down the fort for her while she was on maternity leave. She thought,

Everything will be fine, and I am only a phone call away if Sandy needs anything.

At that moment, Izzy heard a knock at the door, and she said, "Come in," and did they ever come in!

She had worked with twenty-one women for nine and a half years, and talk about pink! Every woman had something pink in her arms. Each one carried a pink package. Sandy had a huge pink cake, Louise, her boss, was carrying a big basket of pink flowers, and Marcy had the pretend pink champagne. All Izzy could see was every color of pink bows and ribbons imaginable. What a beautiful pink baby shower!

Izzy was surprised, elated, and breathless. Tears of joy were rolling down her cheeks when the flashes started; the picture-taking had begun. There was so much love from her family and friends. She was overcome by how wonderful her life was. The baby shower was over by seven o'clock, and Izzy's beautiful pink presents were packed neatly in her car. Before she drove away, she hugged Sandy goodbye and said, "See you tomorrow." As she walked in from the garage door, Michael was waiting with open arms. Izzy fell in love with Michael the first time she laid her eyes on him. He was six feet tall and handsome, with sandy-colored hair and green eyes. He was still dressed in his suit from work. Michael said, "The girls surprised you, didn't they?"

He continued, "Sandy has been excited for months and has called me 1000 times to share all the details and check with me if I thought you would like this or if you would like that and secretly shared all the tidbits about your surprise baby shower. Izzy fell into Michael's arms and told him how much she loved him and was so happy. Michael said, "Let me go unload the car while you sit down, relax, and prop up your feet." Izzy said, "I'm hungry; I think I'll snack on some almonds, get a water bottle, and prop my feet up." As Michael carried in the last of the presents, he asked her where she would like him to place the big basket of pink flowers with the white baby's breath. Izzy replied, "They would look beautiful as our centerpiece on our table." Michael carried the basket of flowers and sat them in the middle of the dining room table. Michael said, "Izzy, we are going to have to get a bigger table or use smaller plates; this basket is huge, and we won't even be able to see each other when we eat." He then opened the refrigerator and put the leftover cake on the middle shelf. "Izzy, where would you like to go to have dinner?" he asked, arranging the refrigerator to fit the half-eaten cake.

Izzy had been craving seafood for months and told Michael, "Let's make it a seafood night." They headed to the garage, and as they got into the car, Izzy said teasingly with a smile, "I must buckle up to take care of this precious bundle I'm carrying."

They got behind a car emitting exhaust on the way to the restaurant. Izzy crinkled her nose as the fumes passed through the air vents. "That smell is making me sick!" Izzy exclaimed.

"They sure do need a new exhaust for that car," Michael said. "I'd pass them if I could."

Within fifteen minutes, they sat at a table in their favorite seafood restaurant, The Conch's Catch. The waitress graciously greeted Michael and Izzy and asked, "May I get you something to drink while you review the menu?" Izzy asked for a Perrier water, no ice, and Michael ordered a bourbon and water.

While waiting for their drinks, Izzy and Michael looked at the menu and discussed the baby shower and upcoming shopping spree with Sandy. Izzy laughed, "I'm ready to buy out the baby department in every store as long as it's pink."

The waitress returned with their drinks and asked, "What can I get you?" Izzy ordered the grilled fish with rice pilaf and a Caesar salad. Michael ordered the hungry fisherman platter.

The waitress came with their food and placed it in front of them. Michael was swirling the ice in his glass, so the waitress asked if he would like another drink. Michael said, "No, thank you. I'm sorry; it's a habit of mine when I have a drink in my hand."

Izzy put her hand over her mouth and chuckled. "Michael, are you ever going to outgrow that habit? You'll have the baby doing that with her bottle."

Michael said, "I promise to stop doing that the minute the baby is born."

As they started to eat their meal, Izzy said, "There must be some kind of nuts on top of my fish; I've never had crushed nuts before with grilled fish."

They ate, talked, smiled, and laughed during their dinner. The waitress came with the bill, which Michael paid with cash. Izzy asked the waitress for a box to take her leftovers home.

Izzy told Michael, "It was so good, but I'm stuffed; I'll have the rest for a snack later."

The minute they returned home from dinner, Izzy showed off all the pink gifts from the baby shower. Michael could not believe how many gifts and how small the clothing was. Michael asked Izzy if Whitney Sue could wear those tiny gowns.

"You can bet she'll be able to wear them, especially these cute little pink booties," Izzy replied with a wink. She then let out a big yawn, tired from her chaotic day.

"That was your third yawn since we got home and your sixth yawn since we left the restaurant; now I am yawning; it's contagious. It's time to tuck my little mother into bed," Michael smiled.

Before they got into bed, they both brushed their teeth. Izzy said, "I sure do like the taste of this new brand of toothpaste."

Michael brushed his teeth, nodded, and replied, "Yes, Izzy." At the same time, he rested the palm of his hand on the counter, where it accidentally landed on the open toothpaste tube and squirted a three-inch ribbon onto the counter. Michael yelled, "Oh no, now I've done it! I just wasted half our good-tasting toothpaste." Izzy chuckled at Michael's mishap and shook her head.

After brushing his teeth, Michael mumbled through the towel as he dried his face, "I sure do hope Whitney Sue has your teeth; they are so straight and white. I don't want our daughter to wear braces like I did." Izzy laughed, recalling pictures he had shown her from his younger years wearing braces.

They got into bed and lay in each other's arms, talking about how happy they were and laughing at how big Izzy's belly was getting. Izzy told Michael, "Even though I could never grow baby's breath, I certainly have grown the real thing: our baby Whitney Sue."

After their tenth kiss goodnight, Izzy told Michael she loved him, and Michael said, "I love you immensely, Izzy, big belly and all." They fell asleep in each other's arms.

CHAPTER 3

He rubbed his temples and said, "Great, another tension headache." Father Frank was sure he had heard at least a hundred confessions that dragged on while he listened, prayed, and pronounced forgiveness. He was in his sixth year at Holy Name of Jesus Catholic Church near Central Park in New York City. It was an excellent assignment for the young priest. The parish had a good mix of active families, older widows, and a fat endowment from deceased wealthy members. But, as in any city the size of New York, there were a variety of misfits, confused and frightened people with problems, and Father Frank had done his best to help all who sought refuge in his sanctuary.

A change in his attitude had come over him slowly. Father Frank had become sick and tired of the city, the crimes, and the inhabitants who never got better, only worse. But, most of the time, he thought he had made the wrong choice for his life's work. After all, he was a priest becoming weaker and weaker by the day, torn between the church and the desire to be a normal man. All the praying in the world did not seem to help him.

Just yesterday, while playing basketball in the park with the junior high boys, he became distracted by the longing to have a relationship like a nearby couple he watched holding hands, laughing, and loving. He could not help himself. After all, he had seen the couple several times and thought the female was extremely beautiful. She had the figure of a goddess with shapely hips that gracefully moved with the spring breeze and long, curving legs gliding with the same elegance as the ballerina he had just seen flying at the ballet. She had the smile of an angel and beautiful, full red lips. She was everything in a woman in which he fantasized. Even after praying for forgiveness for his fantasies of being with her, he lay in his bed alone, lusting over the woman in the park.

Of all his problems, the biggest was Father Frank's feelings of guilt. He was a tormented man, a priest without the faith to endure priesthood. He noticed much too often how women would take a second look at him. His mother told him every day of his young life that he was a handsome man. He took pride in his body. He was fit and very masculine for a priest. He was six feet two inches, with bigger than normal biceps, shiny black hair, and cool blue eyes.

He went out more often, preferring to wear his regular clothes instead of his clerical garb. It took him three times as long to get ready to go out as it did two years ago. He lingered in front of the mirror, sometimes changing shirts, trousers, and shoes four or five times before his outfit suited him.

Father Frank was transforming into a new man, and at times, he did not like it at all. At other times, he allowed himself to enjoy the new feelings that he was experiencing. Father Frank looked good in his outfit. Every woman at the church was in love with Father Frank, married or not; they would flirt with him daily.

What Father Frank needed now after hearing all those confessions, many titillating beyond his ability to endure, was to get far away from the confines of the church. Now, with the perfect outfit on, he left the rectory, hailed a cab, and rode off, destination unknown. He did not care as long as it would get him far away from the church.

Before he knew it, he was twenty blocks away. He paid the cab driver and started walking. He looked and listened excitedly to the sounds of New York City's famous Fifth Avenue. He shook his head in disgust and thought the city's smells and fumes would kill him and everyone else.

He stopped by shop after shop to gaze at the latest clothing styles in the shop windows. His first purchase was at Mike's Nut Shop. The aroma of roasted peanuts filled the air when he walked through the door. He thought to himself, I wish the whole city smelled this good. He purchased a bag of roasted peanuts, assorted nuts, and a pound of his favorite red pistachios. He thought they would at least keep him busy for an hour in his lonely room that night; then, he would have to scrub to get the red dye off his fingers and teeth from the pistachio dye before mass in the morning.

He found a new cologne he liked at the next shop he entered. He purchased the cologne and thought he would head to the nearest bookstore as he left the store. As a priest, he had to be very selective in his purchased books. After all, he would die from embarrassment ten times over if a Playboy magazine or something similar were found in his room or someone saw him making the purchase. Father Frank thought, the games we people play.

As usual, the bookstore was crowded. Father Frank was afraid someone would knock the pistachio nuts out of his hand, and he would be down on the floor scrounging to retrieve them. He looked at the books he thought the church would approve and, being completely bored, left that section and headed for the bestseller section. He took his time and read all the reviews on every bestseller paperback. He wanted to make sure he selected the right book.

After twenty minutes, he had it. He rationalized that he might even find some good messages for a sermon while all the time, he could not wait to read the part about the main character, which was a young woman. Off to the checkout counter he went.

Father Frank stopped into the Petals floral shop and purchased a beautiful bouquet of purple flowers with baby's breath for Mrs. Rossellini, his housekeeper. Purple, after all, was her favorite color.

Father Frank walked several blocks when he spotted a shop called Soap on a Rope. He had to go inside to see what that was all about. It was a bath and body shop for men, and of course, he could not resist buying the soap of the month called "Lady's Wild."

A few stores down the street was a shop called The Chocoholic; he purchased his favorite chocolate there to satisfy his sweet tooth.

Father Frank had enough shopping for the day and hailed another New York cab. After Father Frank told the cab driver his destination, "Holy Name of Jesus Catholic Church," the entire ride, the cab driver talked about how the churches were corrupt, just what Father Frank needed to hear. Just as anxious as Father Frank was to leave the rectory hours ago, he was now just as anxious to return to his room and leave the cab driver and have some peace. After bumping so many people while shopping during the day and the irritating cab ride, he was ready to hide in his room.

After returning to the rectory, he checked everything out and went next door to the house where he and the entire bishops staff lived. Father Frank went to his room, and the first thing he did was to place the book he purchased under his pillow carefully.

It was a rare night off for him. The bishop was delivering the Saturday night service alone, so Father Frank decided to eat early and get a good night's rest. Mrs. Rossellini, the housekeeper, had left a light dinner of seafood salad with crisp lettuce and a huge tomato for Father Frank in the fridge before she left for the day. Father Frank washed his hands with his new soap bar at his sink and enjoyed the wonderful scent. It reminded him of the beautiful woman he admired in the park.

Before getting his dinner, he looked in the cupboards and found a vase to put the flowers he purchased for Mrs. Rossellini. He thought how happy Mrs.

Rossellini would be when she saw the flowers in the morning. He sat in the empty kitchen with his food and a bottle of vitamin water and thought he was glad Mrs. Rossellini had gone for the night. He could think quietly without her fussing around him like an Italian grandmother. Sometimes, Father Frank could understand why her husband had run off so many years ago and left her with the six children to care for alone.

Father Frank's predecessor, two terms before him, had taken the old woman on staff, and she had been there ever since. She kept a neat house, adhered to the meager budget, and prepared good, wholesome food, which was exactly what her duties were; however, she seemed to try to involve herself in the day-to-day operations of the parish as well. Father Frank would find her dusting just outside his office when he completed a confidential counseling session or behind him, straightening pictures when he hung up the telephone in the hallway.

He thought, Before Mrs. Rossellini returns on Monday, I will have to find a better place to keep that new book. He feared that even his briefcase was not safe from her eyes. Father Frank cleared the dishes from the table, washing his glass and plate and placing them on the drain board on the sink. Thank God he had written his Sunday morning sermon on Thursday afternoon. He could go to his room and relax. Father Frank headed for his room, but as he reached the bottom of the stairs, he detoured into the living room and grabbed a bottle of red wine from the bar. Father Frank knew the wine would help him sleep even though it was not a good idea. He would need all his wits to meet the parishioners on Sunday morning, and he had promised himself Saturday night would be wine-free.

As he reached his room, he was struggling with the demons. Good wine and a good book weighed on his conscience. Father Frank got ready for bed, turned on his little light next to his bed, and lit his new candle. Father Frank opened his bottle of wine and poured it into his only wine glass, filling it to the brim. He sat on his bed, ate pistachio nuts, and drank his wine by candlelight. The more Father Frank drank his wine, the more he enjoyed his night and the candlelight.

The combination of the wine and the candle's scent had such a calming effect and made him feel that it was only a matter of time before he was going to leave the priesthood. All he could think about was the gorgeous woman in the park and how good it would feel to lay next to such a beautiful woman. He was inspired to go to the kitchen, take one of the beautiful flowers from Mrs. Rossellini's arrangement, and place it on his pillow.

Father Frank quietly snuck through the house, went to the kitchen, and selected a flower with a sprig of the baby's breath from the vase. He returned to his room without being seen in his pajamas and laughed as he entered. He laid the flower on his pillow next to where his head would be when he slept.

He thought to himself, I love this wine! He poured himself another full glass of wine and looked at the bottle; it was almost empty.

Could he be lucky enough to get another bottle of wine without being seen? He thought, Yeah, why not? So off he went to get another bottle of the good wine. He felt blessed to return to his room without being seen, thinking someone up there must be helping him! Then he thought, I wonder if this is how being tipsy feels, and laughed.

Back in his room, Father Frank decided he had enough of the pistachio nuts, so he closed the sack and put them in the top drawer of his only dresser. He took his new book from the top of his dresser, sat on his bed, and thought, This book is going to be great. He held the book with both hands and placed it over his heart. Father Frank was in love, but not with God! He turned on his light, sipped his wine, lay beside his flower, and stared at his new book. He looked at the cover for several minutes and then turned the pages until he saw Chapter One. He reached for his glass of wine on his nightstand and took a big sip. After swallowing the gulp of wine, he returned the glass to his nightstand. He then picked up the flower, smelled its feminine fragrance, and kissed it. He laid the flower beside his body and picked up his book. While reading the third page of chapter one, Father Frank fell fast asleep.

It was around three o'clock when Father Frank woke up, dazed and confused, not knowing he was in his bedroom. It was like he was in another world, and it took him a few minutes to realize he was still alive. He looked at the clock, looked around the room, and thought, *what happened here?* He jumped out of bed, hid his book and flower, and thought, I need to be at the seven o'clock Mass. Dear God, what have I done? He dumped the residual wine from the bottle and glass and hid them in his suitcase. He rushed to his bathroom and washed his hands several times to remove the red stain from the pistachio nuts. He then looked at his teeth and grabbed his toothbrush and the new toothpaste Mrs. Rossellini brought him.

After brushing his teeth, he thought, *if I had this toothpaste as a child, I would have brushed my teeth ten times a day; this tastes so good. I'm going to have to ask her where she got this.* He then splashed cold water on his face several times. Looking at his face in the mirror, he thought, *this was the first time I felt like I had a life in the past ten years.* He turned off the

light in the bathroom and smiled as he got back in bed.

CHAPTER 4

Michael woke first. He quietly moved around the room to avoid disturbing his sleeping wife. He made coffee, read the newspaper, and showered while Izzy slept. Michael had plans to golf with his friends while Izzy went shopping with Sandy. He was thrilled that Izzy was getting bedroom number two, now better known as the nursery, ready for their baby girl when she arrived. While shaving, he saw Izzy smelling some of the pink items, feeling how soft they were while holding them to her heart. All the time, Michael was smiling.

Sandy arrived to pick up Izzy at ten sharp; Izzy took her last bite of the cinnamon toast that Michael had prepared for her and her sweet little girl, Whitney Sue. Sandy wore her blue jeans and a shirt that said, *Shop Till You Drop*. Sandy was only five feet tall and had beautiful auburn hair with big green eyes.

Sandy said, "I thought this shirt would be appropriate for today's shopping spree."

Izzy said, "I love your shirt, Sandy; I decided to go casual and comfortable today." Izzy wore a straight-line big blue jean dress with sandals. Izzy said, "Nothing tight around my big belly today."

Sandy and Izzy had become best friends from the first day they worked together. Sandy drove, and away they went to the Center Point Mall.

They hit every baby department in every store at the mall. Izzy sought out and touched everything pink she could get her hands on. Sandy must have said at least a hundred times, "Izzy, just look at this. Won't Whitney Sue look precious in this dress?"

By two o'clock on Saturday afternoon, Izzy was starving; after all, she was eating and shopping for two. They stopped and enjoyed their lunch at the food court in the mall. Izzy ordered a fish sandwich with many pickles and a water bottle from The Fresh Catch. Sandy had a cheeseburger, fries, and a Coke from Mel's Burger Place.

During lunch, Izzy and Sandy discussed how they must have looked at thirty cribs, felt two hundred pink blankets, seen five hundred dresses for Whitney Sue, played with every toy in every store, and cuddled every pink stuffed animal they could get their hands on. It was all so overwhelming that Izzy decided she had plenty of time to shop and said, "I'll take some time to think about which of the items I'll purchase later."

Sandy thought that was a great idea, saying, "We can shop again next Saturday."

The ladies ended their lunch and headed back to the shops.

It was time to test new lady perfumes in the cosmetic department. Izzy purchased the latest and sweetest-smelling perfume called Sweetness; of course, it was in a pink bottle.

Then, Izzy and Sandy looked for a new summer maternity outfit for Izzy. Izzy could not find one outfit she liked. Neither Sandy nor Izzy spent much money except for lunch, but they had a wonderful time together, laughing as they had for so many years.

As the afternoon was winding down, they decided to hit the last section in the Center Point Mall and stopped at the first shop, "You Soap Up," a bath shop, where, after smelling every bar in the store, Izzy purchased the latest fragrance of her favorite soap.

The next store they walked by was a bookstore called "Read, Read, Read." Izzy said, "Let's check out the bestsellers. Surely, before the baby gets here, I'll finally have time to read a good book." Izzy stood before the bestsellers' paperback books while Sandy roamed the store. Izzy had one of the bestsellers in her hand when Sandy approached her. Izzy said, "This book looks good. It is about a girl in her twenties who was sexually abused as a child, was on drugs and into prostitution, and then falls in love and lives happily ever after. It says you will not believe the ending. I'm getting the book in hardback in celebration of finally having time to read a book!"

Sandy said, "I love happy endings; what is the book called?"

Izzy turned the hardback book over and said, "The title is Read It and Weep."

Sandy said, "Good title. I want to borrow it when you are finished reading the book." Izzy grabbed her favorite magazine, Persons of Interest, and a newspaper called There Is Good News. They both paid for the purchases and left the bookstore.

They wanted to go into the next shop to buy some candles. They smelled every new scent and both purchased a ten-hour burning candle.

Sandy said, "This is the best buy for the money; I chose the pink carnation scent. What scent is your blue candle, Izzy?"

Izzy said, "The scent is called dusk; very interesting, don't you think?"

Sandy said, "I wonder who sits all day to come up with these names for scents?"

The two best friends headed for the checkout.

Before Izzy and Sandy left the mall, they went into the Chocolate Town store, where Izzy picked out delicious Belgium chocolates for Michael and her. The two friends walked toward the parking lot and got into Sandy's car.

On the drive home, they discussed what they liked best for the baby and her nursery. As Sandy drove up Izzy's driveway, she said, "Izzy, your flower gardens are the most beautiful I have ever seen; I wish I had a green thumb as you do."

Izzy told Sandy, "Why don't you pick a bouquet to take home to enjoy this weekend?"

Sandy said, "That would be great; I will do that on my way out."

Izzy said, "I wonder where they came up with the saying, 'green thumb'?"

Sandy said, "I don't know because whenever I work in the yard, my thumbs are brown with dirt."

Sandy stopped the car, and before Izzy got out, she told Sandy, "I've had so much fun today with you, Sandy; I love you." Izzy then kissed Sandy on the cheek, exited the car, and walked toward her home.

Sandy yelled, "I will call you tomorrow." Izzy nodded her head in reply.

As Sandy drove down the driveway, Izzy watched Sandy get out of the car and pick every color flower Izzy grew. Sandy's bouquet was beautiful.

They waved goodbye and threw kisses to each other.

CHAPTER 5

SUNDAY, MAY 3rd
FLORENTINE
HOMESTEAD, FLORIDA

Florentine was sick and tired of worrying about paying her electric bill. She needed more money to eat what she wanted and always had to wear hand-me-downs or buy her clothing from a thrift shop. She had lived like this all her life, all forty-seven years.

Florentine was born in Cuba and came to the United States at age four. When Castro took over Cuba, her grandfather took the whole family and fled to the United States, where they first landed in Key West. After a few years in Key West, they moved farther north to Homestead, Florida.

Florentine could still remember that day as if it were yesterday. She had never been so scared in her entire life. They only had the clothing on their backs and were on a tiny, crowded boat that went up and down with each wave as they crossed the Atlantic Ocean. She thought she was going to die in the ocean. Each of them brought a rooster and a chicken to trade for food when they reached the US. Florentine did not know which was worse, the ocean waves or holding a rooster the whole way to the United States. From all that Florentine had heard about Cuba, she was now incredibly grateful that her grandfather moved the family to the land of the free.

She packed exceptionally light to start her journey north up I-95 to Palm Beach, Florida. A friend of Florentine's was heading to Fort Lauderdale and offered her to ride with him. When Florentine saw the ad for a live-in cook and housekeeper, she instantly became excited. She had never been close to Palm Beach but always heard it was beautiful. She thought, I can't wait to see beauty in my world again.

Hurricane Andrew took care of any beauty she had ever seen. There was no palm tree left for her to look at, let alone a flower. Andrew took her friends and only family members; she was so lonely. Her friends all left the area, and her mother died a year after Andrew wiped out Homestead, Florida, the only home she ever knew.

Florentine was waiting at the end of the road for her friend. He pulled up right on time, and Florentine placed her bag in the back and climbed into his old, faded grey pickup; away, the two of them went toward the ramp to I-95 North.

Florentine wore the only comfortable pair of shoes for the journey, even though they did not match her outfit. She thought, Soon, I'll be able to buy new shoes and a new outfit. Although I'm nervous about going to Palm Beach, I must stay positive. I'll find work somewhere in Palm Beach, Florida.

They had reached the exit off I-95 to Fort Lauderdale. She thanked her friend and wished him well. Florentine closed the door to the pickup and got her bag out of the back. The pickup drove down the ramp, and Florentine stood on the side of the highway with her bag by her side and her thumb out to hitch a ride. She never imagined herself ever having to hitchhike. She walked down the highway in the hot sun as the cars whizzed by. Florentine took a bottle of water out of her bag and took a long drink of warm water.

She felt like pouring it over her head but thought better as she might need this water later.

Florentine was walking slowly to keep from getting tired. Finally, after walking and thumbing for a ride for thirty minutes, a husband and wife stopped to see if they could help her. The husband asked, "Where are you headed?"

Florentine answered, "I'm headed to Palm Beach, sir, to get a job."

He said, "Hop in, and we'll drop you off there."

Once in the car, the husband and wife discussed Florentine's experience living through Hurricane Andrew. They loved Florida and wanted to move to Florida from Virginia—their trip was to find out where they wanted to live in Florida. Florentine said, "I wish I could help you out, but the only place I've ever been in Florida was Homestead, and I know you don't want to live there."

They talked all during the ride, and before they knew it, they had arrived at the exit for West Palm Beach.

The husband said, "Here you are, Florentine."

Florentine replied, "I'm not going to West Palm Beach; I'm going to Palm Beach, which I think might be the next exit."

They continued their drive a few additional miles until they saw the Palm Beach exit. They slowed and took the exit, driving down the ramp. The wife said, "Good luck with your new job."

As Florentine got out of the car, she thanked them. Florentine said, "You'll never know how wonderful you have been to help me; I wish you only the best when you move to Florida."

As they drove off, Florentine waved goodbye. Florentine thought, How lucky I am; I hope this is a good omen.

Florentine kept walking east and finally saw the Atlantic Ocean. She knew she was close to where the job was located. She was so nervous and began to feel sick to her stomach. She got the newspaper out of her bag and looked at the address. She turned the corner and walked down the most beautiful street she had ever seen. Every home was huge, like pictures she had seen of the White House. Every house had big, tall black gates all around them. She wondered, How do you get in there?

Florentine felt out of place and worried the police would pick her up for loitering. She would put her head down when someone walked by, attempting to hide.

Florentine thought, This is what they call beautiful people, and here I am in this ugly pink shirt, faded blue jean skirt, red sneakers, and a torn black bag; I'm so embarrassed. Florentine was having second thoughts about even applying for the job.

Florentine finally saw house number 698. She was on South County Road and hoped she was going in the right direction as she needed to get to house number 204, the address posted for the job she was seeking. Thank heavens, the blocks were short. When Florentine got to the next block, she breathed a sigh of relief, seeing she was now on the 500 block. Not only was Florentine a nervous wreck, but she was also tired, hungry, and thirsty, even after drinking both bottles of water she had carried in her bag.

Florentine kept walking and finally arrived at house number 204 on South County Road. The minute she looked at the huge home, she hid behind the tall brushes out front, trying to calm herself down. She took out her comb and combed her reddish-brown hair. She looked over her outfit to ensure she looked the best she could. Looking around, she saw the plaque on the front door, "The Kingsleys' Residence."

Florentine moved farther into the bushes. She had now lost all her confidence. What she saw from the bushes was unbelievable to her. The house was at least three stories high, with three beautiful balconies on the second floor. The house was built with a kind of brick she had never seen, and she thought, How beautiful this house is with all the different colors. The roof did not have shingles. It was made from thick, multicolored ceramic tiles. Florentine thought, It's no wonder they need help to keep this big house clean.

After hiding in the bushes for some time, she courageously walked to the front gate. She did not know how to get in as the gate did not move when she approached. Florentine looked all around and finally spotted a doorbell that was a big-lighted circle. As her hand shook, she pushed the doorbell, then thought, What in the world am I doing here?

After spending an eternity at the palace gates, Florentine looked up toward the house. She saw a tall, nice-looking Black man exiting the house and walking toward her. He looked to be about sixty years old with salt and pepper hair. He wore a full black tuxedo with a vest and bow tie. He walked toward her with pride and confidence, coming around the circle driveway to the front gate. Florentine thought He must be the owner of this palace.

When he reached the gate, he said, "Hello, ma'am; what can I do for you?"

Florentine wanted to speak, but nothing came out. She coughed and then tried again, "Hello, sir, I'm here to apply for the job opening for a cook and housekeeper."

The man shook her hand and said, "I'm Mr. Bo, the butler for the Kingsleys." Mr. Bo said, "How did you know where the house was?"

Florentine handed Mr. Bo the newspaper. Florentine said, "Read the part that is circled."

Mr. Bo took a minute and read the ad and said, "Newspapers, they can't get anything right; just wait until they hear from me." Mr. Bo said, "The ad was to have the phone number and not the address, and we are looking for a chef and housekeeper." Mr. Bo asked Florentine, "Are you a chef?"

Florentine answered, "I've never been called a chef, but I have cooked for many people and even cooked at restaurants, "Is that a chef?"

Mr. Bo said, "We must find that out when you cook your first meal."

Mr. Bo liked Florentine immediately and even more after hearing her story about her journey to Palm Beach. Mr. Bo said, "Move back while I open the gate; I don't want it to hit you." Florentine moved back, and for the first time, she felt relief and calmed down.

Once the gate was opened, Mr. Bo said, "Welcome. Follow me to the maid's entrance. Florentine followed Mr. Bo around the big circle driveway to the right side of the house. Mr. Bo walked up five steps, opened the door, and held it open for Florentine, and she entered the Kingsleys' mansion for the first time.

Mr. Bo said, "Have a seat. Would you care for a glass of water?"

Florentine said, "Oh yes, I'm so thirsty and hungry."

Mr. Bo said, "We'll get you back to feeling good, Florentine." Mr. Bo got Florentine a glass of iced tea and a sandwich.

Florentine said, "I'm acting as though I've never eaten before; this is delicious; thank you, Mr. Bo."

Mr. Bo sat down at the servant's kitchen table and said, "I think I'd like to give you a trial run for our opening here at the Kingsleys; you are the first and only applicant."

Florentine said, "Mr. Bo, thank you so much; I promise I'll do a good job for you."

Mr. Bo said, "Okay then, I'll show you your quarters, and as we walk, I'll tell you about your salary and responsibility; just follow me." Florentine followed Mr. Bo up a narrow circular staircase to the third floor. Mr. Bo said, "Many stairs will keep you in top shape." Mr. Bo continued, "You will receive room and board, $125.00 a week, one day a week off, and if all goes well, you will eventually also receive health insurance. You will be required to wear nothing but the maid dresses that Mrs. Kingsley picked out."

The whole time Mr. Bo was talking, Florentine was nodding her head yes.

As they reached Florentine's quarters, Mr. Bo said, "This will be your private quarters. As you see, it is lovely, and everything you will need is here. I will give you time to look around, bathe, and pick your size dress. When you finish, I will meet you back in our kitchen to review your responsibilities."

Florentine said, Oh, Mr. Bo, this is so beautiful. How can I ever thank you?"

Mr. Bo replied, "I'll be happy if you do a good job." Mr. Bo turned and started to walk back down the stairs to the kitchen.

Florentine touched everything: the bright yellow and white drapes, valance, and the matching bedspread. Florentine thought to herself, How lucky I am; I could scream out loud with joy. The lights all matched, white with bright yellow shades. There were three beautiful white dressers with yellow candles, a jewelry box, a live floral arrangement with purple and yellow flowers, and some beautiful baby breath sprigs. The closet was huge, and her quarters were bigger than where she lived in Homestead. She had her very own bathroom for the first time in her life. The bathroom had all the amenities: a tub with shower, yellow and white towels, perfumes, bath crystals, lotions, shampoo, conditioner, and the best-smelling soap that was also yellow. Florentine thought she died and was in heaven. She thought to herself, I must keep this job.

In the medicine chest, there was every kind of medication she may need if she was sick with a cold or headache. The bathroom smelled delicious, and Florentine could not wait to shower as she had only been able to take a bath but now had the luxury to shower.

Florentine undressed and threw her clothing in the wastebasket. She turned on the shower and said, "Mom, I'm taking a shower!" After her shower, she used lotion and deodorant and brushed her teeth. She thought, I love the flavor of this toothpaste; I wonder where they found this.

Florentine was shining from head to toe and could not wait to get her maid's dress on. She got in her bag, took out clean underwear, put them on, and then went dress hunting. The second maid's uniform fit her perfectly. Now, she had to find a brand-new pair of shoes that fit and were comfortable, which took her a little longer than finding her dress size. Finally, she found a pair and was ready to go.

Florentine went into the bathroom to look in the mirror; she could not believe her eyes because she looked very pretty. The last thing she did before going downstairs to the kitchen was to spray perfume on herself; she thought, I better not overdo the perfume, and set the bottle down. She thought, Perfume! I have not had perfume for years! She opened the door and started to walk down the stairs.

Mr. Bo was waiting for her in the kitchen. Mr. Bo said, "Is this the same lady who just walked up the stairs? Florentine, you look beautiful."

Florentine replied, "Why thank you, sir."

Mr. Bo said, "I'd like you to meet Maria; she will assist you with all your duties. Maria has been with us for eight years and can teach you everything you need to know."

Maria said, "Please feel free to call on me for anything you need."

Florentine said, "Pleased to meet you, Maria; I'm sure I'll need your help."

Maria said, "No worries, Florentine, I'll be here for you, and welcome to our home."

Mr. Bo said, "Here we go; this room is our kitchen. Follow me, please." They entered the room adjacent to their kitchen, another huge kitchen. Mr. Bo said, "This kitchen is where all the Kingsleys' food is prepared. This subzero refrigerator and freezer are filled with all their favorite foods, and you will find everything you need in the cupboards and drawers. All these hanging pots and pans should always be cleaned before use. All the plates and the silverware are here; the silver must be polished when taken out to be used." Mr. Bo said, "In this small room pantry, you'll find everything you'll ever need to keep the Kingsleys' home spotless. Mr. Bo then said, "Any questions so far?

Florentine answered, "No, Mr. Bo."

Mr. Bo said, "Great." He then handed Florentine a paper listing the times the Kingsleys like to eat their three meals a day, a list of their favorite foods and snacks, and explanations of what was needed if the Kingsleys had guests. As Mr. Bo handed the paper to Florentine, he said, "You can read this tonight in your room, and now I will show you the first floor of the Kingsleys' home. Mr. Bo opened the door and walked into the dining room.

Florentine said, "Oh, how beautiful!"

Mr. Bo continued walking through the house, "This is the library; Mr. and Mrs. Kingsley love reading. This is the study where the Kingsleys have their cocktails before dinner, which is on your paper. This is Mrs. Kingsley's favorite room, her sunroom. As you can see, Mrs. Kingsley loves plants and flowers. If you look out this window, the bushes were removed so Mrs. Kingsley can see the ocean."

As they continued to walk, Mr. Bo explained, "This is Mr. Kingsley's office, and there are three bathrooms on the first floor other than ours, off our kitchen. The circular staircase gets very dusty and needs to be dusted regularly."

Florentine said, "What a fabulous home I get to clean; it's so beautiful, Mr. Bo."

The front door opened, and Mr. and Mrs. Kingsley entered the foyer. Mr. Bo asked, "Did you enjoy your dinner at the Breakers'?"

Mrs. Kingsley said, "I ate too much as usual; it was delicious."

Mr. Bo then said, "Mr. and Mrs. Kingsley, I would like to introduce to you Florentine; she will be starting in the morning as our new chef and housekeeper." Mr. and Mrs. Kingsley both welcomed Florentine and shook her hand.

"Florentine said, "I'm honored to meet you both and can't wait to start my duties in the morning."

Mrs. Kingsley said, "I'm full now, but by 7:00 a.m., I will be ready to eat again. We look forward to tasting your breakfast." The Kingsleys walked into the study for a nightcap, and Mr. Bo and Florentine returned to their kitchen.

In the kitchen, Florentine asked, "Do they have any cookbooks in the library?"

Mr. Bo replied, "Why yes, they do; feel free to go to the library and get any books you need."

While leaving the kitchen for the library, Florentine said, "Thank you so much, Mr. Bo; this will help me tremendously. I am already calming down!" Mr. Bo laughed out loud.

Florentine walked into the beautiful library with hundreds of books skillfully placed in beautiful, dark, shining wood bookcases. Florentine thought it would take her forever to find cookbooks, but after a while, she realized all the books were placed in alphabetical order. She quickly found the "Cs" and began reviewing every cookbook the Kingsleys had in their library. She chose the best seven cookbooks she thought would help her prepare fabulous meals for the Kingsleys.

As Florentine left the library, she noticed a smaller bookshelf with paperback books. She decided she would look at their selection of paperback books, thinking she needed something to help her calm down at night so she could sleep! She read several prefaces about the book and the back covers of other paperback books. She chose a paperback book to read and walked out of the library. Returning to the kitchen, she shared with Mr. Bo that she had found some great cookbooks and was excited to review them.

Mr. Bo handed Florentine her instructional paper and said, "Happy reading! That's all for tonight; we will meet you in our kitchen at 5:00 a.m. You have an alarm clock in your room."

Florentine said, "Goodnight" to Mr. Bo and Maria and then added, "Thank you so much, Mr. Bo."

With her instructional paper and carrying the eight books, Florentine headed to her quarters. She sat on her bed and thought, what will I make for breakfast? She first undressed and put on her nightgown, turned on the light next to her bed, and started to read the paper. The paper mostly had what the Kingsleys did not like; she read it five times before sorting through the stack of cookbooks, looking for one with breakfast recipes. After looking at the third cookbook, she picked up the paperback book she selected from the library and re-read the back cover. Florentine thought This might be a good love storybook I could read on my day off. Florentine rubbed her hand over the book and thought, *this looks like a brand-new book.* She laid the novel on her nightstand and continued sorting the cookbooks. Finally, she came across a cookbook: Breakfast Fit for a King! That was it! "I'll make one of these recipes for breakfast."

When the alarm went off at 4:00 a.m., Florentine thought, Did I sleep last night? She was still tired, and it seemed like she had just closed her eyes when the alarm rang. She was still nervous, which also made her feel tired. She got out of bed, cleaned up, got dressed, and picked out the breakfast fit for a king, or better yet, the Kingsleys.

Florentine was in the kitchen by 4:55 a.m. with her cookbook. She would make Eggs Diana for breakfast with bacon and toasted bagels. Florentine made coffee for their kitchen crew and began collecting all the ingredients she would need to make breakfast.

Mr. Bo and Maria entered the servant's kitchen simultaneously, and Mr. Bo said, "The coffee smells wonderful, Florentine." They all grabbed a cup of coffee and sat briefly at the small table in the servant's kitchen.

Mr. Bo asked, "What will you make for breakfast? We also eat what the Kingsleys eat, so please make a lot!" Florentine said, "I'm making Eggs Diana with bacon and toasted bagels."

Mr. Bo said, "I can't wait to taste your breakfast."

Florentine got up from the servant's table, returned to the larger kitchen, and began slicing the scallions and black olives. She then cut the parmesan and provolone cheese into small slices, cut five bagels in half, placed them in the toaster, and retrieved ten eggs, butter, and bacon from the subzero refrigerator. She got the plates, silverware, glasses, jelly, jam, and cloth napkins to prepare the Fit for a King breakfast.

Florentine followed every instruction perfectly. She loved the big kitchen and loved using the bacon press to make the bacon flat; she was having so much fun.

It was now 6:45 a.m. Florentine got the juice from the refrigerator; everything was just about ready. At exactly 6:55 a.m., Florentine placed the food on the plates and decorated the plates with little orange slices, thinly cut avocado slices, and placed everything on the serving table. The plates looked beautiful, and she was confident the food would be

delicious. At 7:00 a.m., she pushed the serving table into the dining room toward the dining table where the Kingsleys were already seated.

Florentine said, "Good morning," to the Kingsleys and served them their food. Florentine said, "If you need anything else, please let me know, and I hope you enjoy your breakfast."

As Florentine walked back into the big kitchen, her hands were shaking. At 7:30 a.m., the Kingsleys called Mr. Bo into the dining room. Now, Mr. Bo and Florentine were both nervous.

Mr. Bo entered the dining room, and Mrs. Kingsley said, "Mr. Bo, I don't know where you found Florentine, but she is a keeper; our breakfast was superb. Please tell Florentine how much we both enjoyed our breakfast. Do you know what the egg dish is called?"

Mr. Bo said, "I believe it is called Eggs Diana, and I will certainly tell Florentine, Mrs. Kingsley; I know she will be delighted with your great news that you enjoyed your breakfast.

CHAPTER 6

Mary Kay was so excited as she stepped on the escalator, taking her to the ramp to the fifth deck of the cruise liner. She would soon see and hug seven sorority sisters from Pi Beta Phi! She thought, Can it be ten years since we graduated from the University of Florida?

Mary Kay had arrived early at the port as she wanted to be at the front for check-in for her two-week cruise. She entered the port terminal after checking her bag with the curbside porter. She was amazed at how the cruise line security process was identical to airport airline security.

As Mary Kay passed through the magnetometer, she thought, Cruise liners want to know if you are trying to bring any alcohol onboard; this is where they make most of their money, from people partying at the many bars on board!

She was third in line at the check-in desk. The cruise line attendant reviewed her passport and the medical form she had completed in the waiting hall. Although she had the flu a few weeks prior, Mary Kay checked the boxes, indicating she had not had any coughing or stomach issues. After swiping her American Express credit card for ship incidentals, the attendant took Mary Kay's picture and produced her stateroom card and was instructed that this would be used as her room key, for entering and exiting the ship, and for any ship purchases as cash was not accepted on board. The attendant then placed her card in the front slot section of a clear plastic envelope that contained a ship map and other collateral for the ship amenities.

After having a long lunch at the Lido deck buffet, an announcement came over the ship speakers announcing that guest rooms were now available. Mary Kay looked at her Gucci watch; it was 1:45 p.m. She then pulled out her stateroom key card and the ship map. She headed to the ship atrium to take the elevator up to her deck, carefully followed the cruise liner map, and finally found her stateroom. She became overly excited as she opened the door to her stateroom, as all she saw through the cabin was a double sliding glass door to a balcony overlooking the entire port. She said out loud, "Finally, something has gone as planned, and getting exactly what I asked for, it's a miracle!"

After entering her stateroom, Mary Kay intended to head first to the sliding doors leading to the balcony, but the scent of the fresh-cut flowers filled the air with an overly sweet smell. She was welcomed with fresh-cut flowers and had six bottles of water and a box of chocolate candy. Next to the coffee maker was a silver bowl filled with every flavor of lollipops. She could not believe her eyes when she looked into the stateroom lavatory. To the right of her sink was a 3.4-ounce spray bottle of the latest perfume by Thierry Mugler called Eau De Angel. To the left side of the sink was a top-of-the-line bottle of sunscreen, hand sanitizer, beautiful bars of colored and scented hand soap, a large tube of toothpaste, shower soaps, body wash, shampoo, and hair conditioner. Mary Kay thought to herself, I could live here forever!

Mary Kay looked at her phone; it was only 2:15 p.m., meaning she had plenty of time to unpack without rushing. It seemed that every day of her life, everything she did, she was rushing for one reason or another. She thought, Finally, I can lay back and relax because I have until 4:30 p.m. to meet my seven sisters at the Top Deck Bar to start our two weeks of love, laughter, relaxation, and fun!

Mary Kay was excited about her new home away from home for the next two weeks! She thought to herself, It is time to unpack my suitcase. Mary Kay lifted her heavy suitcase onto her bed and opened it up; she was surprised that everything was a mess and all wrinkled! Under one of the garments, she found a flyer signed by the ship's security team crew member indicating there was a search of her suitcase contents. She thought It was done for security reasons, which is good in our world. She unpacked her suitcase and then placed all her bathroom articles neatly next to all the wonderful items. She then placed her plastic bathroom item holders back into her suitcase and put her suitcase under the bed.

Next, she spotted the book she had brought and placed it on the coffee table. She thought, I bet I never get to read much of this book, but at least I have it if I have the time to read with seven sisters talking all the time! She laughed out loud at the thought of her even bringing a book to read. She should have known better!

She then remembered her jewelry in her purse and thought, I am glad I did not put my jewelry in my suitcase! She walked to the wall safe, programmed the lock using the same numbers she always used anytime she traveled, and placed her jewelry in the safe. She closed and locked the safe.

She headed for her closet to hang up the beautiful dresses she had brought along for dinner. She took the hangers out of the closet to hang her dresses as she liked. Mary Kay could not wait to wear the new sexy silver dress she bought at Nordstrom in New York City! She ran her hands down the front of

her beautiful new dress and thought, You get what you pay for, and I paid a lot for this dress! She then hung up the other eleven dresses she chose to wear on the cruise. Mary Kay then hung up a few of her bathing suit cover-ups that would wrinkle if laid in a drawer and then hung her sundresses to the right of her evening dresses.

Mary Kay placed all fifteen pairs of shoes neatly on the closet floor while thinking, I might have overdone it with this many pairs of shoes and flip-flops! I will buy some new shoes while here and may also have to buy an extra suitcase!

She put her sun hats on the shelf in the closet. The only remaining items were her beautiful and sexy nightgowns and two-piece satin lingerie, and, of course, the adult toys that she placed in the back of her nightstand drawer! She then put her nighties on hangers so they would not get wrinkled. She walked into the bathroom and looked at the back of her bathroom door; yes, there was a hook for her robe, so she hung her robe neatly on the hook!

She was now officially at her new home for the next two weeks. After the unpacking, Mary Kay plopped down on the plush bed while thinking I needed this vacation; being a product analyst at Google has taken a toll on me. Getting my master's degree was tough, but it was nothing compared to my great-paying job at Google. I will never complain because I ended up in NYC, where everything I love happens.

As Mary Kay was preparing to leave her stateroom, she looked in the mirror to ensure she looked perfect. Her long blond hair sparkled and made her light blue eyes more beautiful. With her beauty and bubbly personality, every head turned when Mary Kay entered a room.

Mary Kay then thought it was time to review the ship map to find her way to the Top Deck Bar and not be late meeting her sorority sisters, and she was so excited. After reading the map, she grabbed her purse and left her stateroom early in case she got lost, which, more than likely, she would!

Mary Kay walked into the Top Deck Bar five minutes early, and all seven sisters were already there! They all ran to hug Mary Kay and continued hugging each other for several minutes. One of her sisters said, "We are already on our second cocktail; where have you been?" The ten-year reunion had officially started!

Another one of her sisters said, "Walking in with that Gucci purse, I thought you would be the president or the CEO of Google, just like you were president of our sorority!"

Mary Kay replied, "My position at Google keeps me busier than I like; I can't imagine what the job would entail for the president or CEO!"

The sisters moved from the bar to a table to be more comfortable drinking cocktails and eating appetizers. Most were on their fourth drink, but Mary Kay was only on her second.

One of Mary Kay's sisters said, "Mary Kay, you had better drink fast; we are all ahead of you!"

Mary Kay picked up her drink and downed every drop, saying, "Cheers!"

The bar was filling up with mostly men and a few couples. Mary Kay told her sisters, "You know that all these good-looking men are going to make our cruise more delightful!"

One of Mary Kay's sisters said, "Let us cheer our president like we used to at our sorority parties!"

All seven sisters said, "Cheers, cheers, cheers to our president, Mary Kay!"

Mary Kay replied, "Okay sisters, let's all settle down," all the time laughing. Mary Kay said, "We all have come from different places, different jobs, some married with children, and some of us still single, but we all look the same as we did ten years ago when we graduated; we ROCK!"

As the girls settled down, a handsome man approached their table and said, "Which one is Mary Kay?" The seven sisters pointed to Mary Kay, and Mr. Handsome said to Mary Kay, "Well, do you also drive a pink Cadillac?"

Mary Kay replied, "No, I don't drive an ugly pink Cadillac, and I can't help it. My parents named me Mary Kay, the same as the cosmetic company name. You know, they could have called me Charmin like the toilet paper, and then all I would do is wipe up crap all day!" Everyone laughed out loud!

Before Mr. Handsome returned to the bar, he told Mary Kay, "I hope to see a lot more of you during our cruise!"

Mary Kay replied, "I came on his cruise to relax, not to fall in love!" All the sisters knew it was just a matter of time before Mary Kay would know Mr. Handsome's name, where he lived, where he worked, and his entire life story.

One sister said, "Mary Kay, he is so handsome, no wedding ring and the two of you would look perfect together; may I please be your maid of honor at the wedding!" Everyone laughed!

After signing for the bar tabs, the girls headed for their first dinner at the main dining room on the third deck in the back of the ship.

CHAPTER 7

MONDAY, MAY 4ᵗʰ
IZZY
YORK, PENNSYLVANIA

Michael was dressed and ready to leave early for work to avoid Monday morning traffic. He held Izzy in his arms, and they kissed, and then he gave the baby, Whitney Sue, a love pat. Michael said, "I wish I could stay home with my girls today since we had such a relaxing day of love yesterday. And by the way, our home looks beautiful and smells beautiful because of the beautiful bouquets you have all over the house!"

Izzy replied, "I love you, but since you can't stay home with your girls today, we will have your favorite meal ready for you when you walk in the door tonight."

He said, "You mean I'm finally going to have your famous roast beef for dinner?"

Izzy replied, "Yes, you are; how did you guess?"

Michael said, "What a long day this will be; I will smell the roast beef simmering all day at work." Michael added, "What else will you do today, sweetie?"

Izzy answered, "I'm going to read my new book, enjoy our yard, and enjoy my first day off."

Michael answered, "Izzy, have a wonderful day, sweetie; you deserve a peaceful day at home." They kissed again, and Michael headed out the door to the garage.

Izzy climbed the stairs with her decaffeinated coffee and thought about wearing her most comfortable outfit. After she got dressed, she washed her face, brushed her teeth, tied her long black hair up in a ponytail, and then gave herself a spray of her new perfume before heading downstairs.

Izzy placed her empty coffee cup in the sink and thought, since Michael likes the smell of my flowers in our home, I'm going to fill every vase in this house with fresh-cut flowers from our yard. She headed to the garage, and within twenty minutes, she returned with her arms filled with every color flower from her gardens. She filled the vases and stood to admire them. She placed the vases all over the living room and kept one at the base of the staircase to later take up to her bedroom.

Izzy looked at the clock and thought, It is much too early to start cooking the roast; I think I'll read for a little while. She picked up her new book and laid it on the table beside her big, comfortable chair. She then lit her new candle, went to the refrigerator, and got a water bottle to sip on while reading. She opened the cupboard, got a glass, put it under the ice maker on the refrigerator door, and filled it with ice. As she carried the bottle of water and the glass of ice to her chair, she thought, *even though my freezer has a filter, I am pouring bottled water over ice made from the city water supply*! *Oh well, I cannot do everything right.*

Izzy set her glass and bottle of water on coasters next to her cell phone, sat down, and propped up her feet. She read the book's back cover first, then read all about the author, the titles of all his other books, the copyright of when this book was written, and then the acknowledgments. Finally, she started reading chapter one.

Izzy was having the time of her life. Is that my new candle that smells so good, or is it the flowers from my yard? She thought, I cannot remember the last time I felt so relaxed, but I am hungry. I should eat a light breakfast, but I will snack on some almonds. She got up and got her big plastic tub of healthy sea-salted almonds.

Just as she went to sit back down, her cell phone rang. Sandy called to say all was well at the office, and she missed her. Izzy told Sandy, "I miss you also, but I don't miss work. I'm having a wonderful day at home."

Sandy said, "I will only call back if we need you. Have a great day."

The girls said goodbye, and Izzy disconnected the call as she lounged in the chair, opened the almonds, placed a big handful on her lap, and started eating them and drinking water as she read her new book. She was now in chapter two. Izzy was still hungry, so she warmed up her leftovers and ate every bite while she read. The book was so good that she couldn't put it down despite feeling extremely fatigued.

The next thing she remembered was Michael standing over her, saying, "Wake up, Izzy." He took her arm, and finally, her eyes opened. Michael said, "My girl is having a relaxing day; how long have you been asleep, Izzy?"

Izzy replied, "I think only a few minutes. I can't believe I fell asleep, Michael; what time is it anyway?"

Michael said, "It is six-thirty, Izzy."

Izzy said, "Oh no, Michael! I did not prepare the roast."

Michael replied, "That's okay, honey; we will make it together."

Izzy tried to get up but felt a little dizzy and said to Michael, "I feel dizzy. Will you help me up?"

Michael said, "Izzy, stay there if you don't feel well; I don't want you to fall." With that, Izzy sat back and rested her head on the back of the chair. Michael said, "I'm going to spoil you and make you dinner."

Izzy replied, "Michael, I feel like a terrible wife, sleeping instead of making you your favorite meal; please don't fire me."

Michael removed his suit jacket and laid it on the chair, saying to Izzy, "How could I ever fire my favorite person in the world?" Michael continued, "You just stay right there and relax. Can I get you anything?"

Izzy said, "Yes, the bathroom." Michael approached Izzy and said, "Okay, Mom, here we go; grab my arm and go to the bathroom." Izzy could hardly walk, and Michael was becoming upset. He managed to get her into the bathroom, but she was now extremely lethargic and pale. Izzy told Michael she was having muscle pains, and Michael saw a small amount of blood running down Izzy's upper lip and dripping from her nose.

She sat on the toilet and said, "Michael, I think I'm going to throw up." He grabbed the trash can in the bathroom and held it before her. She gagged and gasped for air; nothing came up, but she was sick.

Michael said, "Izzy, can you breathe?" Izzy shook her head no. Michael said, "I will get my cell phone and call 911. Can you hold on to the wall and the sink until I return?" Izzy nodded her head. Michael raced to his jacket, grabbed his phone, and ran back to the bathroom, where he called 911.

Michael thought, *our front door might be locked*. Michael was not sure and did not know what to do. They couldn't get in if the door was locked, but if he left Izzy, she might fall off the toilet. Michael told the 911 operator his dilemma, and she told him to stay with his wife.

The operator said, "I'll tell the first responder to break down the door if it is locked. Can you get your wife on the floor without hurting her or the baby?"

Michael was sweating and almost in tears as he told the 911 operator, "I'm scared to move her; I don't want to hurt either of them."

The operator replied, "Sir, just stay with your wife and make sure she doesn't fall, and stay on the line until they arrive; they are turning on your street right now."

Michael said, "Thank you, and thank God."

Michael could hear the first responders at the front door. Michael screamed as loud as he could, "We are in here; I can't leave her! Just break down the damn door!"

As Michael heard the noise of the front door crashing down, he also heard a faint whisper from Izzy, "Baby's breath." It seemed like forever, but it was only seconds until they had Izzy on a stretcher with an oxygen mask on her face, taking her pulse and blood pressure.

The medic looked at Michael and said, "Sir, we must get her to the hospital right now; you can ride with us in the ambulance."

The medics pushed the stretcher out the front door and into the ambulance with sirens blaring; Michael started to cry. Izzy's eyes were closed, and she was not responding. They rushed Izzy into a room at the hospital and closed the curtain, but by the time they got her into the trauma unit, Izzy and the baby were pronounced dead.

The doctor came through the curtain, turned to Michael, and spoke slowly and quietly, "Are you Mr. Michael Thomas?"

Michael answered, "Yes, sir."

The doctor replied, "I am truly sorry; neither your wife nor the baby made it."

Michael screamed aloud, began banging on the wall, and exclaimed, "Oh God no, please no, not my Izzy and Whitney Sue; how can this be?"

The doctor kept Michael in the trauma unit while the medical staff consoled him. Michael was unable to compose himself and continued to sob.

The nurse repeatedly asked Michael, "Who can we call for you, sir?" Michael had left his cell phone in the bathroom at home. It took Michael some time, but he finally could provide Izzy's parents and Sandy's names and phone numbers. Michael was unable to contain himself when speaking with Izzy's parents.

While speaking with Sandy, he could only get out: "My Izzy and Whitney Sue are gone. Izzy's last words to me were baby's breath." Michael dropped the phone, becoming hysterical, banging on the wall, and then frantically screamed, "I hate baby's breath," while falling to the floor in a fetal position. As he sobbed, he screamed, "I hate baby's breath, I hate baby's breath." The doctor then administered a sedative and provided intake orders to keep Michael overnight for observations.

CHAPTER 8

Emil Mashaduk was now completely different from the man who flew out of Tennessee. He must have either been a Gemini, the sign of the twins, bipolar, or both. Emil transformed into a clean-shaven, handsome man with sculpted short black hair that shined, manicured fingernails with clear polish, and a smile with bright white teeth. His gal, Cinnamon, in Tennessee, would surely die of a heart attack if she saw him now. He wore a bright red silk shirt with the top three buttons opened, exposing his tanned chest, and a solid gold dollar coin that hung from a heavy gold chain around his neck. He wore beige dress pants, pleats held up by a beautiful dark brown leather belt and matching shoes, and a gold Rolex watch adorned his left wrist.

His room at the Biltmore Hotel was just as flashy as Emil was. Brilliant colors touched every wall, beautiful gold sculptures graced every room, and the bar was fully stocked with the most expensive top-shelf liquors Emil had longed for during his stay in Tennessee. Emil counted eight different bottles of scotch, including his favorite drink, whiskey scotch, Glenfiddich 23 Grand Cru.

The bar was shaped like a scallop shell with gold mermaids on the top and sides of the bar stools. Emil's bed was round-shaped with a headboard that contained a surround sound system with Bose speakers to stream music. He could even vibrate himself to sleep. The marble bathroom was huge, like none he had ever seen. It had a shower, bathtub, and separate Jacuzzi on one side. The other side of the bathroom had a toilet with a bidet, a standard toilet with a cushioned seat, and a separate urinal. The bathroom was stocked just like the bar, with everything Emil needed for grooming to be one of the beautiful people. There were three shelves filled with books and current magazines to read, three soft white bath robes, and huge white towels with the Biltmore logo. The room service was fit to serve the queen of the Nile; Emil thought all this to reward me for a job he did so well in Tennessee and the job he had started in Los Angeles! Emil's job was to kill fifteen million Americans by the time he finished this second job!

Emil looked at his Rolex watch and thought, It is time to go out on the town and look for beautiful women. He thought, What flavor should I look for tonight, a redhead, a blonde? Tonight, a brunette. He grabbed two Cuban cigars and a disposable phone as he headed out the door for his night of fun, good music, and a sexy woman.

CHAPTER 9

Dr. Rudolph Wendt closed his cell phone and walked to his office. On the door to his office, it read: CDC Director. Dr. Wendt closed the door, went to his desk, picked up the receiver to his office phone, and called his secretary, Donna Deplay. Miss Deplay answered and said, "Good morning, Sir; how can I help you?"

Dr. Wendt replied, "Good morning, Miss Deplay. Please have Dr. Hertz and Dr. Wadeson come to my office immediately."

Miss Deplay answered, "Yes, Sir, I will call them now."

Dr. Wendt said, "Thank you and hung up the phone."

Miss Deplay looked like she could have been a basketball star standing beside Dr. Wendt! She towered over the doctor with her six-inch heels and hair in a bun on top of her head; you could spot her coming three blocks away. Her voice was all over the CDC, so you had to be careful what you discussed with her!

Miss Deplay always dressed in beige outfits matching her hair, sported oversized round ruby red-framed glasses, and wore the same pair of beige heels or high-top brown high-heel boots daily! She was always early for work and stayed later than expected.

Dr. Wendt thought she was doing this to get a raise, which he did not intend to give her. He would much rather replace her as she always went overboard in her conversations with people at work, which drove Dr. Wendt crazy! She was overqualified for her job and too many times spoke her opinion. Dr. Wendt tried his best not to talk to her face-to-face. Dr. Wendt heard her tell someone on the phone that she was like the CEO of the CDC because she was the top scientist's secretary! After speaking, she always added a ridiculous giggle and snort that Dr. Wendt found irritating.

Dr. Rudolph Wendt had a slight German accent, and to look at him, you would have never believed he was in charge as director of the CDC in Atlanta. He stood five foot ten inches tall with a pot belly, making his white lab coat bulge in the front. He wore round silver trifocal glasses and the pair of sneakers he bought ten years ago. He always wore gray trousers with a white collared shirt.

Dr. Wendt was appointed to the CDC top position that served at the pleasure of the President of the United States because of his vast knowledge of infectious diseases and his impressive array of doctorate credentials. On the wall behind his desk was an ornate plaque with the engraving: "BOOTS ON THE GROUND – DISEASE DETECTIVES" and was centered between his four certifications: Doctor of Sciences, Doctor of Biology, Doctor of Medicine, and Doctor of Infectious Diseases; all four were from Harvard University in Cambridge, Massachusetts.

Before the final appointment to his CDC position, Dr. Wendt realized he would hold responsibilities for protecting public health and safety through the control and prevention of diseases, so he decided to cut his long hair that he kept tied back in a ponytail and shaved his salt and pepper facial hair, presenting a cleaner image while overseeing the CDC.

Dr. Wendt was a serious man, and it was rare to see him smile.

He yelled, "Come in," when he heard the knock on his door. Dr. Margaret Hertz and Dr. Douglas Wadeson entered his office. Dr. Wendt said, "Have a seat."

Both doctors said, "Good morning," and sat down. Neither Dr. Hertz nor Dr. Wadeson knew why they had been summoned.

Dr. Wendt got right to the point of the meeting. "I believe we may have a profoundly serious problem. We know it is not uncommon to have one hundred undiagnosed deaths in the United States in a month, but we now have 321 undiagnosed deaths in three days. None of the victims had any underlying medical problems in the three days the deaths occurred in seventeen states." Dr. Wendt went on, "Since none of these victims had any underlying medical problems, we elevated the alert mode to CAT 10 and are retrieving blood, tissue, muscles, and organs from the 321 victims for testing to find a common denominator for these deaths. I am putting the two of you in charge of getting all available personnel to stop their current research projects and begin to work on diagnosing these deaths." Dr. Wendt continued, "I don't have to explain to each of you the depth of this problem as we have never experienced this many undiagnosed deaths in the United States in such a short period. I need detailed reports of our findings every hour on the hour until we have this diagnosed."

Dr. Hertz and Dr. Wadeson answered simultaneously, "Yes, Sir, we will get started immediately."

Both doctors stood up, and Dr. Wendt said, "Also, please advise everyone not to discuss these deaths outside of the CDC; we don't need a public panic." Dr. Hertz and Dr. Wadeson nodded in agreement with Dr. Wendt as they left his office and headed to the number-one laboratory.

Dr. Wendt picked up the receiver on his phone. When Miss Deplay answered, Dr. Wendt asked, "Can you get the CIA on the phone? Also, I must ask that you speak to no one about this call."

Miss Deplay answered, "Yes, Sir, I understand." A few moments later, Miss Deplay said, "The CIA is on line one." Dr. Wendt pressed the number one line and asked to speak to Mr. Nelson Whitcomb, the chief of the CIA.

Shortly after the call with Dr. Wendt, Mr. Whitcomb notified the President of the United States.

CHAPTER 10

Mr. Nelson Whitcomb and six other men from the United States security agencies, including the commissioner of the FDA, Department of Health and Human Services, Department of Defense, Central Intelligence Agency, Federal Bureau of Investigations, and United States Intelligence, sat at a round table in a conference room at the Hoover building. All six men were wearing their security badges.

Mr. Nelson Whitcomb started the meeting, "Thank you all for joining me this morning. I have spoken with Dr. Wendt with the CDC in Atlanta, who advised that we may have an epidemic! In the past three days, we have had 321 undiagnosed deaths in seventeen states. I don't have to tell you how urgent this matter is to our United States security." Mr. Whitcomb continued, "The CDC is conducting toxin screening and checking the blood, brain tissue, muscle specimens, and vital body organs to find out what is killing our United States citizens."

Mr. Gephart Tyler, head of the FBI, said, "I feel we must collect data on all 321 deaths, their homes, their cell phones, their computers, their travels, and everything they have done in the past three months of their lives."

Mr. Nelson Whitcomb answered, "I agree. All we have to find is one commonality between our victims, and we can stop these deaths before this turns out to be a full-blown epidemic." We certainly do not want this to be a huge embarrassment to our security bureaus.

Mr. Vincent Walker, head of Homeland Security, said, "We have had no indications of any bio-threats. Mr. Whitcomb and I have been discussing the matter of no unusual chatter for weeks now, which is very unusual."

Mr. James Fieser replied, "All is clear with the NSA, and I agree; let's check out these undiagnosed deaths ASAP."

Mr. Gephart Tyler answered, "I will get our top team of investigators on this immediately; we will go to the home of the first death and continue from

there. I'll brief our team, and we will leave for the first reported undiagnosed death in an hour." Mr. Gephart Tyler looked at his paperwork and continued, "Let me see, our first reported victim lived in York, Pennsylvania, so we will be headed for York in an hour."

Mr. Nelson Whitcomb said, "If anything shows up in any of our departments, we need to get on it right away and hold another meeting as soon as possible. This is at the top of all our lists, and POTUS has already been briefed. The president has asked that no one outside of this room know anything about this epidemic. Let us do our best to keep it from all news reporters."

CHAPTER 11

Mrs. Rossellini knocked on Father Frank's door and yelled, "Father Frank, are you okay?" She finally turned the doorknob, but the door was locked.

Mrs. Rossellini was worried about Father Frank; he did not eat dinner from the night before and did not show up for breakfast.

Mrs. Rossellini started to walk next door to the church. Once inside, she headed for the bishop's office. She knocked gently on the door, and the bishop's secretary came and opened the door. Mrs. Rossellini told the secretary her problem and was immediately ushered in to see the bishop.

Mrs. Rossellini said, "Good morning, Bishop. I'm sorry to bother you, but I'm very concerned about Father Frank." She continued to tell the bishop about Father Frank's dinner and breakfast and how she could not get any response from Father Frank's room.

The Bishop stood up, walked to the front room, and said to his secretary, "Would you please have the head of maintenance meet me at Father Frank's room?"

His secretary replied, "Yes, sir."

The Bishop and Mrs. Rossellini walked side by side to Father Frank's room. Jack, the head of maintenance, was already standing in front of Father Frank's room when the Bishop and Mrs. Rossellini arrived. The bishop said, "Jack, will you please unlock Father Frank's door?"

Jack answered, "Of course." Jack had the master key to every house and church room. Jack unlocked Father Frank's door, and the bishop walked in first. He saw Father Frank lying in bed.

As he got closer, he could see that Father Frank's coloring looked very pale, and Father Frank did not respond when the bishop called his name; the Bishop turned around and said to Jack, "Please call 911." They all left Father Frank's room, and Mrs. Rossellini put her hand to her mouth and started to cry. The bishop put his arm around Mrs. Rossellini to comfort her and said, "The medics will be here in a few minutes; let's sit down and pray for Father

Frank." Together, they walked into the living room, sat side by side, and prayed for Father Frank.

They could hear the sirens, and the medics were in Father Frank's room within minutes. One medic checked Father Frank's pause and listened for a heartbeat, but there was none. The medic squad walked out of the room toward the bishop. The medic who checked for a heartbeat said, "I'm so sorry, Bishop; the man in the bed has expired." Mrs. Rossellini screamed and started to cry very loudly. The bishop spoke to her and entered Father Frank's room to give him his last rites.

One medic told the bishop, "Sir, we have already called this to the police, and they should be here within minutes. Since this may be a crime scene, please keep everyone out of the room. The police will take it from here."

The bishop nodded and said, "I understand, and we will stay here and wait for the police."

When the police arrived, one of them spoke to the bishop and Mrs. Rossellini. He recorded all the details the bishop and Mrs. Rossellini provided, writing it down on his notepad. The other two police detectives and the coroner entered Father Frank's room.

Once inside the room, the coroner examined the body while the police did all the usual detective work: fingerprinting everything, looking in every drawer, and bagging several items. They looked in the suitcase next to Father Frank's bed and bagged the two empty bottles of wine, a wine glass, and the wilted flower for further examination. They checked the closet and looked all over the room for blood but found none. Nothing they could find would indicate this was a possible homicide. It took the police and coroner close to an hour before they walked out and talked to the bishop.

The police introduced themselves to the bishop, told him their findings, and said, "The hospital will get back to you as soon as they know the cause of Father Frank's death."

The hospital never called the bishop but notified the CDC in Atlanta.

CHAPTER 12

Robbie looked at his watch and said, "Oh shit, I'm going to be late." Robbie had followed in his father's footsteps and was in the Navy and stationed at San Diego.

Robbie thought to himself, Dad and I just became friends again after the blow-up about me being a gay black male in the military. Robbie was usually late; he was supposed to meet his father at 10:00 a.m. for a shopping spree for his mother's birthday.

Robbie was stuck on the highway surrounded by big trucks emitting gas fumes when he thought, "This is terrible; I am about to throw up from these damn fumes. Finally, the truck in the left lane pulled to the right lane, and Robbie aggressively passed all the trucks. Robbie thought to himself, Road rage; I have road rage!"

Exiting the highway, he took the first right turn and saw his father waiting there. He parked the car, quickly jumped out, and began apologizing to his father, blaming the trucks, not because he overslept.

His father said, "Are you ready to buy out San Diego for your mom's birthday?"

Robbie said, "Yes, sir, I'm ready to surprise Mom; she will be so excited tonight."

His father said, "Let's go into the shop down the street, Fumes and Bubbles.

Robbie thought, Great, more fumes!

The bells on the door came alive as they entered the store; Robbie said, "That is a nice sound!"

His father said, "Yes, I have never heard bells with that sound before; we are starting our shopping spree off with bells!" They started to look around for just the right gifts.

As Robbie picked up a perfume bottle, the clerk said, "That is the latest scent from Paris; we just got it in."

Robbie replied, "The bottle is beautiful; how do you say the perfume's name?"

The clerk answered, "It's called Chanson, which means 'song' in French."

Robbie said, "We will take the large bottle. Do you gift wrap?"

The clerk answered, "Yes, here are all the wrapping papers we use; you may pick the one you like the best."

Robbie said, "I will take that one with all the purple shades. My mother loves every color of purple."

Robbie's father said with a chuckle, "Robbie, do you think your mother would like this assortment of soaps, bubble baths, and lotions since all of them are purple?"

Robbie answered, "Yes, Mom would love them."

Robbie's father told the clerk, "You can wrap this up with the same paper."

The clerk responded, "Yes, sir." Robbie started to look around in the men's section. Robbie picked out several items, including cologne, soap, deodorant, and shaving cream, all in the same scent. After his father paid for his mother's gifts, Robbie said, "I will take these items, but I don't need these wrapped." Robbie finished paying for his merchandise and exited the store with his father, where they once again heard the bells come alive.

"Where to next, Dad, Robbie said," His dad said, "Let us go to the Last Chapter and buy Mom a book."

Off to the bookstore they went. Once in the bookstore, they looked around for a few minutes when Robbie said, "Hey, Dad, let's get a cup of Shining Day coffee and one of their delicious biscotti covered with chocolate and nuts!"

Dad answered, "Sounds like a plan to me; that coffee smells so good." Robbie approached the Shining Day and got two black coffees and two biscotti. His dad joined him at a table, where they sat and talked while they enjoyed their coffee and biscotti. Once finished, they put their trash in the can and returned to shopping.

Robbie's Dad asked the lady at the information booth, "Can you suggest a good book for my wife?" The clerk made several suggestions and told Robbie's dad where to find the books. They headed to the book section to find the right book for Mom. Robbie's dad ended up selecting three books for his mother.

Robbie and his dad then began shopping for themselves. Robbie bought a CD, two books, and two candles; one large candle for his mother, which was purple, and the other one for him. Robbie's dad purchased a new book about the Korean War. Serving as an admiral during the Korean War, his dad never passed any book related to this war.

Robbie's Dad said at the checkout, "Great idea; I would have never thought

about getting your mother a candle."

As they left the bookstore, Robbie's dad looked at his watch and said, "Are you getting hungry, son?"

Robbie answered, "Yes, I'm starving even though I ate a biscotti."

Robbie's Dad said, "Let's eat at the Wharf's Edge; I love their food.

Robbie replied, "Sounds great to me."

Robbie and his dad walked to the end of the pier and entered the restaurant. The hostess sat them shortly after their waiter arrived at their table. The waiter was a stunning six-foot-tall man with big biceps, shiny black hair, and a beautiful smile with gorgeous teeth. He wore a black short-sleeved shirt with the restraint logo and his name embroidered on the shirt. The waiter introduced himself, and his name was Josh.

Robbie thought he was beautiful, But I had better behave, or my father would kill me. I will have to come back here sometime when I am alone.

Robbie and his dad gave Josh their drink order, and Josh told them about their specials.

Robbie's dad said, "We will get the flowers and chocolates last, so they are nice and fresh for Mom; we don't want the chocolates to melt." As Robbie was about to answer his dad, Josh came to the table and brought them their drinks. Dad ordered his usual scotch on the rocks, and Robbie ordered a martini.

Josh asked, "Are you two ready to order?"

Robbie's dad said, "Yes, I will have the grouper with melted cheese and grounded nuts."

Robbie smiled at Josh and said, "Dido, I will have the same."

Josh said, "Thank you. Enjoy your drinks, and let me know if you need anything else."

Robbie and his Dad both said, "Thank you."

Robbie's dad said, "Son, I'm so happy we spent the day together. This is an incredibly special day for me and your mother."

Robbie answered, "Dad, you can't be happier than I am today; we are family again."

They finished eating, paid the check, and headed to The Beautiful Lady shop. They would buy Mom a beautiful new silk nightgown with a matching robe and slippers. Finding the perfect purple lingerie set for Mom did not take long. The clerk placed the lingerie set in a purple box and wrapped it with purple paper with flower prints. They paid for the lingerie gift and left the store destined for the next shop, The Sweet Tooth.

Robbie's Mom only liked one kind of chocolate, so his purchase would be easy. They asked the clerk for a huge box of milk chocolate almond toffee.

She asked, "Would you like this wrapped?"

Robbie said, "Yes, please; by any chance, do you have any purple wrapping paper?"

The clerk replied, "Yes, sir, I will wrap it for you in purple."

Dad paid the bill, and before they left, Robbie said, "I think I will get a little chocolate for me to eat." Robbie asked for a half pound of his favorite chocolate called All About Nuts. Robbie paid for his purchase, and they went out the door with two more packages.

Robbie's dad told him, "Other than flowers, can you think of anything else we should get for your mother?"

Robbie answered, "No, I can't think of anything else for Mom, but I'm thirsty. Let's go to the drugstore so I can get a bottle of water and some toothpaste."

They walked into the drugstore, and Robbie grabbed a large bottle of water and a new kind of toothpaste with a buy-one-and-get-one-free sale. Robbie walked to the counter to pay for his items and then drank all the water in less than a minute. Robbie's dad said, "Son, you must have been thirsty! Let's get this over with and get to the florist."

Before they knew it, they stood before the White Gardenia. Robbie told the clerk, "We want to purchase a flower arrangement fit for a queen." They first picked out a huge purple vase, and Robbie told the clerk, "We want a lot of different shades of purple flowers, as many as you have, with a touch of other colors."

The clerk said, "How much would you like to spend on the arrangement?"

Robbie's dad said, "Let's keep it around seventy-five dollars."

The clerk said, "It will be fit for a queen."

Robbie and his dad watched as the clerk used her magic. When she was finished making the arrangement, it was beautiful and looked like it was fit for a queen.

Robbie's dad paid for the flowers, and they said, "Thank you so much; you are incredibly talented, miss."

She smiled and said, "Thank you."

They headed for the door and walked to their cars. They talked about how excited Mom would be when they got home. Robbie said, "I will follow you, Dad; see you at home."

Robbie and his dad got in their cars and headed home for the big birthday surprise. Robbie's mother could not believe her eyes when they surprised her with all the beautiful purple-wrapped presents. Robbie's dad opened an expensive bottle of champagne, and the three of them had cheers while his mother opened all her presents.

Robbie's mother must have said thank you a hundred times, saying, "I love everything you two got for me, but the two things I love the most are you!" Robbie walked to his mother, giving her a big kiss and a wonderful love hug.

Robbie's dad said, "Okay, where are we all having dinner? It's your birthday, so you choose your favorite restaurant."

Robbie's Mother said, "This is easy for me; how does The Villa Palma sound to you two?"

Robbie and his dad said, "Great!" simultaneously. They finished the bottle of champagne and were ready to have the best dinner in California!

As they got outside, Robbie said, "I will follow you two because if I take the lead, you will not be able to keep up with me!" They all laughed and were off to dinner.

When Robbie got in his car, he called The Villa Palma, told them three were coming for a birthday celebration, and asked if he could reserve the best table for three. When they arrived at the restaurant, they were escorted to a table with a beautiful view of the Pacific Ocean. Robbie's dad ordered another bottle of champagne. While the waiter retrieved one of the best bottles of champagne, they all looked over the menu. The waiter returned with the champagne, made a big production in popping the cork, poured each of them a flute of bubbly, and then set the bottle in the table side champagne bucket. Robbie's dad ordered the "All In" appetizer, filled with seafood, shrimp, clams, lobster claws, mussels, oysters, and crabs. They were all cheering with the champagne when their appetizer arrived.

Robbie's Mother said, "After I eat this, I won't have any room for a meal!"

Robbie's dad said, "Order one anyway, and you can take it home and eat it tomorrow."

Robbie's parents ordered Blanquette de Veau, their favorite meal at the Villa Palma. Robbie ordered the Black Label sirloin steak dinner and a side dish of mixed vegetables with an assortment of nuts, and Dad ordered another bottle of their best champagne. They ate, talked, and laughed throughout their entire dinner. After eating a small portion of their meals, all three asked the waiter for takeout boxes.

When the waiter returned, three other waiters accompanied him, singing "Happy Birthday" while setting a beautiful birthday cake on the table. Robbie and his dad joined the waiters in singing "Happy Birthday." Everyone in the restaurant clapped, and Robbie's mother stood up and thanked everyone. The cake was delicious, and they needed one more "to-go" box!

Before they parted ways, Robbie said, "Mom and Dad, I have had a blessed day. Thank you both for loving me with all of your hearts!" They all hugged before they parted ways.

As Robbie drove back to the San Diego naval base, he thought about how excited his mom was over the birthday celebration and all the beautiful gifts. Robbie thought to himself, My mom looks like she is my age. Her teeth are beautiful and white, and she keeps her hairstyle up with the latest style. I sure hope I look as young as she does when I am her age.

Robbie pulled into a parking space, got out of the car, and gathered all the bags with the items he had purchased earlier in the day. He was thinking to himself how much fun the day had been. Robbie walked toward his ship and went to his quarters.

Once inside, he unpacked all his purchases and put them in their proper places. He then placed his leftover meal in the small refrigerator beside his bed. As Robbie lit his new candle, his mind wandered to Josh, their waiter at lunch. Robbie thought to himself, I am going back there for lunch as soon as possible; I would like to get to know Mr. Josh.

Robbie put his new CD in his Bose CD player and prepared for bed. After washing his face and hands and brushing his teeth, thinking, This is by far the best toothpaste I have ever had, he picked up his new book and lay on his bed. Robbie thought to himself, a delightful scent from my new candle, great music playing from my new CD, and a good book to read; only one thing could make this better: if Josh were with me. Robbie fell asleep before his CD finished playing.

CHAPTER 13

Ethel Lou was coughing as she was driving her old VW Beetle. The exhaust fumes from the back of the car leaked into her car from somewhere. Ethel Lou thought, I must see if I can find someone to fix my favorite buddy, my hippie VW Beetle.

Ethel Lou lived alone in a one-bedroom apartment with four cats and a seven-foot iguana named Flintstone. Whenever she went anywhere, she would take Flintstone, who would lie on the dashboard of her car. Everyone who passed her always reacted when they saw Flintstone sitting on the dashboard. Ethel Lou loved it when anyone talked to her about Flintstone. Flintstone was the only way Ethel Lou could get attention; she loved her iguana!

Ethel Lou was not close to her family because she could not get along with anyone. She spent most of her life by herself, thinking about what she should be doing but never got around to doing. She pretended she was happy, but she was the opposite. Ethel Lou was very unhappy and depressed most of the time because she did not like her appearance but never took any initiative to change. She had a difficult time keeping a job. It was a lifetime record for her if she was still in a position after two weeks at a new job. She was lazy, bossy, and thought she knew everything about everything. Her low self-esteem made it exceedingly difficult for anyone to get along with her.

Ethel Lou did not have Flintstone with her that day because she was going shopping. Although Flintstone came from a tropical country, she did not want to risk Flintstone getting too hot on the dashboard while she

"

was shopping. Ethel Lou had her food stamp allowance on her SNAP card and was heading for her favorite store, Large Loads. It was not her favorite store, but it was the only one she could afford. All the items at Large Loads came from other retail stores that were clearing out damaged merchandise, nearing expiration, or had poor sales performance.

Ethel Lou pulled her bright yellow Beetle into a parking place, still coughing from the fumes as she exited the car. She was in her late forties with dyed bright orange, frizzy, curly hair. She tipped the scale at 350 pounds or more! No one could believe she fit inside her little car. Sometimes, people would laugh when they saw her get out of her Beetle. It was a sight to see!

Ethel Lou was dressed in a blue-flowered smock with blue shorts and plastic sandals. She usually dressed this way to be comfortable. After all, her life was all about her comfort. When you wear size 5x, it is hard to be fashionable and comfortable at the same time.

Ethel Lou's greatest features were her beautiful face, hands, and feet. The skin on her face gleamed all the time. She would be a stunning woman if she were not overweight and wore her hair in a standard fashion. Ethel Lou was too young to be going through menopause, but she always carried a cloth with her because her face perspired. She was always drying her face and neck.

Ethel Lou entered Large Loads and walked toward the carts. She got her shopping list out of her purse and started to shop. In the grocery section, she got six dented cans of tuna fish and four dented cans of sardines. She put a loaf of bread in her cart, a busted-up twenty-four-pack of bottled water, a dented can of mixed nuts, three bags of rice, several bags of pasta, two jars of spaghetti sauce, a big box of off-brand oatmeal, a dented jar of peanut butter, the least expensive tub of margarine she could find, and a damaged box of chocolates. Ethel Lou thought, I am going to have a feast for dinner tonight, and I cannot wait.

Ethel Lou looked at her store list and headed to find a candle. She always enjoyed candlelight at night. On her way to get a candle, she passed by a big box of books. She rooted around in the box and found three paperback books. Two books were missing the back cover, and the third had a torn front cover. Ethel Lou loved to read, so she was happy finding three books she could get for one dollar. She thought, Now I will have something to do; I will read since my cable was turned off again for lack of payment.

Ethel Lou picked out the biggest orange candle she could find and gave it the sniff test. She thought this candle smelled good, and in the basket, it went. She then got shampoo, a cheap bottle of perfume, a damaged box of soap from one of those expensive bath and body shops, and a tube of toothpaste that she had never seen before. Ethel Lou headed for the checkout

but stopped her cart when she saw the bouquets of beautiful flowers. She wanted a bouquet but thought I shouldn't get flowers; I cannot afford them, but I will treat myself just this once. Having flowers in my apartment will make me feel good. She picked out the only bouquet with orange flowers and baby's breath, as she loved orange.

Ethel Lou got in the checkout line and waited her turn. She thought, I hope they will charge my SNAP card for everything I am buying, even though I can't eat books, a candle, perfume, or flowers! She laughed to herself. I will try to get away with it and wait to see how the clerk handles it. It was her turn to check out, and when the clerk finished ringing up all the merchandise, she handed her the SNAP card. The clerk completed the transaction and handed Ethel the receipt. Ethel Lou grinned and thanked the clerk as she bagged up all the groceries and merchandise.

As Ethel Lou left the store, she thought, "This will be a great day; I will have lots of food to eat, candlelight, books to read, and beautiful flowers". Outside the grocery store, she headed to the racks containing the free ad magazines and papers. She grabbed one of each and threw three magazines and two papers into her cart like she always did, took them home, yet never picked one up to read. As she arrived at her car, she smelled her flowers as she put her purchases on the back floorboard and seat. She sat in the driver's seat with her belly pressed into the steering wheel and headed for home.

Ethel Lou found the perfect parking space close to her apartment. She exited her car with her new purchases and four water bottles and walked to her apartment building. As she unlocked the front door, she thought, I will need a nap after I walk up seven floors with all these bags! There was no elevator at the apartment building where Ethel Lou lived, so the monthly rent on the top floor was the least costly.

Inside the apartment lobby, Ethel Lou unlocked her mailbox and collected her mail, which consisted of junk advertisements. She threw her mail in the bag and the grocery store ad magazines. As she started her walk up the stairs, she would smell her flowers as she reached each floor to help give her the strength to make it up one more flight of stairs.

Finally, she was home on the seventh floor. She unlocked the door to her apartment, and she immediately saw three of her four cats. They were hungry, and Ethel Lou said, "Mommy is home, and I will feed you all right away!" After piling her mail and ad papers on top of the stacks already on her coffee table, Ethel Lou walked through the only path to the kitchen. She grabbed the cat food bag and filled the big bowls with cat food. Before setting the bowls down to the floor, all four cats were there waiting for their food.

Ethel Lou started on the hunt to find her one and only vase to put her flowers in. Ethel Lou said to herself, "Now, where did I put that vase?" She stood still in the middle of the worst hoarder mess in the world! There were boxes, old mail, news magazines, plastic containers, glass bottles, empty flowerpots, bags of trash, broken dishes and glasses, empty cans, and boxes of costume jewelry that Ethel Lou collected. In one corner, the junk was piled up to the ceiling. For the three years she lived in the apartment, she never threw anything away, and the entire apartment smelled like cat urine.

Ethel Lou's apartment had smelled this way for so long that she had become accustomed to the odor and could no longer smell the cat urine. She stepped over numerous items before she got to the closet in the living room, having to move numerous items to open the closet door. Finally, she opened the door, and the contents started falling out of the closet on her and all over the floor! Ethel Lou said, "There you are, beautiful vase!" She returned to the kitchen, filling the vase with water and arranging her bouquet of orange flowers.

Ethel Lou thought to herself, Now where will I sit my flowers? There was nowhere in the apartment to sit anything because everything was piled up on all the furniture! Ethel Lou decided to make room for them in her bedroom. She walked through the only path to her bedroom, moved things around on her dresser, and made a place for her flowers!

While in the bedroom, she talked to Flintstone and said, "Look what I got for us today, beautiful flowers!" Flintstone was lounging on the bed and did not even raise his head. Ethel Lou returned to the kitchen, unpacking her bags and setting the items in the only open space on the counter next to the sink. She opened a can of tuna, made herself a sandwich, retrieved some collard greens from the refrigerator, and joined Flintstone on the bed. She shredded the collard greens and placed them in front of Flintstone, and they both enjoyed their usual meal together in bed.

CHAPTER 14

WEDNESDAY, MAY 6TH
GEPHART TYLER AND THE FBI SEARCH TEAM
YORK, PA

Gephart Tyler rang the doorbell at the Thomas residence. A young man answered the door and said, "Hello, what can I do for you?"

Gephart Tyler said, "We are here from the FBI," as they showed their badges. Gephart Tyler continued, "We are very sorry for your loss, Mr. Thomas; we are here to investigate the cause of your wife's death."

Michael said, "Please come in." All four FBI agents entered the Thomas home. Michael said, "What can I do to help you?"

Gephart Tyler answered, "We have a search warrant," as he handed it to Michael. Just allow us full access to your home, inside and outside, to your computer and your wife's car." Gephart Tyler continued, "Can you think of any reason this tragedy could have happened to your wife?"

Michael answered, "No, I have no damn idea; I don't know anything Izzy did that would have caused her death. You know my wife was pregnant, and my baby girl also died."

Gephart Tyler answered, "Yes, we are aware that your wife was pregnant, which makes her death so much worse than the others; we are so sorry, Mr. Thomas."

Michael answered, "Please call me Michael and make yourselves at home; search whatever you need; everything inside and outside this home is yours. I want to know what happened to my wife and daughter." Michael continued, "My wife Izzy went shopping with her best friend two days before she died; maybe Sandy could help you."

Gephart Tyler answered, "Please call me Gephart, and yes, we may need to speak with Sandy; we will let you know." Gephart turned to his men and said, "Let's split up and start our investigation." Michael sat on the living room sofa with tears in his eyes. He never even looked at the search warrant; he just threw it on the table. He sat and watched everything the FBI did through the flower arrangements people had sent him since Izzy died.

The FBI was taking samples of everything, and Michael watched until they

split up, going upstairs and outside to the garage.

The men were there for six hours, and Michael started to cry when he saw them take some of Izzy's clothing. Gephart asked Michael, "Where is the clothing your wife was wearing when she went to the hospital?

Michael answered, "They are still in a plastic bag in my car. Her jewelry is also in the bag. I just haven't been able to make myself get them."

Gephart answered, "May we please take them with us? Not the jewelry, just the clothing."

Michael said, "Yes, of course, you may take them."

One of the men went to the garage and got the plastic bag. Returning to the living room, he removed the jewelry from the bag and laid it between the flower arrangements on the coffee table in front of Michael. Michael touched Izzy's jewelry and started to cry.

The FBI had taken a hundred bags filled with items from Michael's home. Michael stood up, walked out front, and saw one of the FBI agents taking a sample of every flower from Izzy's gardens. After taking a scoop of soil and placing it into a container, the FBI agent asked Michael, "Did Izzy receive any unlabeled seeds in the mail?"

Michael replied, "I remember Izzy telling me a few months ago about an envelope addressed to her that came in the mail without a return address, and it contained seeds that she did not recognize. She thought one of her friends was secretive, sending her exotic flower seeds for her garden. She was excited to plant the seeds to see what grew. I do not know exactly where Izzy planted those seeds." Michael looked to the right and saw their computer being put in the car's trunk.

Michael walked over to the car and told the FBI agent, "My wife Izzy just took off from her work for maternity leave last Friday. She has a computer in her office; you may want to check that."

The FBI agent said, "Thank you. We will need the address of your wife's office, and we will need to have her friend's phone number.

Michael said, "I will get Sandy's phone number for you." Before Michael left to get Sandy's phone number, he said, "Sandy was my wife's secretary, so I'm sure she can help you out at Izzy's office."

The FBI agent said, "Thank you, Michael."

Michael walked into his home and wrote the address to Izzy's office and Sandy's phone number. He walked back outside and handed the paper to the FBI agent.

Gephart Tyler walked up to Michael and said, "We thank you very much for your help, Michael. One last thing, may we please have your wife's cell phone to send for examination?"

"You may take Izzy's cell phone; I will get it now." Michael retrieved Izzy's cell phone from the end table, where she was asleep when he came home from work on Monday. He returned and handed Izzy's cell phone to Gephart.

As Gephart departed, he told Michael, "As soon as we find anything, I promise we will let you know."

Michael said, "Thank you." The two men shook hands, and the FBI agents entered their cars and left. As they pulled out of the driveway, a florist delivery truck entered Michael's driveway; Michael thought, "I'm going to call Sandy right now to let her know—no more flowers, and give any monetary donations to a charity she thinks Izzy would like. I will also ask Sandy to come and take all of these flowers to people in the hospital who did not get flowers; my Izzy would love this idea.

CHAPTER 15

Dr. Rudolph Wendt walked to the infectious disease lab in his white coat. It was 7:15 a.m., and Dr. Wendt was already hard at work. He had just gotten off the phone from a lengthy conversation with Mr. Nelson Whitcomb from the CIA. As he walked, all he could think about was his conversation with Nelson Whitcomb. Mr. Whitcomb briefed Dr. Wendt on yesterday's meeting with the FBI, FDA, CIA, and NSA. The death rate was increasing at a rapid rate across the United States.

Dr. Wendt entered the dressing room at the lab. He removed his lab coat and put on his gray lab suit, latex gloves, and face mask. Everyone who entered the lab had to protect themselves from the thousands of infectious vials that filled the lab.

Before Dr. Wendt entered the lab, he removed his glasses and positioned his right eye in front of the security eye detector. The security system buzzed, allowing him access to open the lab's vaulted door. Everyone working in the lab acknowledged his presence as Dr. Wendt entered. Dr. Wendt motioned for the top twelve infectious disease doctors in the United States to join him in the conference room. Dr. Wendt sat at the head of the huge, long table as his staff of experts joined him one by one.

Dr. Wendt pulled down his mask and began talking to his staff. "Good morning to you all. I met with Dr. Hertz and Dr. Wadeson yesterday about a critical problem. As of yesterday, we had 321 undiagnosed deaths in seventeen states here in the US," Dr. Wendt continued, "As of this morning, we now have 2,493 undiagnosed deaths in thirty-three of our states. The World Health Organization has notified us that only a few deaths have occurred in other countries. Gentlemen, our world has an immense epidemic, and we are nowhere near any cause diagnosis." Dr. Wendt continued, "I am putting all our staff on red alert, which means we don't leave our lab until we find the diagnosis." Dr. Wendt said, "All of these deaths have occurred in the past five days, and the FBI is starting today to meet with family members of the dead to see if they can find a correlation for these deaths. Also, today, we will receive more blood samples, skin samples, brain tissue, muscle tissue, and samples of vital organs from the victims who have succumbed to this pandemic happening across the United States." Dr. Wendt said, "As you all know, the red alert also means we all wear our full lab gear. No one is to enter this lab without their gray suit of armor and oxygen helmet. Are there any questions?"

Dr. Wadeson pulled his mask down and said, "After our meeting yesterday morning, Dr. Hertz and I checked out twenty samples from one victim with no findings, none at all."

Dr. Wendt replied, "I'm afraid we have a new strain of the disease, biotoxin, or virus spreading all over our country very quickly. Let us all get to work and report all your findings to me ASAP."

Everyone got up and headed for the dressing room to change into their gray armor as Dr. Wendt headed back to his office to contact the Food and Drug Administration to get their perspective and if there had been any reports of tainted foods in any parts of the United States.

Arriving at his office, he asked Miss Deplay, "Can you get the FDA Commissioner on the phone?"

Miss Deplay said, "Certainly, I will call right now."

After his phone conversation with Commissioner David Simmons, he was even further frustrated as there had been no reported cases of tainted food that may be contributing to the deaths.

CHAPTER 16

Mr. Bo was walking back and forth in the servant's kitchen, waiting for Florentine. Mr. Bo looked at the clock; it was 5:45 a.m., yet Florentine still had not arrived. Maria said, "Mr. Bo, you had better go see where Florentine is."

Mr. Bo replied, "Yes, I had better go get Florentine; maybe she overslept," he said as he started to walk up the servant's staircase. Once upstairs, standing outside Florentine's room, he called, "Florentine, are you awake?" There was no answer, so Mr. Bo opened Florentine's door and entered her room. Florentine was still in bed; Mr. Bo touched her lightly, not to scare her, and called out her name, "Florentine, Florentine, it's time to get up." Florentine did not move, let alone answer. Mr. Bo was alarmed as he walked around Florentine's bed to get a better look at her. Slowly and with caution, Mr. Bo touched Florentine's cheek. Mr. Bo screamed out loud, "Dear Lord, sweet Jesus, Oh no!" Florentine's cheek was cold, and her lips were blue. Florentine was dead.

Mr. Bo ran from the room and almost fell, descending the stairs. Once he returned to the kitchen, he told Maria that Florentine was dead. He then started to pace back and forth as he thought, "What in the world has happened, and what do I do? Do I tell Mr. and Mrs. Kingsley before I call 911?" After a few moments, he came to his senses and realized he should advise the Kingsleys before calling 911 so the first responder's sirens would not scare them when arriving at the house.

Mr. Bo started to walk to the Kingsleys' bedroom. He climbed the beautiful spiral staircase to the second floor and went to the only room on the left side, the Kingsleys' spacious bedroom. Mr. Bo lightly knocked on the room and said, "Mr. and Mrs. Kingsley, this is Mr. Bo, and I must speak with you right now."

It seemed forever until Mr. Kingsley opened the door, saying, "Yes, Mr. Bo, what do you need?"

Mr. Bo said, "I don't need anything, but I have awfully bad news. Florentine has passed away during the night, and I wanted to tell you and Mrs. Kingsley before I call 911."

Mr. Kingsley said, "Oh No, Mr. Bo, are you sure she is dead?" Mr. Bo shook his head yes. Mr. Kingsley said, "Go and call 911, and we will be down in a few minutes."

Mr. Bo said, "Yes, sir," as he turned around to go downstairs to call 911.

Mr. Bo went into the office and dialed 911. As he heard the 911 operator state, "911, what is your emergency?" Mr. Bo responded, "One of our servants was found dead in her bed; can you send the police and an ambulance?" After giving the 911 operator the house address, Mr. Bo hung up the phone.

It was only a minute before the police and ambulance were at the front door. Mr. Bo had already opened the gates to the estate and the front door. The first responders came in, wheeling a gurney and carrying their bags. Mr. Bo said, "Thank you for getting here so quickly; please follow me." All nine followed Mr. Bo up the servant's staircase to Florentine's room.

One of the policemen said to Mr. Bo, "We'll take it from here; you may go back downstairs."

Mr. and Mrs. Kingsley were waiting in their dining room for Mr. Bo. Mr. Bo entered the room and said, "They told me to leave Florentine's room and they would take care of everything."

Maria entered the dining room with a silver tray and silver coffee tureen with matching sugar and creamer. Maria said, "I thought you could all use a cup of coffee." Maria poured all three of them a cup of coffee and left the silver service set on the dining room table.

As Maria left, Mrs. Kingsley said, "Thank you so much, Maria; one more thing, would you please call Nadia's and order breakfast to be delivered for Mr. Kingsley and me since you know what we like?"

Maria answered, "I will call right away, Mrs. Kingsley."

After Mrs. Kingsley sipped coffee, she asked Mr. Bo, "What in the world has happened?"

Mr. Bo replied, "When Florentine was not in our kitchen at 5:45, I decided I'd better check on her. I thought she overslept, but when I called her name, she did not respond, so I touched her. She was cold as ice, and her face had already turned blue. I have no idea what happened to her. She was fine when she went to bed last night."

Mrs. Kingsley said, "Mr. Bo, as soon as they open, I want you to call the Deeper Than Clean cleaning service we have used in the past and have everything in that room disposed of, and I mean everything. We can't take the chance that something in her room is infectious and anyone else gets sick in our home."

Mr. Bo replied, "I will call them at 8:00 a.m. sharp, Mrs. Kingsley."

Mrs. Kingsley said, "Since you were in her room and touched her, I want you to shower and dispose of your clothing."

Mr. Bo said, "I'll go right now." Mr. Bo took his coffee and headed to his quarters to shower.

It seemed like an eternity until the police came downstairs, wheeling Florentine's dead body out of the house. Detective Hereford asked the Kingsleys question after question, the same ones they had asked Mr. Bo. None of them knew anything since Florentine had just started to work for them.

Detective Hereford said, "The paramedics can't find a reason for Florentine's death. We have ruled out homicide, but we may have to return to her quarters again."

Mrs. Kingsley said, "Her whole room will be cleaned and everything deposed of by the end of today; we can't take the chance of anything happening to anyone else."

Detective Hereford said, "We have taken cultures, hair, fingerprints, and samples of everything we need. It is okay for you to have the room cleaned." Detective Hereford was not about to argue with anyone who lived in one of the most prestigious homes in Palm Beach.

Before Detective Hereford left, he told the Kingsleys, "You may call the coroner's office tomorrow to see if they found the cause of death. Hopefully, they can share the cause with you so you can put your mind at rest. If we have any further questions, we will call you. Thank you for all your cooperation today." Detective Hereford walked toward the front door and left.

Mrs. Kingsley said, "This is terrible, that poor woman. Florentine was a marvelous chef and a genuinely nice lady. I guess we will have to run another ad for a chef." She continued, "Until we find a replacement and the cause of Florentine's death, I suggest we all eat out or have our meals delivered." Mrs. Kingsley then poured herself another cup of coffee.

CHAPTER 17

THURSDAY, MAY 7TH
EMMA FROM LONDON, ENGLAND AIRPORT
ATLANTA, GEORGIA

Emma was fuming because her secretary did not get her a direct flight from New York City to London. Instead, she would have to layover in the damn Atlanta, Georgia, airport for three hours. Emma was bored sitting in the concourse, as she had already read the newspaper on her flight from New York, so she decided to go into one of the airport bookstores to look for a good novel. After scouring fifteen books, she finally found the right novel and purchased the hardback book. Emma thought paperback books were for poor people to read. She paid for the book and headed out to search for a restaurant that would have decent food.

Emma was used to having the best, the best of everything! She only went to New York City to buy her clothing on Fifth Avenue. Emma always had to be the first to purchase the best new clothing lines to show off her beautiful figure.

As she passed restaurant after restaurant, she finally chose one only because she was extremely hungry. After the hostess seated her, she ordered a very dry vodka martini with lots of olives and asked for top-shelf vodka for the cocktail. After a few minutes, her martini was delivered to her table. Emma sipped her martini as she read the menu. She was delighted to find some dishes she would like and ordered the grilled salmon with a salad and rice pilaf.

Emma was working on her second martini when her meal arrived. She was never nice to a waitress and never said thank you, but she did leave a huge tip on the tab. As Emma left the restaurant, she retrieved the new perfume bottle from her purse and gave herself a spritz; she certainly did not want to smell like fish.

While returning to her departure gate, Emma began searching for an airport shop that sold sundry products, needing a toothbrush and toothpaste as she always brushed her teeth after every meal to keep them beautiful and white. She entered a shop that had everything she needed plus more. She purchased a small kit with a toothbrush, dental floss, and toothpaste. She also bought a magazine, a bottle of water, a small bag of chocolates, and a bag of dried fruit and nuts. After making her purchases, Emma headed for the ladies' room, where she brushed her teeth and disposed of the brush and toothpaste in the waste basket. Emma thought that was the best-tasting toothpaste I have ever used. She then washed her hands and touched up her makeup and hair.

She left the ladies' room and continued walking to her departure gate when she noticed her favorite shop, Bubbles Galore. She went into the shop and smelled every soap and bubble bath bar. She purchased two bars of soap and one bottle of bubble bath.

As Emma left the shop, she looked at the flight departure monitor and saw that her flight was delayed for two more hours. She became irritated and mumbled, "That damn secretary of mine will be fired the minute I get home if I ever do get home!"

Arriving at the departure lounge, Emma took a seat away from the other passengers and began reading the novel. Although there were twenty empty seats in the departure lounge, an older lady with a huge bouquet of flowers sat down next to her. Emma began to sneeze immediately from the scent of the flowers. As Emma got her handkerchief out of her purse, the lady said, "I'm sorry, do you have allergies?" Emma blew her nose and answered the lady, "Yes, I do!" With that, Emma got up and moved to another seat.

As Emma continued reading her novel, she got chocolates from her purse, ate them, and drank bottled water. After finishing her chocolates, she returned to her purse and took out her fruits and nuts. Before long, Emma had completely devoured all the mix.

Emma was extremely bored. She got up to check out the departure board again. Since there was still one hour and 30 minutes before boarding, she decided to get another drink. Emma headed to the nearest concourse bar and ordered another very dry vodka martini and bottled water. While sipping her cocktail, she continued to read her novel. After finishing her martini, she checked her watch and ordered another drink. While sipping her second martini, Emma thought, I am sure glad this novel is so good. It was approaching the aircraft boarding time, so she finished her drink, paid the bartender, and headed back to her gate.

As she approached the gate, she heard the announcement for first-class passenger boarding. She quickly got in line with her boarding pass and passport, presented the documents to the gate attendant for inspection, and entered the jet bridge. After entering the aircraft, the flight attendant greeted Emma and directed her to her first-class seat.

Emma made herself comfortable, arranging the items from her first-class amenity kit and unfolding the blanket for the night flight. She was interrupted by the flight attendant, who asked, "Can I get you something to drink before takeoff?"

Emma responded, "Heavens, no, I've already had four martinis waiting for this damn plane!" Emma retrieved some Lysol disinfectant sheets from her carry-on bag and began wiping every surface around her. She cleaned the pullout tray table, the overhead light switch, the air vent, the call button, and even the seat belt buckle, knowing it was considered the filthiest surface on an aircraft. Then, she took her hand sanitizer from her purse and cleaned her hands. While they completed the boarding process, Emma began reading her novel. Finally, the plane was taxing for takeoff.

Shortly after takeoff, Emma turned on her overhead light so she could see to read and hit the flight attendant call button. When the flight attendant came to Emma's seat, she asked her about the smell of fumes. The flight attendant assured her the fumes were not harmful to anyone, and sometimes, the jet fuel fumes got into the aircraft's ventilation system during takeoff. Emma was unhappy about the fumes and glared at the flight attendant without saying a word. After reaching cruising altitude, Emma continued reading her novel and enjoyed a glass of champagne and a cup of warm nuts.

The attendant began taking the first-class passenger dinner order one hour into the flight. Emma ordered the pecan-encrusted filet of sole entrée, and by then, Emma was on her third glass of champagne. Emma was enjoying her book but could hardly wait to land at Heathrow in London, where there was to be a limousine waiting for her if her secretary remembered to order one!

Five hours into the flight, the flight attendant turned off Emma's light, cleaned off her tray, and put it back into place; Emma was fast asleep. When the plane landed, everyone was busy opening the upper luggage storage bins and getting their luggage together while they yawned and stretched, trying to wake up.

The flight attendant opened the aircraft door, and the passengers began to exit the plane. No one noticed Emma was still sleeping until all the passengers were off the plane. Emma's first-class flight attendant went to Emma and tried to wake her up, but with much surprise, Emma did not wake up; Emma was dead!

The flight attendant said, "Good Lord, I think she drank herself to death!" The flight attendant called the pilot, filling the plane with medics and officials within minutes. After questioning all the flight staff, they were released, and the plane was quarantined.

For the next several hours, everything on the plane was checked, and the officials bagged all of Emma's possessions, everything she touched in her seating area, and all the remaining food left over from the first-class cabin, along with all the stem wear. Emma's body was then taken off the aircraft for the cleaning team to sterilize the cabin. Emma's body was sent to the coroner's office for an autopsy.

CHAPTER 18

THURSDAY, MAY 7TH
EMIL MASHADUK
LOS ANGELS, CA

Emil was having the time of his life and was now intimate with women of every hair color. Emil had a different pet name for each person he met. Every night, he visited a different bar or lounge to pick up a lady for the evening. He was king and in charge! Everyone treated him as royalty. It wouldn't be long until his job was finished, and he would be set for the rest of his life.

Emil had at least thirty pre-paid phones without GPS stashed in his room. All business matters were handled on these pre-paid phones, and Emil never used a phone twice. Anytime a phone was used, he would pitch it in a trash bin in different areas around the city. Emil would always provide the next cell phone number to the team so they could contact him. If they called him on that number, he would provide them with the next pre-paid cell phone number and dispose of the phone. He always waited until he went out at night to discard the phone, which was always far away. He would wipe the fingerprints from the phone, take the SIM cards and batteries out, and throw them away in different locations to ensure no one could trace them back to him. He would not take any chances of someone being able to mess up the rest of his life.

Emil wore different colors and styles of hats whenever he left his room. He also had thirty pairs of sunglasses to wear that would complement his hats and wardrobe. His favorite was a bright red pair of sunglasses to match his bright red silk shirt and hat. Emil would sport around like he was Mr. Joe Cool.

That day, Emil received his new passport and identification cards. Five knocks on the door, and Emil knew to answer it. He thanked the delivery man and reviewed the new passport and ID cards. It would take him a little time to get used to his new name, but with all his money, anyone could call him anything they wished, even an asshole!

Emil could hardly wait to see the news. He would flip from station to station all day, hoping and waiting to hear anything about his job. He thought if not that day, it would be the following day. Finally, on the news the previous night, he heard a segment about people dying across the United States without cause. He could hardly wait for the first report from the CDC in Atlanta. He thought to himself, I hope I am still in the good old USA when the president holds his first Presidential Address regarding the deaths in the United States. I cannot wait to hear what he will say! Hopefully, he will announce an exceedingly high death toll. My mission is to kill fifteen million. The death toll needs to make it to fifteen million!

CHAPTER 19

FRIDAY, MAY 8TH
DR. RUDOLPH WENDT CDC
ATLANTA, GA.

Dr. Rudolph Wendt spent over thirty minutes with Mr. Whitcomb on the phone. Dr. Wendt hated the phone conversation with Mr. Whitcomb, discussing more deaths in more states and countries without knowing any cause. The FBI has already checked over 400 deaths in fourteen different states.

Dr. Rudolph Wendt was waiting in the luxurious lobby of the CDC for the arrival of the top six scientists from Germany. The scientists were coming to assist with the research at the CDC in Atlanta. Dr. Wendt had summoned them as the CDC in Atlanta desperately needed their help.

Dr. Wendt could see the shuttle from the airport arrive. He quickly walked out the front door to greet the German scientists. He stood on the beautiful big CDC carpet that he loved. As Dr. Wendt greeted each scientist, they shook his hand and identified themselves: Dr. Rene Schiller, Dr. Fritz Keitler, Dr. Hans Gruber, Dr Gerhardt Buch, Dr. Arthur Heisenberg, and Dr. Eberhard Rudolph. After the introductions, Dr. Wendt motioned for them to follow him. Dr. Wendt used his security key card to open the front door to the CDC. No one said a word until they were in a secured room. This was a hush-hush meeting, and the United States did not want its citizens to know that their CDC in Atlanta needed assistance from other countries' top scientists. The German scientists had been briefed about the epidemic before they left Germany.

Dr. Wendt said, "Before you go into the lab, I'd like to update you on the latest figures. As of noon today, the death toll has reached over 8,000 people in thirty-eight states and well over 4,000 people in seven other countries." Dr. Wendt continued, "I can't emphasize enough the importance of the work you will be doing. I also want to remind everyone this is classified, and all findings are confidential, and I ask that this be kept under tight wraps. Finally, I want to thank each of you for all your assistance." For the German scientists to access the lab, Dr. Wendt arranged for the CDC IT manager to do a retinal scan on each scientist and program their scans into the security system. Once this was completed, each scientist stood up to the eye scanner and entered the lab individually when the locking mechanism was opened. Once inside the lab, Dr. Hertz and Dr. Wadeson greeted six men. They all got right to work.

Dr. Wendt returned to his office to call the director of Homeland Security. He decided it was safer to call Nelson Whitcomb back instead of asking his secretary, Miss Deplay. It would come out of her mouth if anything leaked from his office.

Dr. Wendt finally got to talk to the chief at Homeland Security and told him, "I'm just calling so you are aware that the German scientists have arrived and are already hard at work.

They answered, "Thank God. I hope these German scientists are as smart as everyone says they are. People are dropping like flies in the United States, and there is no way of telling about all the deceased people who haven't been found yet. Plus, there is no chatter, zero, nothing about this epidemic anywhere. Whomever they are, they are very smart and very successful. I do not doubt that this is bio-terrorism against the whole world."

Before Dr. Wendt hung up the phone, he said, "Please keep me posted, and let's stay in continuous contact and be aware of what you eat." Dr. Wendt hung up the phone as terrible thoughts entered his mind: Food, how could they ruin my favorite, a good steak? With that in mind, Dr. Wendt called the USDA and the FDA, while Homeland Security called the president.

CHAPTER 20

No one in a million years would believe that Lydia had time to go shopping with her friends. After all, Lydia had nine children and homeschooled all of them. Her children ranged from ages seventeen to three, and when the mother wanted to go shopping with her friends, the older children took care of the younger ones. Lydia's family always worked together; they did everything together and loved each other. Lydia instilled in her children from the time they were old enough to know that they were to help their mother with the daily household activities and tend to each other. As a Mormon family, they put God first, family second, and everything else third.

Lydia met her friends at the mall to shop the sale items for her children, her husband, and herself. Even though the family was financially secure, Lydia would only buy items on sale. Lydia and her friends had a set shopping time: the second Friday of every month. Lydia's first thing when the New Year arrived was marking her phone calendar, shopping day, the second Friday of each month.

The friends always met at 10:00 a.m. sharp in the mall at the Beautiful Body shop. They loved treating themselves to lavish soaps, body lotions, and other store items on clearance. They did not care about the scent-of-the-month items; they were only after the sale items. After making their purchases, they left the Beautiful Body Shop and went to their second stop, the Bargain Book Store. Lydia always spent more money at this store buying books for all her nine children, her husband, and herself. Her family had a special time every day set aside for reading. Lydia always lit a candle for her and her husband in their bedroom each night, so she picked out three candles on clearance at the Bargain Book Store.

After leaving Bargain Book Store, Lydia and her friends headed to Bell's Department Store. Bell's always had the best sales on clothing. Once in Bell's, the girls all went their separate ways and met at 1:00 p.m. at Salt Lake Cafeteria, where they always dined for lunch on their shopping day.

Lydia first shopped in the children's department and looked at all the clothing racks marked "Clearance." She found several items for the children and placed them into her basket. Lydia then went to both teenage departments, boys and girls. There, she found some fashionable clothing for her teenage children that was marked down. In the men's department, she found a new pair of trousers and a matching shirt for her husband, also on sale. She placed the two items in her basket and headed for her favorite department: women's wear. With warmer weather coming, Lydia needed some new clothing for summer. She browsed through the first clearance rack and found a few sleeveless blouses. On the next rack, she found two summer shirts. Lydia had now gotten something new for every family member except the baby. Browsing in the baby's department, she decided to get the baby a new toy instead of clothing. She found just the perfect toy: an educational duck that talked and was on sale!

Before checking out, Lydia stopped at the perfume counter. She loved to smell pretty and found a perfume that was on sale with a delightful scent. Lydia looked at her watch; it was 12:50 p.m. She thought I had better go check out; I was starving and did not want to be late for lunch.

Lydia was the last of the girls to arrive at the cafeteria. Her friends were all seated at a table and were engaged in showing off their purchases. After situating her packages on the floor beside her chair, the girls lined up at the cafeteria counter to read the menu board. Lydia decided on the daily special, blackened snapper topped with roasted almonds and sautéed asparagus and carrots.

After Lydia received her plate of food, she headed toward the cashier's stand when she saw the dessert counter. Stopping at the dessert counter, she picked up the plated carrot cake with creamed icing and nut sprinkles and placed it on her tray. Lydia was the last to pay for her lunch, and she joined her friends back at the table.

While enjoying their lunch, the ladies chatted about their shopping adventures. An hour had passed when they left the cafeteria for more shopping. Lydia said, "I need to go to the drugstore; we are out of toothpaste." They all entered Driscoll's Drugstore, and Lydia headed for the aisle with toothpaste to look at the selection of the different products. Lydia found a new toothpaste, which she had never seen before, a green mint flavor toothpaste. The toothpaste was promoted with a "Buy One Get One Free" sale. Lydia went to the cashier with two toothpaste boxes, paid for her purchase, and joined her friends at the store exit door.

As the ladies walked to Sweet Tooth, they were overcome with horrible-smelling fumes and saw several firemen in the mall atrium. Although there was no smoke, the fumes made Lydia and several girlfriends nauseous. The ladies decided to walk outside the mall, waiting for the fumes to dissipate. After thirty minutes, they saw the fire truck leaving and returned to shopping. Most of the smell was gone, and the air was back to normal by the time they entered Sweet Tooth.

As she did every Friday on shopping day, she bought her and her husband a box of dark chocolate-covered nuts; it was their monthly treat. Lydia also bought gummy bears and several candy bags for her children to share. After checking out, the ladies headed for Flower Box. Every day, Flower Box was made up of flower bundles and sold at a discounted price. Lydia and her friends all purchased fresh-cut flowers for their homes.

After 3:00 p.m., the shopping spree ended as some of Lydia's friends had to pick up their children at school. The ladies said "goodbye" to each other, and Lydia said, "See you all next month." As the friends parted, Lydia returned to the drug store to purchase a water bottle for her drive home. When Lydia walked through the front door of her home, you would have never believed that nine children lived there. Their home was clean, everything in its proper place, and without any toys.

Lydia yelled, "Mom's home." All nine children came running down the staircase. Lydia hugged each one separately, looked at them, and said, "Yes, I brought you all something; let me put these flowers in water, and then we'll go through the shopping bags."

Lydia could have been a floral designer; her bundle of flowers looked beautiful in the vase she picked to put them in. She cut some stems and arranged the flowers until they looked perfect. She placed them in the middle of their dining room table every month.

The children were patiently waiting in the living room for their presents. Lydia walked into the living room, picked up all the shopping bags, and took them over, where she sat on her chair. One by one, she gave her children their gifts. The children were overly excited and loved the items she purchased for them.

Each child kissed their mother individually and said, "Thank you."

Lydia said, "Look what time it is; it's our reading time. I hope you all enjoy your new books. The children took all their new items to their rooms and settled in to read their books.

Lydia walked to the kitchen to get food from the freezer for that evening's dinner and then returned to the living room. She picked up her candle and the clothing she purchased for her and her husband, walked upstairs to the bedroom, and laid the clothing on the bed. She then put her new candle in the holder and sat on the bed to remove her shoes. Lydia placed the shoes in her closet and put on her slippers. She then returned downstairs, sat on her living room chair, and read her new book. You could have heard a needle drop in her home; it was so quiet.

CHAPTER 21

Robbie's best friend Stanley was used to it taking thirty minutes for Robbie to get up in the morning after calling him six or seven times! This morning was a little different; no, it was much different. After calling Robbie for thirty minutes, his friend Stanley opened Robbie's door to his quarters, went to his bunk, and shook him. Robbie did not respond. Stanley felt Robbie's forehead; it was ice cold. He pulled his hand away as fast as he could.

Stanley would roll Robbie's body over but thought, I better not disturb anything. Stanley rushed from Robbie's quarters to find the chief petty officer and told him about Robbie.

Within ten minutes, the navel medics were in Robbie's room. He had been dead for hours; Rigor mortis had already set in. Next, the NCIS officers arrived and took samples, fingerprints, and everything that belonged to Robbie for testing. The local police were then notified. When the police finished their examinations, the Navy chaplain came to give Robbie his last rites, and the medics then covered Robbie's body. The body was then taken to the Navy Infirmary.

The Navy chaplain, a good friend of Robbie's father, called him to share the horrific news about Robbie's death. Robbie's father immediately said, "I will be right there." The Navy chaplain waited in his office for Robbie's father.

When he arrived, the two men shook hands, and the Navy chaplain said, "I am so sorry for the loss of your son. Robbie was loved here on the ship and had a wonderful future ahead of him."

Robbie's father replied, "Yesterday was my wife's birthday, and Robbie and I were together all day long, and he seemed fine and happy. How could this have happened?" Robbie's father continued, "We had lunch and dinner together; he and I did the same thing all day. His mother will be devastated when I tell her Robbie is gone."

The Navy chaplain said, "They will do an autopsy on Robbie later today. Would you like to see your son?"

Robbie's father shook his head no and said, "I don't think I could take it right now."

The Navy chaplain said, "The local detectives and NCIS are investigating Robbie's death as we speak; as soon as I know more, I will call you at home."

Robbie's father cried and said, "Thank you. How could this have happened to our only child, our only son?"

The NCIS and the local detectives inspected every inch of Robbie's quarters and found nothing suspicious. They could not find a reason for the death of Robbie. At the autopsy, the pathologist conducted a routine inspection of all organs and a thorough examination of Robbie's body surfaces. The pathologist meticulously inspected for skin punctures to rule out any possible injections that could have introduced poison into Robbie's body.

He found no surface wounds or punctures anywhere on his entire body.

After the autopsy, samples of Robbie's organs, skin and muscle tissues, and blood samples were all sent to the CDC in Atlanta, Georgia. Yet one more death to add to the many undiagnosed deaths in the United States.

CHAPTER 22

SATURDAY, MAY 9TH
ETHEL LOU
KANSAS, MO.

This had become a monthly ritual for Ethel Lou's landlord; her rent was late. He would bang and bang on the door until Ethel Lou finally answered. After three minutes of banging, he walked to the end of the hallway and looked out the window to see if her Beetle car was in her parking spot. It was parked right out front in her designated spot, and now the landlord was mad. He returned to Ethel Lou's door, banged some more, and screamed her name, but she never answered. Kyle, the landlord, was sure Ethel Lou was ignoring him because she did not have the money for the rent again.

Kyle had waited long enough. He took his key to her apartment, unlocked the door, and entered the apartment. The stench in the unit was unbearable, he thought. Does she ever clean this place? Cats came from everywhere and swarmed around his legs. They were all thin and hungry. Kyle went to the bedroom and could not believe his eyes. It did not take him long to realize that Ethel Lou had been dead for days. He ran out of the room, closed the door so the odor did not get out into the hallway, and ran to his office to call 911.

The police department was right down the street, so it did not take them long to arrive at the apartment complex. The sirens blared from the police car, the medic's truck, and the fire department truck. He thought I did not report a fire; why are they here? Twelve first responders entered the apartment complex lobby, and Kyle said, "Upstairs, apartment 710." All twelve men, including two medics pulling the stretcher, rushed up the stairs to Ethel Lou's apartment. Kyle lit a cigarette and said out loud, "This is my first death and no rent; oh, shit!"

Two detectives went into Ethel Lou's bedroom to check on the corpse. One detective immediately came out of the room and exclaimed, "No one is going to believe this one; a dead, really big lizard is lying next to the victim on its back with its feet up in the air. We will need a body bag for the lizard!"

Bruce, the lead medic, peeked around the corner into the bedroom and said, "Holy shit, I will go get a body bag; who in the hell would sleep with a lizard?" As Bruce left the apartment, he shook his head and said, "Who in their right mind would sleep with a damn lizard?"

Several of the first responders left the apartment as soon as they could. As they were leaving, they opened the only window in the apartment, but it did not help with the strong smell of death, nor the smell from the cats and the litter boxes. Two men vomited as they exited the apartment. One of the policemen asked the attending medic, "What do you think she died from?"

The medic replied, "This one probably died from the fucking Lizard Flu!"

They looked over the body, checking for any knife or bullet wounds, but found nothing. Performing an extensive check on this corpse was a difficult task, not only because of the smell permeating from the dead lizard but also because Ethel Lou was morbidly obese with skin that draped down her chin, back, stomach, and thighs. To make matters worse, dead fruit flies were all over the white sheets. Hundreds of dead fruit flies, food morsels, and lizard scales were all over the bed and pillows!

One medic said, "She probably ate all her meals in bed with the lizard beside her. Look at all the dried-up greens over the bed; isn't that what lizards eat?" Just then, the medic threw up all over Ethel Lou! After wiping his mouth with a cloth and trying to clean off Ethel Lou, the medic said, "In twenty years, I have never gotten sick to my stomach attending to any death and believe me, I have seen a lot of terrible things!"

One of the medics yelled, "We need help in here! We will not move this one out of the bed and onto the gurney! She sure is a big one! We will need at least four of us to carry her fat ass down the stairs!" Two men removed the lizard in a body bag. After dropping Ethel Lou's body to the floor, the four medics made several attempts and finally got her body on the gurney. They had to zig-zag between the boxes and the trash to get her body to the door.

One of the medics said, "This is going to be very interesting trying to get her down seven flights of steps; please go slow; we certainly don't want her body to fall on one of us; that would be instant death for whomever she fell on. Please go slowly!" It took the medics thirty-five minutes to get her out of the apartment complex because they had to rest on every floor as they carried her body down the seven flights of stairs.

One of the Medics said, "I hope we don't get charged for all the damage to the walls the gurney made when we got off balance!"

One other medic said, "We will talk about this for the rest of our lives!"

After the body and the lizard were moved out of the apartment and were on their way to the coroner's office, the smell was not as pungent, but the detectives were still covering their noses and breathing through paper towels. They had to examine the room and dust for fingerprints.

As the detectives left, they told Kyle, "We don't think this is a homicide, but if you want to know the cause of death, you can call the coroner's office tomorrow; he will know more." The lead detective handed Kyle his card as they left the building with the stench lingering from Ethel Lou's apartment. Kyle returned to his apartment and called the Humane Society to arrange for them to pick up the cats. He returned to Ethel Lou's apartment and looked around until he found the cat food. He grabbed a large bowl sitting on the counter, filled it with cat food, and placed it on the floor. Three cats surrounded the bowl to get their share of food. He filled another container with fresh water and sat it down for the cats. He looked at the litter box and thought, I am not about to touch that mess; I will leave that for the Humane Society. Kyle scratched his head when he thought, "Where is the fourth cat? Kyle looked everywhere but couldn't find cat number four!" Kyle said, "She must have gotten rid of it, lucky kitty!"

Kyle then went to the refrigerator to clean out the food so that when the electric company turned off the electricity, the food wouldn't decay and make the place smell worse! He got a big bag and started throwing the food out of the refrigerator and into the garbage bag; he thought there was not one damn thing he would ever eat there! Kyle got the second trash bag and opened the freezer. Kyle said, "OH MY GOD, there is a dead cat in the freezer; I think I will throw up now!" When he removed the cat from the freezer, Kyle looked around to find towels or something to protect his hands. With much hesitation, Kyle found two dirty rags and removed the dead, frozen cat from the freezer! Kyle said, "It feels like this small cat weighs forty pounds, DEAR LORD!" Kyle then closed both bags and said, "I am getting out of here before I die!" Kyle picked up both bags and started down the steps to the trash bin.

The coroner completed Ethel Lou's autopsy the following day. Suspecting what killed Ethel Lou may have come from the lizard, an autopsy was also done on Flintstone. Samples of both Ethel Lou and Flintstone's organs, tissue, and blood were sent to the CDC in Atlanta, Georgia. The coroner separated the lizard samples with a note to the CDC toxicologist that these were reptile specimens.

CHAPTER 23

Emil was like a kid going to Disneyland for the first time. All the idiot newscasters were discussing the unexplained deaths in the United States and referred to it as overkill. Emil laughed out loud and said, "An overkill; just wait to see the overkill figures when we are finished!" Emil laughed again; all his organs, especially his heart, must have been made from stone, and his blood had to be made of ice!

The news stations were preempting their programming to report the latest death counts at the top of each hour. Emil was excited that the reports indicated the death count was now over 10,000 in the United States alone. He thought, *my work is going well.* Then he said aloud, "These damn idiots in the US." As a reward for the progress of his work, Emil thought, I am going to celebrate tonight with the company of two ladies."

Emil continued flipping from channel to channel with his remote control to hear the reports. It pleased him to hear the top anchor from the KTLA network report, "All these deaths, and no one can explain why this is happening." With this being reported by the top news channel in Los Angeles, Emil thought he should ask for additional money for doing such an extraordinary job.

Emil was scheduled to fly to Bali on Monday and thought, I only have two more days here before I fly out of this damn stupid country. He hoped that when he arrived in Bali, there would be US television programming so he could continue to monitor the US situation and the American people's climbing death toll. He hoped the death count would reach fifteen million. Our goal is only fifteen million.

Emil looked at his gold Rolex watch and thought, It is time to go party. He walked around the room and gathered up three disposable cell phones that needed to be disposed of. He wiped his fingerprints off all the phones, took the SIM cards and battery out, wiped them clean, and placed all the parts in a different plastic bag. Emil then went into the bathroom to ensure his hair was combed perfectly and doused himself in his favorite cologne, wanting to smell good for the ladies. Emil checked to ensure he had his key card and cigars and walked out of his room with the biggest smile. While walking to the elevator, Emil said, "Here I come, ladies, get ready!"

CHAPTER 24

SATURDAY, MAY 9ᵀᴴ
DR. RUDOLPH WENDT CDC
ATLANTA, GA.

It was a grim time at the CDC in Atlanta. Dr. Wendt asked Miss Deplay to take a week off. Dr. Wendt had talked to several of the world CDC organizations and was disappointed that they had yet been able to determine the cause of deaths in their respective countries. His scientists were getting worried about what they ate and drank, so they decided to eat the same food items they had eaten for the past two days for every meal because no one at the Atlanta CDC had died.

Dr. Wendt was tired and weary. He was so sick of talking to anyone; it was the same conversation every time, with no new findings. He held his breath and hoped the president did not call him. What could he say? What else could they do? He was outsmarted, and Dr. Wendt did not like it. Everyone at the CDC was homesick for their families, but a red alert meant you did not leave the CDC for any reason. Dr. Wendt had several inspirational meetings with his scientists in the past few days. He praised their intelligence and said everything he could to inspire his scientists to find the cure so no one else would die. It was becoming hard for him because he lost all hope of finding the source of the deaths. Dr. Wendt was scared for his family and friends but kept true to the red alert rules: you speak to no one outside of the CDC except the leaders of our country, and that was one of his primary responsibilities.

Dr. Wendt spent every hour he could in his gray suit in the lab. He was incredibly determined to discover what was causing the death of the people in his country and worldwide. They ruled out airborne transmitted viruses and any plagues. They tested every food item the victims had consumed but still found nothing. One of the German scientists came up with the theory; it had to be specific to humans because no animals were dying. This was a profound finding but still nowhere near determining what was causing the death for so many and so quickly. No one at the CDC had heard about

Flintstone, the seven-foot lizard! They knew it had to be something humans did, what they ate, smelled, or digested, but what? Everything they tested came up negative. Dr. Wendt and his scientists had tested everything they could get their gloves on, or so they had thought.

Dr. Wendt hoped and prayed that his staff would be more positive the following day. Being positive would make a big difference in more favorable findings. Dr. Wendt was focused on keeping the morale up at the CDC.

Before Dr. Wendt went to bed on his little cot in his office, he again had his same meal: Steak, baked potato, and green beans for dinner with city water to wash it all down. With every bite, Dr. Wendt believed they were one bite closer to finding the cause of all these deaths.

As Dr. Wendt tried to fall asleep, he wondered what the president of the United States would say the following night when he gave his Presidential Address to the citizens of the United States!

CHAPTER 25

Lydia's husband was the first one up; he was so used to leaving for the factory he owned at 6:30 a.m. Monday through Friday. There was no way he could sleep past 6:00 a.m. Since this Mormon family did not drink coffee, Lydia's husband poured boiling water into his teacup for his morning green tea. He then turned off the security system and opened the front door to get the Sunday morning newspaper. He sat in his chair in the living room and started looking over the newspaper while sipping his tea.

Starting at 8:00 a.m., the children would begin joining him in the living room. All nine children were now awake, and he said to the children, "Your mother has overslept this morning; go jump on the bed and tell her to wake up!"

After being upstairs for a few minutes, the children came down the staircase one by one and said, "Dad, she won't wake up."

Dad said, "I bet she is playing a trick on you kids; I will go up, tickle her, and make her laugh until she gets up!"

Dad walked up the stairs, and all the children followed him. Once in the bedroom, he said, "Lydia, you are a sleepy head this morning," and started to tickle her." There was no response. Lydia's husband looked at her face, touched it, and then his face turned white. He felt like he was going to faint. He turned to the children and said, "I don't think your mother is feeling well; you all go have breakfast while I see what I can do for your mother.

The children left the bedroom and walked downstairs. The two eldest children prepared breakfast for them all.

After the children had left the bedroom, Dad rolled Lydia over on her back. He knew she was dead as her coloring was blue, and her body was stiff. He put his hand over his mouth and said, "Dear Lord, no, not my Lydia."

It took him a few minutes to regain his composure before going to the phone.

He first dialed 911 to report the death of his wife, and then he called their church bishop. Dad sat down next to Lydia, held her hand, kissed her on the lips, and said, "Lydia, we all love you so much; just how are we going to live without you?" Dad then slowly walked back downstairs and walked out to the front porch. He did not want the children to see him crying. How would he tell them their mother was gone and now in heaven? Just then, the fire trucks, medics, and police arrived. Dad thought, Thank heavens, there is also our bishop.

The children heard the sirens and raced to the front door as their bishop approached the front porch. The bishop returned the children to the kitchen while Dad talked to the police.

The medics raced upstairs and found Lydia had no pulse. One of the medics radioed to have the coroner come to the site. The police called detectives, which were there in ten minutes. A search was conducted in the bedroom while they waited for the coroner.

One of the policemen knew Lydia's husband and told him, "We can't find anything that looks suspicious. After the coroner inspects Lydia's body, she will be transported to the coroner's office, where the pathologist will examine Lydia and hopefully find the cause of her death.

Lydia's husband said, "Do you think this is the same thing that's killing others in the US?

The policeman replied, "I don't know, but I do know that this killing spree in the United States has got to stop." The policeman said, "Let me know when it's okay for us to take her downstairs.

Facing back his tears, Dad said, "Just give me five minutes to get the children and bishop gathered, and then you can take our Lydia."

Dad knew he was now facing one of life's hardest situations. He asked all the children to come to the living room with him and their bishop. As the children settled in the living room, they knew something was wrong. Dad had tears streaming down his cheeks, and he was shaking. The bishop sat beside Dad and wrapped his arm around his shoulder as he shared the sad news that his mother was gone and was now at peace in heaven. The younger children were confused and began crying, while the older kids started to cry after hearing Dad's words.

CHAPTER 26

SUNDAY, MAY 10th
PRESIDENT OF THE UNITED STATES PRESIDENTIAL ADDRESS ON
TV WASHINGTON, DC.

It was 7:55 p.m. prime time, and every TV station in the United States was ready to air the president in five minutes. At 8:00 p.m. EDT, President Hamilton R. Bennett stood behind the pressroom podium and began addressing the nation.

"Good evening, my fellow citizens across our great nation. I feel it necessary to address you all, making you aware of an epidemic sweeping across our country over the past ten days. As of 7:00 p.m. EDT tonight, we elevated our US terror alert to the highest level."

I want to assure everyone that our top scientists, medical professionals, and agency leaders in our country and across the continents are working to identify this unknown enemy that is killing the US population.

"As I speak to you this evening, our Homeland Security has no findings of physical terrorism but has not ruled out bioterrorism. The United States is the intended target of this fatal epidemic. Today, I have appointed our director of Homeland Security to head up my Epidemic Team and advisor to the White House. The director has advised me that the epidemic is not airborne; it is not a new viral strain or the plague. What we are facing is something new and never recorded."

"At the CDC in Atlanta, Georgia, our top scientists, who have been working day and night on this epidemic, have yet to find anything abnormal in their testing. Whatever the killer host is, it enters the body, causes death, and then leaves the body. We have been unable to identify and examine any victims before they succumbed to the killer host."

"The United States is offering a reward of one million dollars to the person who can give us information about the possible cause that is afflicting this insane and inhumane epidemic on our fellow citizens. We have established a hotline for any citizen feeling ill to contact us. I cannot stress enough the importance of calling our nation's hotline. We have one thousand representatives ready to take your call. Write this toll-free number down and memorize it: 1-800-555-5555. If you are feeling well one minute and ill the next, please dial this number. It could save your life and the lives of thousands. Please, we need everyone's help."

The CDC has become aware that whatever is causing all these deaths in our nation does not affect animals, only humans. Until we have some clues about this killer, the Center for Disease Control advises everyone to eat what they ate the past two days until we find the answers. If you are still healthy after eating the foods you ate the past two days, then whatever you ate will not afflict you. So, we request that from here on, all you eat is what you have eaten two days ago. Also, not only what you ate two days ago, but what you did two days ago. Write down everything you did two days ago and stay with that program every day until this epidemic is over.

"At the CDC in Atlanta, all they drink is the city water. The city water has been checked across the United States and is safe to drink. If you have been drinking city water, continue to drink only that and nothing else."

"I am immediately mandating a "Stay at Home" order nationwide. Unless it is an emergency, please do not leave your home. Those essential persons must continue to work, like doctors, nurses, firemen, police, and grocery store employees. If your work role is non-essential, you must stay home. All schools, colleges, and universities across the United States are closed until further notice."

"Eat what you ate two days ago, only drink city water, do not leave your home unless it is vital, and stay tuned to the news for further updates."

"If you see anything or anyone who looks suspicious, please call 1-800-555-5555. No problem is too small. We will take all your ideas and advice; it just may be your call that will stop this epidemic, and we need everyone's help. We are all in this together."

"The United States has made it through many prior crises; we all must stay united and work together as we have always done here in America, the Beautiful."

"One more time, the number is 1-800-555-5555. Thank you, and goodnight.

"God bless the United States of America; God bless the world."

95

CHAPTER 27

Emil was pacing back and forth in his room. He was pissed! The Presidential Address had screwed up his last night of partying in the United States; he must start late tonight! He looked at his watch and thought, "Only forty more minutes, and I will see the president of the United States of America look like the asshole he is."

"So much for the great United States of America," Emil exclaimed as he laughed out loud. "They may think they have a democracy and are the greatest country in our world, but they cannot figure out why so many wonderful citizens are dying!" Emil raised his arm and patted himself on the back, thinking, Great Job, Emil!

Emil poured himself a tall glass of scotch over ice and was now sitting in front of the TV with the remote in his hand. He could hardly contain himself and anxiously awaited the president's national address announcing that the death count was fifteen million citizens, just fifteen million! He took in every word the president of the United States had to say. When the president mentioned animals, Emil said, "Oh shit, we forgot their animals; oh, how they love their precious doggies and cats!"

Emil was very disturbed when the president said to stay at home. If people do not go out, we may not reach the fifteen million people dying in the United States. Even though no one was supposed to go out, Emil was sure he would find places open in Los Angeles where there would be beautiful, frisky women!

The Presidential Address ended, and Emil headed out the door for his last night of partying in the good old USA. Emil ensured he had his key card, cigars, and disposable cell phones. As he headed to the elevator, he thought, "Two women might kill me tonight, but what a great way to die!"

CHAPTER 28

MONDAY, MAY 11TH
AMERICAN CITIZENS
ALL OVER THE USA

On Monday morning, the chatter began, but it was different from the kind that Homeland Security listened to. The national hotline was overloaded with so many calls that people were getting busy. Some people had to dial the number on their cell phone twenty times until their call went through. The American citizens were in a panic.

Jade made a call to her best friend, Rose. "Damn, Rose, I had the worst-tasting TV dinner I have ever eaten three nights ago. Does this mean I can only eat that same meal until this crisis is over?"

Rose replied, "By what the president said, that is all you are to eat; this is unbelievable; what did you eat the day before then? You did not die. I hope it is something you like since that is all we will be eating."

"Great idea, Rose; what did you eat two days ago?"

Rose answered, "You're not going to believe this. I had a frozen pizza that I bought at the convenience store, and it was terrible."

Jade said, "Maybe you should return to what you had for lunch two days ago. We are in a real mess here! We will either drop the pounds or drop dead!"

Rose added, "I hate the taste of our city water; it's awful! What in the world could be causing all of these deaths?"

Jade said, "Are you going to stay home?"

Rose replied, "No, how can we stay at home? We must get the same thing we ate and go grocery shopping."

Jade said, "They have this big sale at the mall, and I was going to go shopping today; I wonder if all the stores will be open."

Rose answered, "I don't know, but I'm not going to find out; I'm going to the grocery store. Maybe we should all eat dog food!"

Jade said, "The baby's crying, so I have to go. Please be safe, my dear friend; I could not live without you. I love you."

Rose said, "Give the baby a hug and kiss from me, and I love you too, and please be safe." The two friends ended their call and thought about what they would do: go shopping or stay home and eat what they had in the house.

Rose mumbled, "Shit, this is a mess."

All over the United States, family and friends were having the same kind of conversations. What to do, what to eat?

Rose grabbed her purse and headed for the door; she told her husband, "I'm going to the grocery store to stock up on the items you and I can eat."

Her husband said, "Get some liquor and beer and buy some movies so we have something to do. I am off work, so we can party, sweetie pie." Rose kissed her husband goodbye and left to do her shopping.

As Rose pulled into the grocery store parking, she said, "Holy shit!" There was not one open parking place, and people were in a long line that stopped at the end of the parking lot. Rose said out loud, "I'm going to have to stand in line just to enter the grocery store, and then there is the chance they may not have the items I need once I get inside." Rose thought this was far worse than going to the grocery store when a major hurricane was headed for Florida.

The grocery stores were the only things open except for emergency responders, doctors, and nurses. Every grocery store in the nation was facing the same dilemma.

Rose thought Everyone in the United States must be shopping at my grocery store! The malls were empty as all the retailers were closed. On her drive to the grocery store, Rose noticed that every business parking lot was empty, and all offices and retail stores were closed. The only thing that opened was grocery stores; who knew how long their food supplies would last?

Rose parked in the parking lot across the road from the grocery store. After parking her car, she dashed to get in line. It was 10:00 a.m. when Rose called her husband to tell him she hoped to be home for dinner eight hours later. He could not believe what she told him about the grocery store madness.

After hanging up from Rose, he turned on the news. The news was not good and showed coverage of people in the grocery stores shoving each other and even fistfights breaking out over the last items shoppers sought. He thought This is bad; we all know better than this; we must share and have patience until we get through this crisis. He flipped to the next station, and people were breaking the windows at a bank, thinking they could get their money. He thought to himself, The ATM must be out of cash. We are headed for big trouble. He called Rose back to tell her what he saw on the news and told her to be careful, to get something to eat anything, and not use her cash; use her debit or credit card.

The next thing he saw on the news were people using tire irons to beat on the gas pumps. They were breaking windows at the closed gas stations. He thought, Oh God, this is going to be unbelievably bad! He called Rose again, telling her about the gas stations and telling her not to waste any gas. Rose told him, "In all this time, I have moved forward about three feet; we may be eating dry cereal with city water substituted for milk!" Rose's husband was upset and wished he had gone along with her. He would never let her go alone again.

As Rose stood in line, she thought, I wonder what the president ate two days ago! She started to talk to the people in line; they all agreed this was a disaster, and everyone was scared for the near future.

One lady told Rose, "Just a few days ago, life was beautiful; maybe we have all just taken our wonderful lives for granted."

Rose agreed, saying, "Until I heard the president's speech last night, the worst thing I had on my mind was the Monday Night Football game; my favorite team is playing or was to play tonight, and I was worried they would not win. I feel very stupid now." All the people in line had now begun conversations with the other people nearby.

Maybe this is one good thing coming from this crisis because not one of us would have ever spoken to each other if not for this crisis, Rose thought. The scenario in front of Rose reminded her about the new song she was writing, "Everyone's Hand Fits Into Another Hand."

Rose suggested that they all hold hands because now they were all one; no one had an edge on anyone else; they were all just fighting for their lives for another day on our marvelous earth.

Rose arrived back home at 6:45 p.m. with a few grocery items, which were not what they had eaten three nights ago or even two nights ago. She was frightened that she could not stick to President Bennett's advice, but it was better than having nothing to eat. Although it was important to bring the food home, Rose thought it was more important to bring with her a feeling she had never felt before: "All men are created equal," which she felt was a very good feeling.

When Rose entered the grocery store, the liquor, wine, beer, and movie rentals were gone. Their dinner consisted of broccoli, popcorn, and Vienna sausages from a can. Neither one complained, and both hoped and prayed that they were still alive the next day to eat the same thing together!

With no movie to watch, Rose sat beside her husband and shared her experience standing in line for hours and what she witnessed inside the grocery store. They held hands and talked for hours, getting to know each other again. They were still madly in love. They occasionally watched the news as the evening grew later and continued to have deep conversations.

CHAPTER 29

MONDAY, MAY 11TH
EMIL MASHADUK
LOS ANGELS, CA LAX AIRPORT

Emil was standing in line to go through security. He was nervous about his new passport and driver's license. He was holding his breath and anxious that he would not encounter any problems. Emil wore a T-shirt, shorts, and sandals like everyone else at the airport. He fit right in, just like he had planned to do.

On the way to the airport, Emil was happy he had mailed his jewelry and other personal items to his new address in Bali because no FedEx facility was open. Emil did not want to carry these items on his airport journey. He wanted no evidence of any wrongdoing. He even had a ticket in coach, no first class for Emil; he did not want to stand out from the others on the plane or at the airport.

Arriving at the security checkpoint, Emil handed the security officer his passport and boarding pass. After scanning the passport, Emil said, "Thank you," as the man returned his credentials. He walked to the end of the line and took a deep breath; this was the last stop, and he would be on the plane to paradise for the rest of his life. He removed his sandals, placed them in a plastic bin, put his change in a bowl, and walked through security. No sound; he was free to move on. Emil put his sandals back on, put his change back into his shorts pocket, and walked to the tram. As he waited for the next tram, he was smiling and was about to burst with excitement. He did it, and he was on his way to freedom. Emil thought This is about as good as it gets, as good as the two women last night; what a night we three had!

The tram stopped, and Emil got in and held onto the railing and, in minutes, was at his gate waiting to board his plane to Bali. When he arrived, the United States could not touch him because Bali had no extradition treaty.

The gate agent called for group three, so it was Emil's time to board the plane. He found his seat and asked for a blanket and a pillow.

After the plane took off, Emil smirked and closed his eyes as he thought, I will sleep the whole way to Bali and dream of my new life with all the beautiful new women with tanned bodies I will meet in Bali. Goodbye to the damn, stupid United States of America; I know we will reach fifteen million deaths, just fifteen million, and I will be the happiest man on earth, just fifteen million!

Later that night, at 8:00 p.m., all flights were canceled in and out of the United States of America.

CHAPTER 30

Nelson Whitcomb dialed the direct number to Dr. Wendt at the CDC in Atlanta, Georgia.

Dr. Wendt answered his phone, "Hello, Dr. Wendt."

Whitcomb said on the other end, "It's me again, Nelson; I'm calling to tell you that we now have deaths in all fifty states."

Dr. Wendt replied, "How many more?"

Nelson answered, "A few minutes ago, we were up to 1,473,000 deaths, and the calls are coming in nonstop."

Dr. Wendt answered, "Are all of these deaths undiagnosed deaths?"

Nelson replied, "Yes, at this point, I'm only giving you the undiagnosed deaths. Other deaths have been diagnosed; however, these are not included in our numbers."

Dr. Wendt asked, "Are these diagnosed deaths unusual or abnormal?"

Nelson said, "No, just the normal, heart attacks, cancer, and so on."

Dr. Wendt replied, "Why can't we catch a break with just one thing that would give us our first clue?"

Nelson responded, "I am so sorry to report nothing out of the ordinary except for the 1,473,000 deaths and believe me, every death is being examined, and every coroner in the United States is aware of the problems. They all have been told to give every death a full autopsy, even if there was an obvious cause. Every pathologist is going that extra mile for every death." Nelson continued, "Every lab in the United States works twenty-four hours daily; nothing unusual. Gephart Tyler and the whole FBI team have found absolutely nothing."

Dr. Wendt sighed and said, "There should be a new word other than epidemic for all these deaths!" Dr. Wendt continued," We are at our wit's end here at the CDC; everyone is tired, homesick, and sick of continuously eating the same food daily. I have run out of words to say to our scientists; I am trying my hardest to keep their morale up. I have given at least fifty inspiring speeches, but I am not an inspirational speaker but a scientist! We have no one to replace these scientists because they are the top scientists in the world."

Nelson answered, "You must find a way to keep their morale up! They are so important to the citizens of the United States, and we need them desperately."

Dr. Wendt said, "Nelson, maybe it would be a good idea if you did not call me so often with bad news! I need to keep my morale up to help the others here; let's establish that you only call if there is something new and important to report?"

Nelson answered, "Good idea, Dr. Wendt; the next time you hear from me will be when I have something new to report other than the death count."

Dr. Wendt said, "Thank you, Nelson, this will greatly help us all. Goodbye." Dr. Wendt hung up the phone before Nelson had time to speak.

Dr. Wendt walked to the lab and announced to all the scientists, "If I could have everyone, please take off your lab gear and meet me in the library." Dr. Wendt walked to the library and checked the TV to make sure he could get a good reception.

The scientists walked into the library one by one and took their seats. Dr. Wendt said when all thirty-nine were present, "Take a deep breath, everyone. isn't it great to be out of that lab?" Dr. Wendt said, "Let's all take our two hands and clap for each other for working all these long, hard hours and eating the same food you had two days prior." Everyone in the room started clapping, which continued for several minutes. Dr. Wendt said, "I know exactly how you all feel; remember, I'm also here twenty-four hours a day. Let's all stand and give yourselves another applause. Hopefully, it will relieve our stress and tensions!" Everyone stood and clapped for another five minutes, and then Dr. Wendt spoke again, "I thought it would be good for all of us to watch a little TV, or better yet, the news. I'm hoping if you see the news, it will bring your spirits up and make you all realize just how especially important you all are." With that said, Dr. Wendt turned the TV on.

All forty of them sat and watched the news in total amazement. None of them could believe what they heard or saw about their country and work. The six German scientists were concerned about their country. No one in the library could believe the death count.

After an hour of watching the news, Dr. Wendt said, "I realize what you have just seen and heard is devastating, but I also realize we are the only ones on this earth capable of finding the cause of this epidemic." Dr. Wendt continued, "Let's clap for ourselves the whole way back to the lab, and one more thing, do what I do; with every bite of food you eat, keep telling yourself that we are one bite closer to the cause or the cure. Good luck to you all; let's get back to work!" Some of the scientists were still clapping as they walked back into the lab.

Dr. Wendt was successful as he raised their morale; positive attracts positive!

CHAPTER 31

There was now chaos across the United States. People rioting in the streets, and grocery store deliveries were a mess. The grocery stores were getting fresh food deliveries, but everyone needed help finding what to eat. Most citizens tried to help each other; some people were genuinely nice and traded food, but most were rude and impossible to speak with. People were pushing, shoving, swearing, and fighting to get the last of the meat supplies at their grocery stores.

Police across the country were now stationed at grocery stores for crowd control and ordinances, trying to resolve problems before they escalated and keeping the peace. In bigger cities, the National Guard was called upon to protect the grocery stores and their patrons while they shopped. The United States was now in dire straits. Food shopping in the United States has become dangerous for its citizens. Most grocery stores implemented limited hours and designated lines for shoppers. So that all patrons would have the opportunity to get their grocery and toiletry items, designated lines were set up for families with children and lines for the disabled and elderly. All other patrons outside of these categories were to use the general admission line. To ensure necessary items were available to all, grocery stores limited their customers to one item per family per day for any one product.

A news report televised a scene from one of the stores that had become so chaotic that a policeman shot blanks in the air to control the angry crowd. One lady standing in line screamed in a shrieking voice to the crowd, "You are all spoiled! Help each other out and stop fighting; do any of you think

I have enjoyed eating sauerkraut for the last four days?" The news reporter ended the segment with the comment, "How could our United States of America get this bad?"

In some neighborhoods, families worked together by combining their food supplies and sharing with each other to have variations of the foods everyone had eaten in the prior days. Family members would shop and replenish the products consumed from the community food supply. Neighbors provided childcare for others, and everyone was available to help in their community with any needed assistance.

CHAPTER 32

The one thousand operators hired to answer the government helpline, 1-800-555-5555 had now turned into four thousand operators. Every operator was courteous and treated every call with the utmost urgency, but the operators' nerves were wearing out. Some people called and blamed the operators for having to eat the same food, others called about their sick dog or cat, and some asked for directions to a grocery store with what the person was supposed to eat.

The government helpline was out of control. One person called to see if they knew how long they would have television programming. Another person called to see what the president ate two nights ago! One man called to ask where he could buy beer and if the beer was safe to drink. Another person called to ask what he should do when his car ran out of gas; the operator who answered that call screamed, "WALK, DUMB ASS!"

One operator stood up and quit after this phone call: "Miss, can you tell me that if my cable goes out, they will come and fix it?"

The calls went on and on. "If I have a sore throat, should I go to the CDC in Atlanta or call my doctor?" "Do you think they will still have the bus trip to Branson, Missouri, on the 20th of May?" "Miss, I think all groceries and cigarettes should be free."

The president, Hamilton R. Bennett, had an in-depth discussion with Miss Lydia Peabody, the head of the government helpline. They even discussed shutting it down, but the president thought it would be better to keep it up until his next Presidential Address the following Sunday.

President Bennett said, "Our United States citizens are scared, and we need to keep the number up if it's only to help calm people down a little.

The government helpline is their only way to vent or feel secure; anyway, it's giving them something to do." The president suggested hiring more operators and having shorter shifts for the operators.

Miss Peabody stood and said, "Thank you, President Bennett," and shook his hand goodbye."

The president sat in his desk chair in the Oval Office, thinking, "What is happening here? This has got to be terrorism, but I bet the terrorists never dreamed all these other problems would occur in our country. They are all probably laughing their asses off."

CHAPTER 33

WEDNESDAY, MAY 13TH
THERE ARE MANY MORE DEATHS, MANY MORE PROBLEMS
UNITED STATES OF AMERICA

They had their first death in Cuba. The death count was rising at an unbelievable rate in several countries. Hundreds were dying each day in other countries, but still nothing like the United States was experiencing, where the death count was now over 4,500,000. Everyone was scared to death; some people could not take anymore and killed themselves. This added to the overall death count in the United States.

Some people did not have cell phones, landline phones, water, or even electricity before this epidemic started, and many people needed more money to buy food. This had happened in the past few days since Sunday night's Presidential Address to the nation. Gangs all over the US hijacked grocery store tractor-trailers and sometimes killed the driver. They sold the food, making lots of money. Now, every grocery store tractor-trailer that left the warehouse had armed guards to protect the drivers and the food.

Grocery store warehouses reported an uprise in theft daily since Monday. The food losses were enormous when food was needed so badly by so many in the United States.

Most grocery store owners gave their employees the food they needed to compensate for their long hours of work and dedication, helping in this tragic time. Some employees shared the food they were given with others in need. Most people shared food at home but were not supposed to eat. Some neighborhoods started a morning food table to share food.

Other than the undiagnosed deaths and the epidemic that was from one end of the United States to the other end of the United States, everything was happening as usual. There were the bad people, and there were the good people. The only difference was that the bad people got worse, and the good people became kinder. That is the best way to describe the citizens of the United States. Store after store was being looted; TVs and laptop computers were the hot items. Although no sofa was left at a famous furniture store in LA, not one dining room table was taken from the store.

All available National Guard units were to start protecting against looting across the United States in the morning. It would have been easier if every store in the United States had steel bars across the windows, like in New York City. Unfortunately, it was a little late for that idea.

Nursing homes across the nation turned every TV off. They did not want elders to know about the negative things happening in the country. The parents of these elders in nursing homes were the ones who entered the United States through Ellis Island and worked their hands to the bone to start this great country. Many of their lives were negative, and if they could remember, why make them feel worse or sad?

Most parents kept their children away from the TV because the only thing left on TV was the depressing news. Many parents repeatedly played children's movies to entertain their children and read the same books to them. They played games and cards and worked on math problems, anything to help their children since their world had changed for the worse. The government hired men to go door to door to see if anyone was dead inside homes. They couldn't have the National Guard do this because they were so busy protecting the little food left at the warehouses. No new food was coming from anywhere, so when it was gone, it was gone.

CHAPTER 34

Dr. Wendt's worst fear was coming true: his first call from the president of the United States.

Dr. Wendt said, "Hello, Mr. President; what can I do for you today?" Hamilton R. Bennett had nothing to say except praise for the CDC and asked if they discovered anything new. Dr. Wendt answered, "Yes, sir, we have been working on the demographics and their characteristics and have found that very few victims are children, and only a handful are from impoverished areas."

The president replied, "Very good, Dr. Wendt; where are the victims mostly from?"

Dr. Wendt said, "Most of our victims are from the middle to upper-class citizens in the United States."

The president answered, "What do the middle and upper-class citizens of the US do that children and people in impoverished areas don't do?"

Dr. Wendt cleared his throat before answering, "Well, Mr. President, that is what we don't know, but we are testing everything we can think of that those children don't do or eat and what the lower income don't do and eat. Currently, I'm sorry to say, we have no idea yet."

The president replied, "I'm going to start a committee in five minutes to think of what children and people living in impoverished areas don't do that middle to upper-class citizens do. I will be back in touch the minute we can figure it out, and you call me directly if your team comes up with any answers."

Dr. Wendt said, "Thank you, Mr. President; we can surely use the help here at the CDC." They both said goodbye at the same time and hung up their phones.

Dr. Wendt raced to the lab and yelled, "Back to the library right now." First, Dr. Wendt had them clap for themselves, and they all watched the news together for thirty minutes.

Dr. Wendt turned the TV off and said, "Okay, fellow scientists, please come to the front and grab a piece of paper and a pencil." One by one, the top scientists in the world took a piece of paper and a pencil. When they were all back in their seats, he said, "We have found no animals, very few children, and people from impoverished areas not dying; now we have to figure out why! Let's put our brains to work in another way. What do middle and upper-class people do that animals, children, and lower-income citizens don't do?" Dr. Wendt continued, "Walk to a desk if you wish, move around, walk anywhere, chew your pencil, but please think; we must solve this; after all of our work, we must be the ones to solve this!"

Almost every scientist got up, moved, walked, or sat elsewhere. Finally, one scientist yelled, "I got it; it's bottled water!"

Another scientist said, "No, that is not right; it's got to be nuts."

A German scientist stood up and said, "You know I have heard a lot about the chemicals in your water; could it be fish?"

Dr. Wendt replied, "If it is fish, then people in the impoverished areas would be dying as they fish all the time for food, but we need to explore this theory further."

This continued for hours until Dr. Wendt said, "Okay, which ones do you think it is?" The entire group just stood there and said nothing. Dr. Wendt said, "We have forty different ideas; the one you chose will be the one you test. Let's find the source. See you all in the lab."

They worked longer than twenty-four hours on their ideas. Every type of bottled water was sent to the CDC, every kind of fish was sent to the CDC, and every kind of nut was sent to the CDC. This continued until the next night, and no one could find anything wrong.

Dr. Wendt said, "I'm getting old, and I'm so tired and not even hungry for my steak. Let's all call it quits for now. A good hot meal and a good night's rest may give us the answer. Goodnight to all; see you at 8:00 a.m. Also, if anyone wants to watch TV, please feel free to turn it on as this may also help you to think.

Dr. Wendt walked very slowly back to his office. On his way, he picked up his meal. He sat down on his cot, forcing a bite here and there. This was the first time he was baffled in his career, and he disliked it. With all his studies and spending his life helping the United States when they needed him the most, he couldn't figure the damn thing out. He put his plate on the desk and lay down to think.

CHAPTER 35

THURSDAY, MAY 14TH
MARY KAY

Mary Kay's sisters did know her well! Within the first week of the cruise, Mary Kay had three dates with Mr. Handsome! On her third date with him, she knew everything there was to know about him and was having the time of her life. After the second date, Mary Kay thought, I don't know what love is, but I think it might be Mr. Handsome!

On their third date, Mr. Handsome took her to dinner, and she got to wear her expensive dress. She looked like a princess.

At dinner, Mr. Handsome told Mary Kay, "Mary Kay, I think I am falling in love with you, and I can hardly wait to get you back to NYC for you to meet my family and friends!"

Mary Kay reached for his hand and held his hand to her lips, and then she kissed his hand. Afterward, she said, "The feeling is mutual, Mr. Handsome!"

Every day on the cruise was nonstop, from early morning to late night. Mary Kay and her sisters had now been to every shop on the cruise ship, buying everything they wanted and then finding it for less money on the first port they visited. Of course, the eight sisters had to buy something on every island they visited.

Their first port was Port-au-Prince. They had a great time during their stay on this island. They purchased beach bags, and some moms bought jewelry for their children. They each bought the same sun hat to find each other while shopping. They all especially loved the salted ice cream and the piña coladas. They were going to buy postcards but then decided they would never have time to send them, so they were onto the next street of shops. They loved the stores at Port-au-Prince that carried real sponges from the sea, everything made of sea salt, including beautiful skin face masks and luscious leg creams.

Mary Kay said, "This cream smells so good I think I could eat it!"

Even though the beaches were crystal clear, and you could see the bottom of the ocean, no one wanted to go to the beach as they were having such a great time shopping and eating!

One of the sisters said, "It's almost 1:30 p.m. Don't you think we should eat lunch soon?" They all agreed and started to look for the perfect restaurant. It did not take them long to find the perfect spot, and all eight ladies walked into Let's Taste Port-au-Prince! The ladies each ordered something different and shared eight tastes of Port-au-Prince. Since they had to return to the ship by 5:00 p.m., they hurried the waiter along to return to their shopping.

They all purchased long silk scarf swimsuit cover-ups; they loved them and couldn't wait to wear them to the pool the next day!

One of the sisters said, "Aren't we going to St. Croix tomorrow"?

All of the other seven sisters said, "NO!"

One of the sisters said, "We need a day to relax by the pool; I don't know when I have ever been this tired, plus we must all wear our new silk scarf swimsuit cover-ups!"

Mary Kay said, "If I do anything other than relax at the pool, I am going to buy myself another suitcase to get all this new stuff in!" All eight sisters laughed! Mary Kay said, "Okay, we are not going to St. Croix tomorrow, but how about St. Martin's the next day? The island I want to see is Barbados, but that's not for another five or six days!"

One of the other sisters replied, "Let's figure all this out tomorrow after we have a good night's sleep!

It was time to board the ship, and all eight ladies stood in line to get back on the ship. Security inspected all their shopping bags, looking for famous island spirits, as no liquor was to be carried on board! They returned to their cabins and prepared for dinner at 8:00 p.m.

One of the sisters said, "Mary Kay, are you not meeting Mr. Handsome for dinner tonight?"

Mary Kay replied, "No, I already told him tonight is a night off, and he is to hang with his friends. He's also tired like we are, and we all need a night off to relax in our cabins."

At 8:00 p.m. sharp, all the girls met for dinner in the specialty dining room. Mary Kay said, "I think I need toothpicks to keep my eyes open while we eat!" Everyone agreed with her as they ordered their drinks!

That night was a very special night for the sisters. One by one, they each talked about their last ten years. Mary Kay said, "To think I thought my job was hectic; I just can't imagine chasing three precious children around all day!" Mary Kay continued, "I am paying for dinner tonight! I want you all to know how much I love each of you and how blessed I feel that you all love me!" Mary Kay paid the tab, and all eight sisters said a big thank you, loved and hugged each other, and said, "Sweet Dreams!"

When Mary Kay entered her cabin, it was 9:55 p.m., and she felt one hundred years old. She hurriedly removed her clothing except for her underpants and put on a big, comfy T-shirt she brought along. She then lit the new candle she had brought that day, smelled the fresh flowers they had replaced in her room earlier, and thought, I should go out on the balcony and breathe fresh air, but I am too tired to open the door.

Mary Kay went into the bathroom to brush her teeth; the entire time she was brushing her teeth, she was thinking about how much she loved this new toothpaste and would buy some for herself when she got back home. She thought I was brushing my teeth longer now that I had this wonderful new toothpaste; I love the taste of it.

As she crawled into bed, her foot hit the paperback book she brought along lying on the floor, and she laughed, saying, "I knew I would never have time to finish this book; I think I am still on chapter one!" She picked up the book and tried to finish at least the chapter she was on; Mary Kay finally found the page where she stopped reading and started to read the rest of the chapter. She hoped she could at least finish this chapter before she fell asleep.

At 11:45 p.m., Mr. Handsome, who shared ten shots with his buddies, was having difficulty walking and ran into the walls several times on his way to bed when he thought, I must kiss Mary Kay goodnight. After walking into the walls fifteen times, he remembered the old saying, he's doing the weave; yes, I am doing the weave! He got to Mary Kay's cabin door, knocked, and knocked on the door. He just wanted to kiss her goodnight! He knocked and knocked, but Mary Kay never answered the door.

After thirty minutes, he thought he should have someone check on her; he thought that no one slept that sound! He looked for the first steward he could find and finally spotted one, telling him his dilemma. They walked together to Mary Kay's cabin and knocked.

Mr. Handsome told the steward, "I know she has to be there. We have to make sure she is okay. The steward had to call his supervisor to get permission to use his master key to open Mary Kay's cabin door. After explaining the situation to his supervisor, the steward was permitted to enter the cabin.

He said, "Sir, wait here and let me go and peek in the room!"

Mr. Handsome was not about to wait outside the room, so when the steward unlocked the door, Mr. Handsome just about knocked over the steward! Mr. Handsome said, "Mary Kay, it's me with a goodnight kiss for you! Mary Kay didn't move, not at all. Mr. Handsome touched her, and she still didn't move.

The steward said, "Sir, you will have to wait outside! Right now! GO!"

The tears were already falling down Mr. Handsome's face, and he said repeatedly, "OH GOD, PLEASE NO!"

The steward called the cabin supervisor and duty manager, and within minutes, six men were standing outside Mary Kay's quarters! Two police took Mr. Handsome away from the cabin while the rest of them stood watching the ship's doctor.

After briefly examining Mary Kay's body, the ship doctor said, "Oh Jesus, mercy, here we go again, not again! The ship needs to be quarantined immediately, just like the last cruise; what is happening? Last year, we didn't have to quarantine the ship one time!

CHAPTER 36

"**G**ood evening, fellow citizens of the United States. My initial plans were to address the nation on Sunday night, but I have found it necessary to speak to you all tonight. Our great country and you great citizens are being tested like no other time in our nation's history. I don't have to go into details, and I'm sure most of you have seen the news and know what tragedies have occurred in our country. We now have over four million undiagnosed deaths, a terrible loss and tragedy to our country and citizens. Our country is experiencing tragedy after tragedy, and we must stand together as the great nation we have always been.

"I have no choice but to place a curfew on our nation. No one is to be on the streets from 8:00 p.m. Eastern Standard Time until 8:00 a.m. Eastern Standard Time. Due to all the looting, I must take action. Starting tomorrow morning, our grocery stores in the United States will open at 9:00 a.m. and close at 7:00 p.m. to help enforce this curfew. I regret having to say this, but if you are caught on the streets during our curfew hours, you will face a felony charge that will come with jail time.

"We must unite during this tragedy to help our fellow citizens. I am ashamed that so many of our fellow citizens have decided to take advantage of this bad time our country is facing. I beg you all to check in on your neighbors, see if you have anything they need, trade food, games, books, whatever you must do to peacefully make it through this dilemma.

"We live in the best country in the world, and I'd like to see all my fellow citizens continue to keep our country the best country in the world.

I promise we are working nonstop on solving this epidemic and will continue to do so until everyone in our great nation is safe.

"Don't forget to call 1-800-555-5555 if you have any information about these tragic deaths nationwide. We are raising our reward to five million dollars for information leading to this epidemic's end." "Good night, and God bless!"

CHAPTER 37

Emil was sitting on the beautiful white sand in Bali, looking at the beautiful clear blue water while sunbathing his body. Emil's disposable phone rang. He answered his phone, "Yeah, it's great here, boss, but not so great in the United States." Emil laughed aloud. "Who would have ever thought that all this turmoil would have happened in the greatest country in the world?" Emil continued, "Did you hear the president last night?" There was a pause before Emil replied, "Yes, it was wonderful, and we are getting there, but I never thought we'd cause all of these other problems; I feel so sorry for the citizens of the US." Emil laughed aloud again. "They would all be in hell if it was up to me!" Emil turned off his phone and threw it in the sand.

Emil thought, A lousy five-million-dollar reward, what a cheap president! That's only a drop in the bucket compared to what I have made!

On the second day, Emil purchased a fabulous nine-bedroom home on the beach at the end of Bali. The home should have been on the front cover of Home Beautiful magazine. The first thing he did after moving in was to have every toilet seat covered in fabric. Emil was living the good life with beautiful, tanned women everywhere you looked, and Emil had already shared last night with one of them.

The first thing Emil did every morning was to swim twenty laps in his spacious pool. The pool deck had huge stones with every color of blooming plants decorating the pool deck. There was an inside shower at the pool and a changing room with lockers for his guests. This was Emil's favorite place in the house.

Sometimes, he'd sit on the pool deck for hours with a drink in his hand and think of his time in the United States. He did not have many good memories of the United States. Whenever he thought about Cinnamon, he felt like throwing up! He'd look at his marvelous home thinking, I hardly did any work, and here I am, a multi-millionaire. The big man pays well!

He loved watching all the news about what the United States was going through. It made him feel like he was God and did not feel sorry for any United States citizens. His only concern in the world was that they made their quota of fifteen million undiagnosed deaths in the United States!

CHAPTER 38

FRIDAY, MAY 15TH
ROSE AND HUSBAND

This was certainly a test for true love. Rose and her husband were just about stuck together, literally! They lived in a small home, so it was hard to be apart. They were up to well over one hundred games of cards; they played every game they had in the house at least twenty times and watched every movie they owned ten times. Rose's husband, who did not like to read, enjoyed reading. All that was airing on the TV was terrible news, and they could only take so much.

Rose told her husband, "Let's do what the president asked us to do last night: meet our neighbors and see if we can help anyone."

Rose's husband looked at his watch and answered, "Okay, it's after 8:00, so we're allowed outside on the streets; let's go."

Since they only knew one neighbor, this was a great idea. They started across the street from their home and started knocking on doors. Everyone was delighted to have company; everyone was as bored as they were. At every home they went to, they asked the people to meet in the middle of the street at 11:00 a.m. Everyone was excited; they had something new to do!

They went to all sixteen houses on their block, and everyone answered the door and said they would be thrilled to meet at 11:00 a.m. Ten minutes before 11:00, every neighbor stood in the middle of the street. Three were elderly people, and there were about a dozen children. They all exchanged names and what they could eat; they all talked about the deaths and everything happening in their lives. They were having a great time, better than any party some had been to.

One lady came up with a great idea: "Since we are all sick and tired of eating the same things, let's swap our food; what did not kill me won't kill you!" Everyone thought that was a wonderful idea, so they went to their homes to collect their food.

Rose said to her husband, "Isn't this wonderful? We did a great thing, and our reward is eating something new today!" He agreed as they walked into their home to get their food.

Everyone met in the street with their food, and the swapping began. These people were having fun for the first time in days. They all took their new meals home, met in the middle of the street, and decided to get together to play poker, sports in the streets, whatever anyone could think of.

Before Rose and her husband left to go eat lunch, Rose said to everyone, "This has been wonderful to meet you all; please, let's all help each other out, and let's get back together after lunch; we can swap movies, games, books, anything anyone can think of." They all agreed and were excited to head home to eat a new lunch.

While Rose and her husband were eating, Rose said, "You know, honey, we would have never met our nice neighbors if all of this had not happened in our country. Just think what we have been missing all these years; like my sister used to say, when the world hands you lemons, make lemonade!"

CHAPTER 39

SATURDAY, MAY 16TH
PRESIDENTIAL COMMITTEE CALLS
CDC

Miss Lydia Peabody dialed the direct phone number of Dr. Wendt at the CDC.

Dr. Wendt answered the phone, "Hello, Dr. Wendt."

Miss Peabody said, "Hello, Dr. Wendt, this is Lydia Peabody calling from the special presidential committee. I'm calling to tell you that we have not come up with one item that either children or people who live in impoverished areas do not do that middle and upper-class people do. The president has asked me to call you to see how you are doing."

Dr. Wendt replied, "All of our scientists have been working nonstop on this puzzle, and I have nothing new to tell you."

Lydia Peabody said, "Dr. Wendt, do you think it would be a good idea if we all worked together on this instead of testing the same things twice?"

Dr. Wendt answered, "Yes, that would be a great idea."

Miss Peabody answered, "How do you think it would work best? Should we come there or fax what we have been testing?"

Dr. Wendt replied, "It would be best for us to work together at the CDC. Fresh faces and ideas may be the key to uncovering the problem."

Miss Peabody added, "Would we stay there or just come for the day?"

Dr. Wendt answered, "We have plenty of room here; I think it would be best if you came here and stayed. We have plenty of sleeping facilities. We must know how many will come and what you need to eat."

Miss Peabody replied, "This sounds like a great plan; hopefully if we put our minds together, we may be able to resolve this catastrophe."

Dr. Wendt said, "Should I expect you all today?"

Miss Peabody said, "I will round up our team of twelve and fax our menu. We will plan on being there by 1:00 p.m."

Dr. Wendt said, "We will be ready and waiting for you. See you all at 1:00, goodbye."

Dr. Wendt called housekeeping and their chef. He then walked to the lab to tell his scientists about the coming team.

Dr. Wendt was delighted that more resources would be working on the case. If they found the problem, it would be here at the CDC, which made him very happy. He spoke with everyone in the lab and told them all to be at the library at 2:00 this afternoon. He called it "The Meeting Of The Minds!'

CHAPTER 40

SUNDAY, MAY 17TH
PRESIDENTIAL ADDRESS
WASHINGTON, DC

The president's approval rating has been at an all-time low! No president has ever been this disliked in our nation's history. The only reason the citizens of the United States were going to watch the Presidential Address was because there wasn't anything else to do or to talk about. Everyone could watch and listen to the president again!

At 8:00 p.m., President Hamilton R. Bennett said, "Good evening, fellow citizens." Although you are hearing all the latest about our nationwide epidemic, I must give you the latest information.

We still have not found the cause of this worldwide epidemic. In our country, the death rate has risen to over seven million. I have started a special committee at the CDC in Atlanta, Georgia. Together with the scientists, they are working nonstop on the cause of all these undiagnosed deaths.

"Let's all pray tonight that they soon find the cause. What we have come to realize is that no animals, very few children, and people living in impoverished areas are not dying. The question is, what have the people who have died done or eaten that the above don't do or eat? When we answer that question, we will solve this epidemic. If you have any ideas, please call our helpline at 1-800-555-5555. One of you just may come up with the answer."

The president continued, "Our jails across the United States are filled with the homeless and people who have no food to eat; the curfew I put on our country has helped our country's homeless and hungry people. When I set the curfew in force, I was unaware that so many citizens of our great country had no money, food, electricity, or phones. The curfew was a good thing since looting is way down, and the hungry and poor people in our nation have three square meals daily. The new inmates are starting programs to help them find work and homes when they are released. This is a good thing. We have hired thousands of social workers to help these people get back on their feet.

"Since I did not die from what I ate twelve days ago, every inmate at every jail has the same things to eat as I do: a hamburger, macaroni and cheese, baked beans, and drinking only city water. I must admit that a hamburger, macaroni and cheese, and baked beans used to be one of my favorite meals, but when this epidemic is over, I will not eat any of the above for at least a year!"

"As I'm sure you have seen on the news, our tractor-trailer drivers delivering our food from warehouses are much safer now. Another good report is we have had no new hijackings."

"I have heard of many neighborhoods across our country that are having street parties and meeting each other. They trade food, movies, books, and games and entertain each other. This is a very good thing! Hopefully, this will continue long after our epidemic is over."

"It seems that our country is greater since the start of the epidemic. It has brought our citizens closer to each other, which is a very good thing. I feel very confident that we will solve this epidemic very soon."

"Until then, keep up the good work you all have been doing, and pray that there are no more deaths in our nation as we continue to work on discovering the cause."

"Good night, and God bless.

CHAPTER 41

MAY 18TH
EMIL MASHADUK
BALI, INDONESIA

Emil sat at his pool, drinking coffee and reading the tiny Bali newspaper. He stopped reading the paper and looked out over the marvelous, beautiful Indian Ocean. The water was calm and flat this morning; Emil looked at every beautiful shade of blue. He thought to himself, "All those poor people in the United States will never get to see what I'm seeing this morning."

When Emil heard last night that the death count was over 7 million in the United States, he jumped up and clapped with joy. He thought that way too many good things were happening in the United States. We didn't plan on the people uniting. Shit, street parties, just how much fun can that be? How nice are neighbors meeting neighbors? What a crock of shit this is!

So, the president of the United States eats hamburgers, macaroni and cheese, and baked beans all day. Good for the president; I hope he has a lot of gas and a severe shit problem, not to mention a sore ass! How much longer will their food supplies last? Knowing this dick of a president, he probably has food flown in or shipped in from other countries.

Emil thought, "We have forgotten the animals, children, and poor in the ghettos. I can understand the animals but not the children and the poor. Hmm, next time, we'll know better!

Fifteen million, please, just fifteen million!"

It was getting time for his usual morning drink before he did his laps in his pool. He rang his bell, and Kastria, his beautiful dark-skinned woman, appeared at his side. Emil said, "Good morning, my dear; you look ravishingly beautiful this morning. I love to look at your jet-black shining hair, my dear." He took her hand and said, "Would you please be my guest this morning and join me for a mimosa?"

She answered, "Why yes, Emil, I'd love to join you; I'll be back in a moment with two mimosas."

The two of them sat and talked while they enjoyed their drinks. Emil then did his laps in his pool and headed for a long walk on the beach. As Emil walked in the sand, he thought, "What a life; everyone in the world should live this way except for United States citizens!"

CHAPTER 42

Dr. Wendt, his scientists, and the "new" committee had been brainstorming for two days with no new clue. The only good thing is that the CDC scientists had new faces to look at and people to talk to. They divided into new different groups every four hours. Dr. Wendt thought it would only take one idea from one of them, and before they knew it, they would have the answer. So much for that!

Dr. Wendt called a meeting for everyone at 4:00 p.m. in the library. Dr. Wendt said when everyone was there and sitting, "Ladies and gentlemen, I have an idea; let's all think of only things people touch, like paper products, soap, plants, and newspapers; the list is very long."

One committee member stood up and said, "How could it be something people touch?"

Dr. Wendt replied, "People could touch something toxic and touch their mouths and ears or wipe their eyes; it may be something we touch daily. Let's all form new groups and work on this idea."

Dr. Wendt continued, "As of an hour ago, the death count has reached eight million of our fellow citizens; we must not overlook any possibility; good luck and think!"

New groups were formed, and all sixty-one headed in different directions.

Dr. Wendt thought to himself, "This is about to kill me; what in the hell could be killing all of these people, and why is it so difficult to find the answer?"

Dr. Wendt walked with paper and pencil to the kitchen; he would write everything touched in there. Even though his chef hadn't died, it didn't mean it wasn't a different brand or color of one of the items in the kitchen!

Just as Dr. Wendt walked into the kitchen; his mind went to toilet paper; he thought, If you wipe with toilet paper that has toxic chemicals on it, it could enter your body through the vagina, urethra, or anus, better known as an asshole, which is what I feel like today!

Dr. Wendt turned around, left the kitchen, and would meet with every group to give them his latest thought, which may be the answer.

One scientist in the first group he spoke with said, "Dr. Wendt, children use toilet paper all day long in every home in the United States. Could those homes with children use a different toilet paper than all the other homes?"

Dr. Wendt answered, "Yes, you are correct. Okay then, what do adults use in that region of the body that children don't?"

Dr. Wendt went to every group and told them his latest thought, and the scientists replied. Dr. Wendt also told every group that they were meeting at 4:00 in the library the following afternoon, but they were to call him if they found a solution before then.

As Dr. Wendt walked away from the last group, he finally felt good; they were getting close to solving this damn problem.

CHAPTER 43

TUESDAY, MAY 19TH
DEPRESSED US CITIZENS

Every United States citizen was depressed, sick, and tired of the news. Way too many cried when they saw the latest death count. It certainly was a grim time in the United States.

People were still having street parties but less fun than they first were. All everyone talked about now was the death count, thinking of things that children and people in the ghettos didn't do; they were all bored, and most of them never thought they would ever miss their jobs, but for most, they did, and they were missing their work and daily routines.

One person thought it a good idea for all of them to go to another block and meet new people with new everything. Not one person wanted to do that.

The grocery store discussion was getting very bad; there was less food in every store every day, and the people were getting scared. They even talked about staying in the streets past eight o'clock so they would have three meals daily in jail!

They all agreed they had to devise a new plan to lift their morals. Everyone had seen each other's movies and read their books, and they were sick to death of the games and playing cards. Poker would have been fun if they had any real money to bet.

Some men talked about things they could be doing around the house: painting, putting on new roofs, and making repairs; if only they had known to get the supplies, they could have fixed every problem in every home on their block and their block would be the most beautiful for miles!

One man came up with the idea that they all swap books again. Not many were interested in that.

One woman said, "There is no way I could concentrate on reading a book with all this mess going on in our country, but I sure do miss the newspaper every morning!"

The elderly man in the neighborhood said, "Let's pull our home repair supplies together; maybe we have what we would need to repair one of our homes. Everyone clapped; they decided to meet at 8:00 a.m. with their repair supplies.

Before they parted and ended their street party, which was no longer a party, one lady said, "Let's all smile and be happy that none of us have lost anyone we love in this epidemic; we all still have our health, food, family, and friends, and some people have it a lot worse than any of us do."

They hugged each other and returned home to do nothing except clean, work in their gardens, or watch the news.

CHAPTER 44

D r. Wendt looked at his watch; it was 3:45, so he started to walk to the library. Everyone joined him from every direction at the CDC when he arrived.

After everyone was seated, Dr. Wendt said, "Did we solve our problem?" One of his scientists stood up and said, "There are only two items that only adult men and women use that children don't use other than medication for herpes or medication for venereal disease; the first is an intimate moisturizer, and the second is prophylactics. We have also discussed that these are items that people in the ghetto wouldn't often use because of the cost of these items, and the children who have died may have found one of these items and played with them."

Dr. Wendt said, "Excellent, great job; now let's order every brand of intimate moisturizer, prophylactics, and all medication used for herpes and venereal disease to be delivered to the lab immediately."

Dr. Wendt started clapping, and everyone in the room joined him. Finally, they may have the answer.

Dr. Wendt then asked Dr. Hertz and Dr. Wadeson to start making calls to have every brand of these two items sent to the lab ASAP.

The scientists were getting back into their grey suits and entering the lab when the items started arriving. One by one, each scientist took one of the items and started testing.

Dr. Wendt knew this would take days, so he decided to help. He wore his gray suit and took the next brand that entered the lab. Everyone in the lab was excited and working at a fast pace.

Dr. Wendt was unaware that the phone in the main office of the CDC was ringing off the hook.

By 3:00 in the morning, Dr. Wendt walked to the dressing room, took his gray suit off, put it in the big red hazardous bin, and put his lab coat back on. He then walked to the kitchen and got his food; everyone else had eaten except for him. He carried his now boring meal to his office, set it on his desk, took his lab coat off, and sat down. The minute he sat down, he heard the answering machine beeping in Miss Deplay's office. He stood up, opened the door to her office, and pushed the button on the answering machine. The first ten calls were unimportant, but when Dr. Wendt listened to the eleventh call, excitement ran through his body. It was from a coroner in Warwick, Rhode Island, and he was calling to tell the CDC that in the past two days, he had twenty-three women from Warwick who had died from undiagnosed deaths. Dr. Wendt thought, Finally, a breakthrough. He felt like jumping for joy. He dialed the number the coroner left, but no one answered.

Dr. Wendt listened to the rest of the calls and continued to dial the number to the coroner in Warwick, Rhode Island. After dialing the number twenty times, Dr. Wendt walked back into his office and thought, I guess there are still people in the United States that sleep at night, and I already know I won't be one of them tonight!

CHAPTER 45

TUESDAY, MAY 19

GUNTHER GOES TO GRANDMA'S

Dr. Wendt's hands were shaking for the first time since this catastrophe started. It was 6:30 a.m and he was sitting in his office alone, trying to drink his coffee. With each sip, he felt like he was going to throw up. He used to love coffee, but now he hated it; now he hated everything except for his family! There certainly wasn't much Dr. Wendt liked anymore; he was worried, felt defeated, and was now worried about his mother, whom he had called for two days every chance he got, but she never answered. His brain was working nonstop to make everything in his world right again. He had had it but must keep up the appearance that everything would be all right!

Dr. Wendt said, "Just why in the hell does everyone think I am the only one to end this catastrophe in the United States?" He took a big gulp of coffee and reached for the phone."

He dialed his son's phone number: one ring, two rings, three rings, and by the fourth ring, his son finally answered. Dr. Wendt said, "Good morning, son; how is my Gunther doing?" They spoke back and forth for a while when Dr. Wendt said, "I was worried your phone wouldn't work; so far, that is the only thing in the United States that still works!" Dr. Wendt continued, "I have tried to call your grandmother off and on for the last two days, and she never answers, and I am worried about her! Gunther, would you please drive to South Carolina to see if she is okay or needs anything? Maybe bring her home with you, son." Dr. Wendt continued and said, "And please call me the minute you find her; I am so worried about her."

Gunther replied, "Of course, Dad, I will go and see how everything is with her." Gunther continued, "I think she needs to come home with me, and yes, I will call you the minute I get a hug from Grandma!"

Dr. Wendt replied, "Well, this takes one thing off my mind, thank you. When can you leave?"

Gunther replied, "I just got out of the shower when I heard the phone ring; as soon as I get dressed, I will head to her home. Do you think there will be a lot of traffic?"

Dr. Wendt replied, "At this point, I would have no idea at all. With people breaking into food trucks and taking all the food, you should expect anything, son. Do you still have the gun I bought for your twenty-first birthday? If so, please take it along just in case."

Gunther replied, "Yes, I would never part with such a wonderful present, and I will have it with me. I will not call you because you are so busy until I get a hug from Grandma! Also, Dad, all you can do is what you can do, so please keep yourself focused on that; no one can solve every problem in the world!" Gunther continued, "Please, Dad, calm down. I got this, Dad, and I will call you soon. I love you!"

Gunther quickly dressed and started to pack; he knew he didn't have enough gas to return home from his grandma's, so he packed more clothing than he normally would. He got his toiletries from the bathroom, his computer, and all his chargers for his electronics. Gunther didn't want to tell his dad he would pack more than normal, not to worry him with one more thing. He stood there momentarily, thinking, Do I have everything I need? The only thing other than the gas situation was cash. He packed up his car and was ready to leave for Grandma's in South Carolina. He first went to his bank and used the ATM, which did not work, and of course, he got no money.

Gunther was now on the interstate that would take him to South Carolina. After five minutes, he realized he was the only one on the interstate in both directions. Gunther thought This was weird; there were no lights, and most streetlights were out. Not one car, pickup truck, bus, and no police, nothing! I could drive fast and not get into trouble with the police, but then I would use more gas, which is not a good idea.

As Gunther continued to drive, he was surprised to see no fast-food signs lit up, and nothing was open! Gunther thought, *this is certainly a lot worse than I ever thought, and I will be the first to admit that I am scared. Thank heavens I brought my gun along.*

Gunther decided that some good music would help the drive, but he found out quickly that there wasn't any music on any station, not even the AM stations. All he heard was news about the millions of people dying and that no one had any food; the same things he heard on his TV at home. Suddenly,

Gunther remembered he forgot to get the food he was to eat. He thought, I guess I will have to share Grandma's food!

Gunther started talking out loud to himself. "This trip made me aware of how so many others have felt in their lives, like when a Negro man with his family was let go from a plantation, where did he take his family, which way, and how did he find food for them? A lonely soldier walking alone in a foreign land with no compass, bloody, hungry, and thirsty." Gunther continued, "This is eerie, scary, dark, and I must pee, but I am too afraid to stop!"

Gunther finally saw the sign: South Carolina. I am here, Grandma, and there are no other cars in South Carolina and no lights. It must be like this all over the United States!

Gunther noticed bright lights coming up on him in the rear. Great, I am not the only fool in this world! The vehicle was nearing very fast, and right before it hit Gunther in the rear end of his car, it went around him very fast until it was out of sight. Gunther thought to himself, *what in the heck was that all about?* It wasn't very long until the vehicle approached him with bright lights that were blinding him. When the vehicle was about to hit his car, it came to a screeching halt. Gunther could then see a driver and a passenger, a black flag on both sides of the big pickup truck with skulls on the flag.

Gunther thought, I am dead, and he immediately got his gun from the glove box in his car.

The passenger exited the truck with a gun and started walking toward Gunther's car door! The big man with a long black beard told Gunther, "Roll your window down, please; we mean no harm; we are just looking for food to feed our families."

Gunther rolled his window down and said to the man, "I have no food to give you."

The man replied, "I am going to search your car inside with my flashlight, and then I want to look in your car trunk!"

Gunther said, "As long as you are not going to hurt me, be my guest; I will open up my trunk." The man used his flashlight, and the inside of Gunther's car lit up.

The man found no food and said, "I am going to look in the trunk; remember, we mean no harm to you." The man was back there for only a few minutes, but it felt like hours to Gunther. The man said, "Thank you for not lying to me. I opened your bags, and you have no food, and we thank you for your time!"

Gunther said, "You are welcome, and I hope you can

find food for your family. I am like you; I have no food either!"

As the man walked away, he said to Gunther, "Safe travels, and we hope you also find food." With that, the man got back into the pickup truck, and they backed up and then drove past Gunther's car.

Gunther was so upset he wasn't sure if he could even drive. Gunther just sat there for a while until he thought he could drive safely and thought to himself, What the hell has happened to our world? How can this be, people only wanting food for their families? What has happened to our great country? No wonder my dad is a freaking mess. This may be good; people may realize how good they have it in the USA!

Gunther put his gun back into the glove box of his car and headed off to Grandma's again. Gunther said, "Thank heavens, only three exits to Weeping Willow Way; I love the name of Grandma's Street. I grew up with a big, beautiful weeping willow tree in my backyard that I played under for years; what a great memory."

Gunther said, "I am here and seeing people in the streets having fun!" I will park my car at Grandma's and start looking for her. I no sooner got out of my car than I heard and saw Grandma calling my name in excitement and rushing toward me!" They fell into each other's arms and kissed each other.

All of Grandma's neighbors were outside, so Gunther had to meet each one of them before they could go into Grandma's house! Everyone hugged and shook his hand, and some women kissed him.

One woman said, "We just love your grandma; she is the pillar of this street and organized us to share everything we have: building supplies, games, books, food, sewing, and kids' trading stuff. I could go on forever, but your grandma saved us all from being scared to death over what has happened to our country!"

Gunther looked at his grandma and said, "Good job, Grandma!"

Grandma said to him, "Why are you here, son?"

He answered, "Well, we couldn't get you on the phone, and we were worried about you since we love you so much!"

Grandma said, "See, I told you about my wonderful family, and he is one of them!"

Gunther told Grandma, "We had better call Dad and tell him you are safe and I am here with you."

Once inside Grandma's house, Gunther plopped down on a chair and took a deep breath. He thought, I must forget about my drive here, or I will never drive again! Gunther got up, called his dad, and handed the phone to Grandma. She was smiling, and Gunther was certain that his dad was too. I couldn't see the moon, but it was a miracle I got here alive! I will never do this again, ever! I am staying with my grandma!

Grandma and Dad ended their conversation, and Grandma handed Gunther the phone. He told Dad, "This is a miracle. I turned into Grandma's street, and everyone in the neighborhood was in the middle of the street talking, laughing, and having a great time!"

Dad asked him, "When will you bring Grandma back here?"

He calmly said, "Not until this thing, whatever it is, is over, and I am going to stay here with Grandma and take care of her." Gunther continued, "It's a great place, and the people are lovely, and I already feel at home here!" He didn't want to upset his dad about his drive down here! Gunther promised Dad they would call him every other day as long as they could, but if he didn't hear from them, not to get upset because some people here no longer had a phone.

Gunther no sooner hung up the phone that Grandma wanted to know what he was supposed to eat; he told her he couldn't eat anything right now, but he would take a big glass of cold water! I now feel safe again, and this is where I will stay. Gunther then said to Grandma, "May I use your bathroom? I have had to go for hours now!" Grandma laughed, and afterward, Gunther felt so much better!

CHAPTER 46

D r. Wendt kept looking at the clock. Finally, it was 8:00 a.m. As Dr. Wendt dialed the number to the coroner in Warwick, Rhode Island, he realized he had forgotten his name. The coroner finally answered the phone, and Dr. Wendt said, "Hello, this is Dr. Wendt from the CDC returning your call."

The coroner answered, "Thank heavens, I have been waiting impatiently for your call. I assume you know from my message that we have twenty-three women who have died from undiagnosed deaths in our town of Warwick, Rhode Island."

Dr. Wendt said, "Yes sir, you have assumed correctly; this is the first group of deaths we have gotten. what are the ages of the dead women?"

The coroner answered, "The death age ranges from twenty-five to sixty years old."

Dr. Wendt replied, "Please tell me your name before we go on."

The coroner answered, "My name is Patrick Gilhooly, and I have been the coroner for Kent County for twenty-six years."

Dr. Wendt said, "That is a very unusual name; no wonder I could not say it correctly. Is it okay that I call you Patrick?"

Patrick answered, "You certainly may, Dr. Wendt; now, what do we do about all these deaths?"

Dr. Wendt said, "A group of us will come to you as soon as we get packed; I will call the United States Air Force and get us up in the air ASAP. Do you know of anything these women have in common?"

Patrick answered, "Unfortunately, no, but with your approval, I can call our best detectives and have them start an investigation."

Dr. Wendt answered, "Of course, you have my approval. We need all the help we can get, and would you please give me your address?"

Patrick said, "I'll be waiting at the Kent County Memorial Hospital morgue."

Dr. Wendt said, "I'll have my secretary call you with our landing time, which I hope will be later this afternoon."

Patrick answered, "I look forward to meeting you and helping all I can."

Dr. Wendt said, "Thank you, sir; you have made my day!"

Dr. Wendt dialed Miss Deplay's phone number. When she answered, he told her he needed her ASAP. Miss Deplay replied, "I'll be there within the hour."

While Dr. Wendt was waiting for Miss Deplay, he walked to the lab and yelled the good news finally a group of deaths. He called the names of three of his top scientists and told them to meet him in his office right away.

The three scientists entered Dr. Wendt's office. Dr. Wendt said, "I would like all of you to go to Warwick, Rhode Island, with me. I have a good feeling about this and need your help, so go get packed to leave today. And one more thing, you may all call your families to tell them where you are going, not why you are going but where you are going. You all deserve to speak with your families. We will meet back here in two hours."

While he was having his meeting with his staff, Miss Deplay showed up. Dr. Wendt immediately walked into her office and told her he needed a plane for nine people flying to Warwick, Rhode Island. Miss Deplay said, "Yes, sir, I'll take care of it immediately." Miss Deplay was so happy to be back at work!

Miss Deplay knocked on Dr. Wendt's door and said, "You are to meet an Air Force jet at Hartsfield-Jackson Atlanta Airport at 3:15 sharp."

Dr. Wendt said, "Thank you, Miss Deplay, and it is good to see you again."

Miss Deplay replied, "You have no idea how good it is to be bad here at work."

Dr. Wendt said, "Please, no one is to know that we are leaving, okay?"

Miss Deplay said, "Yes, sir. I will keep it under wraps!"

Before Dr. Wendt left for Rhode Island, he ensured all the other scientists kept testing the products they were working on and the medications used for the two diseases. Dr. Wendt then called the CIA with the news. They were excited with the news and said, "Dr. Wendt, I will call the president and the FBI. I'm going to join you there and bring the FBI along. This is big, and we need all the help we can get."

Dr. Wendt answered, "We are meeting the coroner in Warwick, Rhode Island, at the Kent County Memorial Hospital morgue, and our flight leaves Atlanta at 3:15 this afternoon.

Nelson replied, "We'll be right behind you; see you in Rhode Island.

All four were on their way to the Atlanta airport. Dr. Wendt said, "Let's keep our fingers crossed that this is it, and let's solve this disaster!"

CHAPTER 47

WEDNESDAY, MAY 20TH
CDC SCIENTISTS LEAVE FOR WARWICK RI

On their walk out to their airplane, Dr. Wendt turned to his traveling buddies and said, "I don't know about all of you, but my brain is on overload, causing a think ache! I'm going to sleep the whole way to Rhode Island; someone, please make sure I get off this plane when we arrive.

The four scientists got to fly in the best United States Air Force jet. They all felt very special. Every seat was larger than a first-class seat on a regular airline. They all took a seat and buckled up. The pilot came to brief them on their flight to Rhode Island. Major John Foster said, "Welcome aboard your flight to Rhode Island; I am honored to be your pilot. This jet flies so fast we will land in an hour and fifteen minutes; sit back and relax; we are ready to take off."

Dr. Wendt turned to Dr. Hertz and said, "There goes my long nap; guess I'll have to sleep rapidly!" It seemed like they just took off when they were landing. A huge Air Force van was waiting beside the plane to take them to the Kent County Memorial Hospital. They walked into the hospital within fifteen minutes and took the elevator to the morgue.

Dr. Wendt knocked on the door to the morgue and then walked right in. He could not wait to get started. Patrick held out his hand and said, "Welcome, Dr. Wendt." The two men shook hands, Dr. Wendt introduced his scientist, and Patrick introduced his staff and detectives.

Dr. Wendt asked the detectives, "Have you found anything out about our twenty-three deaths, anything in common?

Detective McGuiness answered, "Nothing yet, but we have just started our search."

Dr. Wendt replied, "Is there any way we could visit each victim's home?"

Detective McGuiness answered, "I'm sure all the families would approve, but as of yet, none of the victims have been buried.

"Dr. Wendt said, "We are under the gun here; we must search these homes and speak with the families ASAP. What we do today may save thousands of lives tomorrow."

Detective McGuiness replied, "What is the best way to do this?"

Dr. Wendt answered, "Just go start knocking on the doors, one by one, and explain our predicament. We should get started instead of waiting for the CIA and the FBI. I'm sure all these families have seen the news and would happily help us!"

Detective McGuiness said, "Whose house do we go to first?"

Dr. Wendt answered, "Let's start with the youngest victim and go from there."

Patrick said, "Our youngest victim is Sara Sue Ridgewell; she was twenty-five, married with no children, and lived at 321 Greenwich Avenue. The next youngest is Barbara Perrone, age twenty-seven, who was married with children and lived at 741 Warwick Avenue."

Dr. Wendt said, "Can we split up, and half of us go to Ridgewell's home and the other half to Perrone's?"

One of Dr. Wendt's scientists said, "Dr. Wendt, I think that the same group should go to each home; it would be easier for one group to see or find a commonality."

Dr. Wendt answered, "I have to agree with you; one group visits all the homes until we find what they have in common."

Detective McGuiness said, "I'll take your group to every home, and my other detective can bring the other members of your group if you wish."

Dr. Wendt said, "Sounds like a plan to me; we will have more flying in from the CIA and the FBI. I'm not sure how many of them will be coming, but they will be coming to your lab, Patrick. Please have them call me when they arrive."

Patrick replied, "Sure thing, Dr. Wendt."

Dr. Wendt motioned to his scientists, and the four of them joined Detective McGuiness in his car. The other detectives followed in their cars.

Detective McGuiness pulled his car into the driveway at 321 Greenwich Avenue. Dr. Wendt and Detective McGuiness walked to the front door together, and Dr. Wendt rang the doorbell. A young, handsome man answered the door. He said, "Hello, what can I do for you?"

Dr. Wendt replied, "First of all, we are so sorry for your loss; I am Dr. Rudolph Wendt, head of the CDC in Atlanta, Georgia. We are here because your wife was one of the twenty-three women who died from an undiagnosed death in Warwick in the past two days. We want permission to search your home to see if we can find a commonality between the twenty-three deaths. We hope to solve this epidemic going on in the United States of America. This is the first group of people and our first chance to investigate the potential cause."

The young man said, "I'm George Ridgewell, Sara Sue's husband, and I was unaware that twenty-three women had died here in two days. and you are most welcome to search our home from head to toe; please find the cause."

With that, George went to his mother and cried. Detective McGuiness waved for the rest of his detectives to join them in the search. Dr. Wendt asked George, "While they search your home, can you please tell me if your wife was a member of any women's group?"

George replied, "Sara was a nurse at the local hospital, and many nurses would get together for what they called girls' night out. Sara also went to the local gym for workouts. Sara was home most of the time. She wasn't at work and loved working in her gardens. Other than that, I can't think of anything else right now, but I'm not exactly thinking straight either."

Dr. Wendt answered, "Thank you, and if you think of anything else, please call the coroner's office at the hospital." George nodded his head. Talk about an invasion of privacy; the men searched every drawer, the refrigerator, in which they took specimens of food, all closets, the basement, the garage, and the whole house from top to bottom, and they didn't find or see anything unusual. They were finished and ready to leave the Ridgewell home three hours later. They had at least sixty different-sized bags with them when they left.

Dr. Wendt walked over to George and shook his hand, saying, "George, you will never know how much we appreciate you allowing us to search your home. Again, we are all so very sorry for your loss. We will be back in touch when we solve the problem."

George said, "Thank you, and good luck. If I must live without my Sara, I'd like to know why."

Dr. Wendt walked out of the front door to the car and was feeling like hell and very disappointed.

Once in the car, Detective McGuiness said, "I think we should have asked to take their computer. There is no telling what we may find on the computer. It is already after eight, and I think it's too late to visit the next home; remember, we all are on a curfew."

Dr. Wendt said, "You are correct; please take us to a hotel where they have room service."

Detective McGuiness replied, "Dr. Wendt, there are no hotels open, let alone with room service; the only place I can suggest to you all is to go back to the hospital to get rooms and eat in the cafeteria."

Dr. Wendt said, "About the computer, you are right. We should have asked to take it. I thought about it but thought it may be too much for the family."

Dr. Wendt continued, "I have been locked in the CDC so long I have forgotten all about the curfew, the hotels, and the food. Please take us back to the hospital."

When they returned to the hospital, they all went to the morgue. Nelson Whitcomb and two FBI agents were waiting for them. Nelson Whitcomb said, "Dr. Wendt, I was just about to dial your number to let you know we have arrived." Dr. Wendt and Nelson Whitcomb shook hands.

Dr. Wendt said, "It's good to meet you finally."

Nelson Whitcomb answered, "It seems like I already know you, Dr. Wendt, and I would like to introduce you to our top partners, Mr. Sean Miller and Mr. Gephart Tyler from the FBI."

They all shook hands, and Dr. Wendt answered, "I would like you to meet Detective McGuiness from Warwick and my scientists Dr. Hertz, Dr. Wadeson, and Dr. Schultz from the CDC in Atlanta."

Nelson Whitcomb said, "Hello to everyone, and I think we should have a quick meeting. Is there a room where we can all sit down, Patrick?"

Patrick said, "Follow me."

They all left, walked down the hallway, and entered another room on the right. The room had a huge table with chairs, a water dispenser, a coffee pot, and a snack machine.

Everyone took a seat, and the meeting began. Nelson Whitcomb started, "Have you found anything we need to discuss, Dr. Wendt?"

Dr. Wendt said, "We have only searched one home and didn't find anything, but we think we should investigate the computers from all twenty-three homes."

Nelson Whitcomb replied, "That's a definite, and I think we should get a search warrant for every home, which includes all computers and any of the homes inside and outside."

Gephart Tyler from the FBI said, "All I need is the names and addresses of all homes, and I can have the search warrants in an hour, if not sooner."

Patrick stood up and said, "I'll get your names and addresses." Patrick returned with two pages of names and addresses and handed them to Gephart Tyler. Gephart Tyler left the room and called the home office in Washington, DC.

While Gephart Tyler was gone, they discussed starting early at 8:00 to search for the second home. Dr. Wendt asked Patrick, "I'm hoping you have rooms in the hospital for us and a hot meal that's safe to eat!"

Patrick said, "I'll get right on it, Dr. Wendt!"

As Patrick left the room, Gephart Tyler said, "It's all taken care of; they will be faxing all twenty-three search warrants to Patrick's office." Patrick stopped and said, "How do you know our fax number?"

Gephart Tyler replied, "Patrick, this is the FBI; we know everyone's fax number, cell number, home phone number, and computer addresses!"

Patrick replied, "I had better go make sure there is enough paper in the fax machine; I don't have a secretary; I may need some help to keep the fax machine filled with paper if I'm going to go get you all rooms and food."

Gephart Tyler said, "I'll sit at your fax and keep it filled with paper."

Patrick said, "Thank you, and would you all like to be served dinner here or in the cafeteria?"

Dr. Wendt replied, "I have eaten steak, baked potato, and green beans. I'd sure like to visit the cafeteria. I'm sure all the food here is safe, right?"

Patrick said, "Yes, we haven't had one patient die in our hospital."

Dr. Wendt said, "Okay, lead the way to the cafeteria, Patrick."

Before they all walked to the cafeteria together, Patrick went into his office to give Gephart Tyler directions so he could meet them all in the cafeteria after he received all twenty-three search warrants.

As they entered the cafeteria, Dr. Wendt said, "I'm so hungry for different food that I don't care if it does kill me."

The entire cafeteria staff was busy getting everything ready for the men. They usually close at eight o'clock. They all went through the line, and the men's trays were filled with a little of everything! All the men sat together at a long table and ate without saying a word!

Most men were finished eating when Gephart Tyler entered the room with twenty-three search warrants. Gephart Tyler said, "Here they are, all twenty-three of them; I'm going to get something to eat."

When Patrick entered the cafeteria, Gephart Tyler had just sat down to eat and said, "Your quarters are ready for you!"

Nelson Whitcomb said, "Thank you, Patrick; as soon as Gephart Tyler is finished eating, we'll follow you to our quarters. Let's meet at the cafeteria at 7:00 a.m. for a good hot breakfast; we will be very busy tomorrow!"

Gephart Tyler said, "I have called the local FBI, and they will be spending the night in their lab testing all the specimens you took from the first home; I'll stay in the morgue until they come and get the bags of goodies!"

When Gephart Tyler finished eating, they cleared their trays and headed to their rooms. Gephart Tyler said, "I'll see you all at 7:00 a.m. sharp."

Dr. Wendt walked into his room and turned on the TV to watch the news, but he didn't hear much. He was asleep ten minutes after he lay down on the hospital bed.

CHAPTER 48

Detective McGuiness and his partners joined Dr. Wendt and his group at 7:00 a.m. in the hospital cafeteria. Dr. Wendt said, "I wish everyone were this prompt; let's eat breakfast and get to work."

Detective McGuiness said, "Where to first, Dr. Wendt?"

Dr. Wendt looked at his paperwork and said, "We are going to the Perrone home at 741 Warwick Avenue. Oh, how I dread this one; they have children!"

They all reached 741 Warwick Avenue in two police cars from the Warwick police department. They all got their supply cases out of the cars and followed Nelson Whitcomb. The supply cases had every size of a plastic container, four different envelopes, four different sizes of paper bags, and four different

plastic bags. Each case also had fifty face masks, fifty pairs of latex gloves, long Q-tips, and wooden sticks longer and wider than a Popsicle stick.

Mr. Nelson Whitcomb rang the doorbell; a cute little boy with blond hair answered the door. The father was right behind his son, grabbed his arm, and said, "How many times must I tell you not to open this door?" He let go of his son's arm, and the little boy ran off crying. Mr. Perrone said, "What do you want?"

Nelson Whitcomb handed Mr. Perrone the search warrant. He said, "We are investigating your wife's death because this is the first group of people who have died simultaneously in the United States. We are trying to find a commonality between the twenty-three women's undiagnosed deaths that occurred here in two days."

Mr. Perrone asked, "What can I do to help? I have three little children here without their mother."

Nelson Whitcomb replied, "I first meant to tell you how sorry we are for your loss, and you can help us by allowing us to search your home; we are looking for why so many women have died, your wife being one of them."

Mr. Perrone answered, "How long will this take? I need to feed the children breakfast."

Nelson Whitcomb said, "I have no idea how long this will take. I promise we will stay out of your way."

Mr. Perrone replied, "Come on in, and please excuse this messy house."

Before Nelson Whitcomb entered the house, he waved for the rest of them to come. Once inside, Dr. Wendt said, "Mr. Perrone, I have one question for you: was your wife a member of any women's groups?"

Mr. Perrone said, "Not that I know of; she was with the kids every day, all day long."

Dr. Wendt said, "Thank you so much." By then, all the men were searching for everything in the home. Everyone wore gloves and filled plastic bags, paper bags, and containers with anything they thought was suspicious.

They all got out of the home as quickly as they could. They searched everything they searched at the first home but did it much faster. The kids were everywhere and into everything, and the little girl kept crying for her mother.

As one of the men was carrying their computer out of the front door, Mr. Perrone yelled, "You can't take our computer!"

Nelson Whitcomb answered, "Yes, we can, sir; it's clearly stated in the search warrant, and we can take anything we need to take, and we may have to return."

Mr. Perrone yelled, "The damn government!" He then turned and walked away.

Dr. Wendt couldn't get out of the house fast enough. Once they were in the car, Dr. Wendt said, "Detective McGuiness, let's pick the next home with no children; I can hardly stand it; it is so sad for those children."

Detective McGuiness said, where to next, Dr. Wendt?"

Dr. Wendt looked at his paperwork. Dr. Wendt replied, "1349 Elm Street, Amy Fusco, twenty-nine, with NO children!"

Detective McGuiness put the police car in drive, and away they all went, with the second following to the third house. Dr. Wendt told Detective McGuiness, "I'm so glad Nelson Whitcomb and the FBI are in charge of this now; it's very difficult for me to talk to the victims' husbands; that is not my forte!"

Detective McGuiness pulled next to the curb at 1349 Elm Street. The second car followed. They all got out of the cars and got in the trunks of the two police cars for more materials to put in their cases to use in the search.

Nelson Whitcomb walked to the front door and knocked on the door; there was no doorbell.

An older lady with grey hair answered the door. Nelson Whitcomb asked for Mr. Fusco. The lady walked into the kitchen and got Mr. Fusco. Mr. Fusco walked to the door and said, "Yes, how can I help you?"

Nelson Whitcomb replied, "I am Nelson Whitcomb with the CIA in Washington, DC; I have a search warrant for my team to search your home because your wife was one of the women who passed away from an undiagnosed autopsy."

Mr. Fusco answered, "Yes, sir, this is a mess. By all means, come in." Nelson Whitcomb waved his team to join him, and they entered the Fusco home individually.

Dr. Wendt walked over to Mr. Fusco and said, "Mr. Fusco, we are so sorry about your loss. May we speak for a few moments?"

Mr. Fusco answered, "How can I help you?"

Dr. Wendt replied, "Are you aware of any women's clubs your wife was a member of?"

Mr. Fusco answered, "Well, my wife went to the gym to work out almost every day, but I don't think she was a member of any women's club there because she went at different times during the day. Amy was a member of the choir at our church, the Methodist church on West Shore Road, but that's the only group I know that she was in, but men are also in the choir."

Dr. Wendt then asked, "What were your wife's hobbies?"

Mr. Fusco answered, "Amy was happiest in summer when she could work in her flower gardens; she read many books and loved to sew."

Dr. Wendt said, "Thank you so much, Mr. Fusco, and again, we are so sorry for your loss, and we'll be gone as soon as possible." Mr. Fusco shook Dr. Wendt's hand and walked back into the kitchen.

The Fuscos lived in a large home, so the search took much longer than the last. When they were finished, they quietly left the house. Once they were all back at the cars, they decided to take the items seized to the FBI lab in Warwick and then go and eat lunch.

Gephart Tyler said, "I don't think we have room for another computer in the cars; I think we need another car from here on in."

Detective McGuiness said, "We did not get the computer at the first house, the Ridgewell home at 321 Greenwich Avenue, and we need to go get that one after lunch, and I'll call the dispatcher for a third car." They all agreed and discussed that another search of the Ridgewell home should be done when they get the computer. They all agreed, got back into the cars, and followed Detective McGuiness to the FBI lab in Warwick. Once there, they placed all the specimens they took at different places. They numbered every bag of specimens. They certainly didn't want to mix things up. They labeled them by numbers, the Ridgewell home being number one.

CHAPTER 49

They ate their lunches in thirty minutes; they had no time to waste. They walked out of the hospital toward the cars. Detective McGuiness said," I'll lead the way since I know my way around Warwick. They all got into the cars and were on their way to the Ridgewell residence at 321 Greenwich Avenue. Two cars pulled into the driveway, and the third parked along the street. Gephart Tyler handed Nelson Whitcomb the search warrant, and they all got their cases of supplies, and away they went to the front door.

Nelson Whitcomb rang the doorbell and waited. Finally, a little old lady answered the door. Nelson Whitcomb told her, "We are here to see Mr. Ridgewell."

The lady answered, "One moment, please."

Mr. Ridgewell came to the door and said, "Hello, you are back. Have you found the reason my wife died?"

Nelson Whitcomb answered, "No, Mr. Ridgewell, we haven't solved the mystery yet. May we come in?"

Mr. Ridgewell said, "Why, of course. I'm so sorry, come; you all come in."

Nelson Whitcomb handed Mr. Ridgewell the search warrant and said, "We must search your home again; we will work as quickly as possible; this time, we have FBI agents with us." The FBI agents showed Mr. Ridgewell their badges.

"My name is Nelson Whitcomb, and I'm with the CIA." The two men shook hands.

Mr. Ridgewell said, "Go for it, search anywhere you would like, and take anything you need; by what I hear on the news, this is really out of hand. I hope and pray you find what you need here."

With that, the men went in different directions. They took a little of this and a little of that and had over one hundred plastic and paper bags filled and out at the car within an hour. They asked for the clothing his wife was wearing when she died, and Mr. Ridgewell got it for them, and as he handed it to Mr.

Whitcomb saw his computer go out of the front door. Mr. Ridgewell saw one of the FBI agents taking pieces of every plant his wife grew. By four o'clock, they were finished, and the last thing they took out of the home was Sara Sue's clothing.

Mr. Whitcomb walked toward Mr. Ridgewell and said, "You'll never know how sorry we are for your loss, and we thank you so much for your cooperation; we'll let you know when we find something."

Mr. Ridgewell said, "For the sake of our great nation, I hope you find something very soon."

The men walked out of the front door, nodding to Mr. Ridgewell. They walked to the cars, and Gephart Tyler said, "I think it's time to check all our samples; it's too late to go to another home today. Let's take all of this to the FBI lab here in Warwick and find the solution."

Detective McGuiness said, "Follow me, men."

CHAPTER 50

All the men were eager to work if they had to work all night. They couldn't wait to find the commonality between these twenty-three deaths. They split up and took different specimens to check. They were all like little kids in a toy store, excited and determined to get what they wanted: the solution to the deaths.

This FBI lab was very different from the CDC in Atlanta. They had no gray protective suits, a protective helmet, and pure oxygen to breathe. At this lab, they only had face masks like people wear to mow their grass and latex gloves to protect themselves.

Dr. Wendt said, "Gentlemen, please be very careful not to breathe in any toxin or touch any specimens or samples with your bare hands. Remember, we have no idea what substance the killer may be, so please be very careful."

Gephart Tyler said, "I'll be the one to check the computers if that is okay with everyone else." All the men agreed he should be the computer man. Gephart started with the Ridgewell computer, which was labeled number one. Gephart plugged in the computer and started it up; it took forever. Gephart thought, They must not have much memory in this computer, and it's very slow, way too slow.

Finally, the hard drive kicked in, and Gephart started his search. Gephart knew every trick to find a needed password; his first search was everything that the Ridgewell family looked at on the Internet. The search found lawnmowers, air plants, halogen lamps, air purifiers, New York City, the Florida Keys, Amazon books and CDs, candle shops, nursing clothes, outdoor furniture, and so on—nothing that was useful to the investigation!

Gephart now went to their emails, normal chitchat between friends and family; Sara Sue emailed a lot to her nursing friends, nothing associated with a group or anything suspicious. Mr. Ridgewell was a great husband, with nothing on his email except love notes he wrote to his wife about what nightgown he would like to see her in that night. He decided to close down computer number one and get computer number two, the

Perrone computer. Gephart walked back into the big lab where everyone was busily looking for that key that unlocked the door to the deaths.

Gephart said, "No luck. I'm getting computer number two, and I hope this one works faster and has more information!"

Gephart picked up computer number two and walked back into his little room. He plugged computer number two in and waited. Gephart thought, Doesn't anyone have a fast computer here in Warwick? Finally, the computer was awake, and Gephart went to work. When he checked the Internet, all that was there were safe toys for children, cheap clothing for children, "What is ADHD", "What do I do if my child gets a fever over 104", "How do I get my son tested for ADHD", and free government services for parents with children.

Gephart said to himself, "Oh shit, how boring can a person's life be?" He first checked the husband's email; Mr. Perrone was a little kinky, to say the least; the only contacts he emailed were women, and some of those emails were way out of bounds for a married man. Gephart thought Mr. Perrone probably gave his wife a venereal disease. Gephart thought, I certainly hope his wife never saw these emails, the scumbag!

Barbara's emails were normal for women: chitchatting with friends and mostly complaining about her stupid husband. She talked to a friend about a new fish recipe, and the scent of a candle instantly took the fish smell away. She told a friend about a new book she was reading and all her new flowers blooming in her yard. She complained to another friend that she bought nuts to make a new dessert, but her husband ate just about every nut before she had time to make the dessert.

Gephart thought, What bullshit? Nothing here either. He rubbed his eyes and looked at his watch for the time. He thought, No, it can't be 9:00 already; no wonder my belly is growling. This is taking too long. He then thought I'm afraid to see the death count for the past two days while we have been here in Warwick.

Gephart picked up number two and headed for the main lab. He said, "Hey, is anyone making any progress?" The top team was all very busy; all looked at him simultaneously, and they shook their heads no. Gephart said, "Same here, fellows, nothing; I thought we would have the answer by now. Are we doing something wrong?"

Dr. Wendt answered, "No, we are doing nothing wrong; we have just been outsmarted by the bastards who did this to us!"

Nelson Whitcomb said, "I believe we are all tired and hungry; let's hit our favorite restaurant at the hospital and call it a day. I know I've had it."

On the way to their cars, they discussed how much they hated seeing the TV that night; the wonderful news, how many more must die before they found the cause?

Dinner at the hospital cafeteria was very quiet and somber. All the men were very disappointed and getting depressed. They all parted and went to their rooms at the hospital; maybe a good night's sleep was just what the doctor would have ordered.

Once in his room, Dr. Wendt said, "I don't want to do this, but I must," and he turned on the TV. As soon as he saw the count, he turned off the TV. A million more had died in the United States, and the CDC director for our country had no clue how these citizens had died. Dr. Wendt cried himself to sleep that night; this whole thing reminded him of his grandparents' stories about the Holocaust they lived through in his native country, Germany.

CHAPTER 51

After breakfast, they all walked together quietly to the cars. Gephart Tyler said, "House number four, Doris Auger at 218 Beach Street, she was thirty and had one child."

Detective McGuiness said, "Follow me." Ten minutes later, they pulled up to 218 Beach Street.

They exited the cars, got their cases, and headed for the door. Nelson Whitcomb rang the doorbell. He must have awakened Mr. Auger because his hair was a mess, he was barefooted, and he was wearing a white T-shirt with pajama bottoms when he answered the door.

Nelson Whitcomb said, "Good morning, sir; I'm sorry we woke you up; I am with the CIA, and the other men are with the FBI; we have a search warrant to search everything inside and outside your home because of your wife's death, which we are all so sorry."

Mr. Auger took the search warrant and said, "Please come in and find the cause; let's stop this crisis."

Dr. Wendt followed Mr. Auger into the kitchen as he said, "Mr. Auger, are you aware of any women's clubs your wife was in? We are desperately trying to find a commonality between the twenty-three women who died here in Warwick."

Mr. Auger answered while making coffee, "Right off the top of my head, I can't think of any time my wife met with a group of women other than a Tupperware party or a Home Interior party; the women here were really into stuff like that."

Dr. Wendt then said, "What hobbies did your wife have?"

Mr. Auger answered, "You can tell by looking at our yard that she loved yard work and flowers, she liked to do needlepoint and sew, she loved to cook and was always making new dishes for dinner and the best desserts, but it was hard for her to do much with a three-year-old boy."

Dr. Wendt said, "Thank you for your time, and if you think of anything else, please let me know."

Mr. Auger, waiting patiently for his first cup of coffee, replied, "I certainly will; after I drink my coffee and awaken, I may think of something else."

Dr. Wendt left the kitchen, and Mr. Auger poured himself a cup of coffee, went to the den, and turned on the TV. It was loud, and all the men could hear the depressing news while they were at his home.

There was no little boy, so he must have spent the night with Grandma or someone else. They searched the boy's room first.

The men searched the cars, took flowers from the garden, soil from the garden, samples of food in the refrigerator and boxes in the cupboard, and cleaning supplies. They searched under beds, took samples in the bathroom, looked in every drawer, took paint samples, opened every box, searched the office, and took the computer.

Four hours later, Mr. Auger was still drinking coffee and watching the news, flipping from station to station. Nelson Whitcomb entered the den and told Mr. Auger, "It looks like we are finished here. Thank you for allowing us to search your home; we will let you know if we find anything of importance, and again, I'm so sorry about your loss."

Mr. Auger replied, "Thank you, and I hope you have found the answer to all these unnecessary deaths." The two men shook hands.

As the men walked to the cars, Detective McGuiness said, "Lab, then lunch?" Everyone agreed. They drove to the lab, dropped off what was now number four, and headed to their only restaurant for lunch, the hospital. They all got their lunch, and while eating, Gephart Tyler said, "I feel lucky today; I just have a good feeling. Let's all hope I'm right!"

Lunch was over, and they were headed to house number five. Detective McGuiness said, "Where to next?"

Gephart Tyler said, "Maggie Ciamlse, 914 Oak Street, she was thirty-three with two children."

When they arrived at the Ciamlse home, Nelson Whitcomb told Gephart Tyler, "Would you please be our spokesman for this house? I'm getting tired of saying the same thing over."

Gephart Tyler said, "Yes, I will happily take over for you."

The men walked to the front door with their cases, and Gephart Tyler rang the doorbell three times before anyone answered. It was a girl around twelve who answered the door. Gephart Tyler said, "Hello, we are here to see your father. Is he in?"

The girl replied, "Yes, just a moment; I'll get him." The men stood there for several minutes until Mr. Ciamlse came to the door. He must have been working in the yard and had on old clothes and dirty hands. Mr. Ciamlse said, "What can I do for you?"

Gephart Tyler replied, "I am from the FBI, and we have a search warrant to search your home inside and out."

Mr. Ciamlse answered, "Is this because my wife died and all the other deaths?"

Gephart Tyler said, "Yes, sir."

Mr. Ciamlse said, "Please come in; our home is now yours; my girls and I will stay out of your way."

Gephart Tyler said, "Thank you, sir; we are so sorry for your loss."

Mr. Ciamlse went to talk to his daughters, who were watching a movie, and then he went outside in the backyard.

The men all went in different directions and started their search, and Dr. Wendt walked back to talk to Mr. Ciamlse. Dr. Wendt said, "Mr. Ciamlse, I'm sorry to bother you, but I need to ask you a few questions."

Mr. Ciamlse said, "Fine, go right ahead and ask." Mr. Ciamlse stopped working in the flower garden and stood up and faced Dr. Wendt.

Dr. Wendt said, "Are you aware of any women's groups your wife was in or anything she did with women? We are looking for a commonality of the twenty-three women who died here in Warwick."

Mr. Ciamlse said, "My wife volunteered at the library three mornings weekly. She also was a garden club member, but she didn't always go to that; she loved to be in her gardens. I'm trying to keep them up for her. She didn't like those parties where they sold stuff, so she never went to one. Maggie did swap recipes with other women every week. Maggie was a great cook and made the best desserts. She stopped doing a lot of things as the girls got older. They took up most of her free time."

Dr. Wendt said, "Thank you, and if you can think of anything else, please let me know."

Dr. Wendt returned to the house and asked the girls the same question. They had nothing new to add except the weekly soccer picnics, where the moms got together and made goodies for the girls to eat after their games. Dr.

Wendt said, "Thank you, girls, and I'm so sorry for your loss; please let us know if you can think of anything else."

Dr. Wendt walked out the front door and went to the car to review his list of things the women had in common. Gardening seemed to be the only commonality between the women other than cooking and desserts. Dr.

Wendt thought, All women cook, don't they? Dr. Wendt was at his wit's end; he was sure they would finish the culprit at the first home. Dr. Wendt called the CDC in Atlanta to see what was happening there. Miss Deplay directed his call to the lab. Dr. Wendt was told that they had now checked every feminine moisturizer, every brand of prophylactic and every medication for herpes and venial disease, feminine wipes, and toilet paper with no positive results at all. Dr. Wendt slammed his cell phone shut and just sat there and shook his head. Dr. Wendt thought I have never in my whole life felt as helpless as I do right now! Dr. Wendt stayed in the car until all the men were finished searching and joined him.

When all the men were finished putting their cases and the three computers in the cars, Gephart Tyler said, "Why don't we take number five to the lab and then go eat and return to the lab? That way, maybe we can work longer tonight at the lab?"

Nelson Whitcomb replied, "That sounds like a plan to me."

They all got in the cars and headed for the lab. Once there, they unloaded all of number five and headed to the hospital for dinner. The men finished eating the delicious hospital food and were returning to the FBI lab in Warwick. Once inside the lab, they got right to work.

Gephart Tyler said, "I'm taking the number three computer." Off he went with the computer to his little room. He plugged up the computer, turned it on, and waited as usual. Finally, it was up and running. It was the same old bullshit on the Internet, nothing that looked suspicious; time to check the e-mails.

Amy Fusco's emails were mostly to her family and friends from Rhode Island. She must have missed her family, Gephart thought. She must not be from Warwick. Mr. Fusco's emails were mostly work-related; nothing about nothing exciting anywhere Gephart searched. He unplugged the number three computer, returned it to the lab, and placed it with the rest of the number three stuff.

Gephart Tyler spoke, "Did anybody find anything yet?" Everyone shook their heads no. Gephart picked up computer number four and took it into his room, plugging it up and waiting for it to come alive. He first checked the Internet, and they only ordered one item from the internet: a book from Amazon. This was the second computer that went to Amazon and looked at books, but the other one also looked at CDs and brought nothing. The rest of the search on the Internet showed nothing.

Next, he went to Doris Auger's emails; mostly, they were just friendly chit-chat, but one excited Gephart. The email was from one of the other women who died; he remembered her name from getting the search warrants. It was about a new women's online book club that had just started up called The Warwick Women's Book Club.

The lady who sent Doris the email was trying to get her to join; maybe that was why Doris brought a book from Amazon. Gephart got back on the Internet to see if he could find the book's name. Finally, he found it; it was called The Third Chapter. It was shipped three weeks ago, so Doris would have already received it. Gephart didn't remember seeing any book in the Auger home, but maybe someone else in the group picked it up.

Gephart got up and walked into the lab. He said, "Did any of you see a paperback book called The Third Chapter at any of the homes we searched?"

Everyone answered, "No."

Gephart replied, "I have found a commonality between this book and Amazon. They have recently started an online women's book club here in Warwick."

Dr. Wendt replied, "If it's online, none of the husbands would think about it even if their wife told them about it; all we ever asked was if they were a member of any women's club, which usually means the women would all meet."

Nelson Whitcomb said, "This is very interesting, but how could a book kill people?"

No one else said anything, so Gephart walked back into his room, unplugged the computer, and was eager to get to number five hooked up.

He carried number four into the lab, placed it with all the other number four stuff, picked up one of the three number five computers, and carried it into his room. This one was a newer laptop and was up and running in a flash. Gephart went straight to the Internet, and what a surprise he saw. Gephart thought This must be one of the girl's laptops; they had often been chatting to a dating service online! Gephart thought, Do I tell the father this? I think yes! All the emails were about boys, dates, and typical stuff you would find on a teenager's computer.

Gephart returned number one of the number three computers and placed it with the other five. He picked up number two of the three computers and returned to his room. This computer was not a new laptop, and it took several minutes until he saw any life in this old computer. Gephart was hoping that the other laptop was the other daughters and this one was the parents. Gephart was excited. Finally, there was one thing someone had in common. First, he got the Internet up, and there it was, a book order from Amazon; he kept looking, and yes, it was called The Third Chapter. He couldn't wait to get on Maggie's emails. He read twenty-five emails before he found it, an email that Maggie sent to every woman she knew in Warwick, asking them to join her online women's book club. The e-mail was dated April 8th and said that the first book they would read was The Third Chapter. The email continued to say that on June 1st, they were to email each other with their comments on the book.

Gephart got so excited; he looked at the email addresses and saw some names for which he got search warrants. Gephart stood up and rushed to the lab screening, "I've got it, I've got it! It's a book called The Third Chapter. I know at least eight women I got search warrants for who were on the email list for The Warwick Women's Book Club."

Everyone else dropped what they were doing and rushed into Gephart's little room. They were all around the computer trying to read the email. They had to take turns because too many could read it simultaneously. Gephart said, "I will print this out and make everyone a copy." Gephart hooked up the printer, and in a few minutes, everyone had their copy to read.

Dr. Wendt thought he was about to have a heart attack. He said, "A book? How could a book kill someone?" Dr. Wendt then screamed, "THE INK! Damn them; it's the ink. Whoever they are, they put poisons or something in ink, and it enters the reader's body through their fingers and hands." Dr.

Wendt continued, "DAMN, THEY ARE SMART TO HAVE FIGURED

THIS OUT!"

Gephart said, "Detective McGuiness, would you and your men please go to all twenty-three homes, get those damn books, and wear the heavy latex gloves?"

Detective McGuiness said, "It's after midnight; isn't it too late?"

Gephart said, "Hell no. Go get those books before anyone touches them."

Detective McGuiness said, "Okay, men, let's go; I'll call in more help; I'll need the addresses of the twenty-three homes." Detective McGuiness and his team ran out of the building.

Nelson Whitcomb called the president of the United States' direct line. The president answered, "Hello."

Nelson said, "Hello, Mr. President, so sorry for the late call, but we've got it; it is a book. We are rounding up all twenty-three books right now, but Dr. Wendt thinks someone put poison in the ink that goes through the skin on the reader's hands and fingers and kills them. Mr. President, I can't tell you how excited we all are here in Warwick."

President Bennett replied, "Great work, I'll get the press on this ASAP; no one is to get near a book. Thank God, Nelson. Tell your staff a job well done."

Nelson said, "I'll call you back as soon as we test the first book. Good night,

President Bennett."

President Bennett replied, "I'll be waiting for your call, and thank you, Nelson. What great news!"

President Bennett got out of bed and called his press secretary. Within ten minutes, the president's press secretary was there and saw the president in his pajamas!

President Bennett said, "Thank you for rushing here. We believe we have solved the cause of the undiagnosed deaths, and we need to get it out to the news media everywhere, and I mean everywhere, every other country in the world."

John Murray, the president's press secretary, asked, "What is it, President Bennett?"

Shaking his head, President Bennett answered, "It is books, and the ink has some kind of poison or something in it that enters through the skin on the reader's fingers and hands."

John Murray said, "Oh my God, who would ever think of something like that?"

President Bennett said, "Tell the news media to tell everyone not to touch any books, and I mean no books, not even the covers of the books, but if they must move a book because of children, they should wear heavy latex gloves and then dispose of the gloves without touching the outside of the gloves."

John Murray said, "It will only take me five minutes, and everyone in the world will know not to touch a book of any kind, even an old telephone book."

CHAPTER 52

John Murray rushed to his office and started writing a press release to all the White House reporters. Within five minutes, everyone who reported the news on every radio and TV station worldwide would have this critical information. While John Murray was typing the press release, he thought he saw someone reading a book.

John Murray's press release:

THE KILLER IS BOOKS

The president of the United States has just reported findings from the CIA, FBI, and the CDC that books contain poison in the ink that penetrates through the skin of the reader's fingers and hands and eventually kills the reader.

Please report these findings to everyone in the world. No one is to touch a book, an old telephone book, or the book's cover. They are to leave all books where they are until further notice. If they must move a book because of children, they should wear heavy latex gloves and then dispose of them in a safe place immediately without touching the outside of the gloves. Also, put the books in a sealed plastic bag and place them up high in their home.

We will release more information as soon as it becomes available. John Murray, Presidential Press Secretary

CHAPTER 53

SATURDAY, MAY 22ND
EMIL
BALI, INDONESIA

Emil was waking up and still lying in his bed. He looked out the window and saw nothing but a beautiful blue sky and huge white puffy clouds. He lay there awhile and thought about how wonderful it was here in Bali. Not one bad day here yet; everything was perfect, and he was enjoying his life.

He finally decided to get up and have his coffee served to him on his pool deck. After he got out of bed, he put on his swim trunks and a sleeveless T-shirt. He walked down the circular staircase and yelled, "Good morning." That was his normal morning yell for his coffee to be served on the pool deck.

His beautiful, tanned woman servant met him at his favorite table on his pool deck with a silver urn of coffee, a little silver creamer filled with his favorite half and half, and the newspaper.

Emil said, "Good morning, my beautiful woman; how are you today?"

She answered, "Today, I am wonderful, Mr. Emil." She poured Emil's coffee and put half and half in it.

Emil replied, "Good, my dear, and thank you."

Emil thought getting a morning newspaper with yesterday's news from the United States would be good. I hope I soon get used to the difference in time from Bali to the United States.

At the bottom of page one of the newspaper, Emil read the headline: OVER 12 MILLION DEAD IN THE UNITED STATES. Emil smiled to himself. Only three more million, and we will have done it!

Just then, his servant came to the pool desk and said, "Mr. Emil, I am watching the TV in the kitchen, and they have found the cause of all the deaths in the world; you may want to see it."

Emil said, "Damn it," got up, grabbed his coffee, and went to the den where his Seventy-five-inch plasma TV was huge on the wall. He picked up the remote, and there it was in big, bold letters from the president of the United States press secretary: THE KILLER IS BOOKS! Every station had the same thing on. The wonderful United States had finally figured out what was causing all the undiagnosed deaths.

Emil said to himself, "Well, good for them!" Emil thought We could still kill 15 million; I know it! We will do it because they have no idea about the second book! When they tell the name of the first book, the second book will still be read by readers because they will only think it's the book called "The Third Chapter."

CHAPTER 54

SATURDAY, MAY 22ND
"STREET PARTY"
ROSE, HER HUSBAND, AND ALL THEIR NEIGHBORS

Everyone in the neighborhood was in the middle of the street, hugging each other, laughing, and talking about the latest news. Books, who would have ever thought the killer was a book?

Rose yelled, "It can't be any of our books because we have swapped each other's books back and forth for weeks now, but I'm certainly not going to touch another book; let's burn them all!"

One neighbor lady said, "Who has heavy latex gloves?" Ten people raised their hands. Rose said, "Okay then, let's get our gloves and start burning books."

One man said, "That may not be a good idea; if one of us has the killer book and we burn it, we may be harmed from the smoke and the fumes."

Rose replied, "I guess you are correct; we will just share our gloves and put our books into sealed plastic bags and away from all the children. I have two pairs of heavy latex gloves; I'll get a pair to give to one of you.

Rose said, "This is so exciting; not only did they find the cause of the deaths, but we also have something new to do today!" Rose continued, "Also, we will need a lot of plastic bags; let's all share them. I'm sure some of us have more books than others."

Rose approached her home and got her two gloves and plastic bags. When she entered her home, she stood still momentarily and looked at their bookcase filled with books; she couldn't believe this had happened and had a feeling that she had never felt before. She entered the kitchen, got her supplies to share, and joined the street party, which was a party this time!

Rose said, "Let's meet back here in two hours to see if anyone needs help removing the books or more bags." Rose grabbed her husband's hand and said, "Honey, let's get rid of our books!"

Once inside their home, Rose's husband said, "I'll put the gloves on, and you hold the bag."

Rose answered, "Please be careful."

Before they were finished throwing out every book they had in their home, they had three huge plastic trash bags filled with books; they ran out of the small plastic bags. They put the bags with the books in their garage next to all the trash building up since they had no trash pickup for weeks.

Rose said, "This garage smells terrible. Let's move our car outside so it doesn't start to smell."

It was time to meet back in the street; Rose took her huge trash bags in case anyone needed them.

One of their neighbors said, "I would have never dreamed we had so many books; I'll take one of those bags, Rose, and thank you."

They all thought it would be safer to put their bags of books in their garages; at least they were out of their homes.

The oldest man in the neighborhood said, "I'm going to miss my books; I love to read. I wonder how long it's going to be until we can buy books again?"

Rose's husband yelled, "We can eat anything we want to now." Everyone was smiling and laughing.

Rose yelled, "Finally, we can regain our lives!" They all hugged each other; they were all one happy family by now!

CHAPTER 55

No one had slept a wink the previous night; they stayed at the lab and waited to get their hands on the first book. Finally, Detective McGuiness and his crew returned with sixteen books, all with the same title, The Third Chapter.

Dr. Wendt said, "Okay, men, let's get to work." Dr. Wendt continued, "Gephart, could you arrange for me and my team and ten of these books to be flown to the CDC lab in Atlanta ASAP? We have much more up-to-date equipment in our lab at the CDC."

Gephart replied, "I'll get right on it."

Everyone else was standing there; none knew where to start or how to find the poison in the books. Dr. Wendt looked at them standing there and said, "Would you all like to go with me to the CDC in Atlanta?"

One by one, they answered, "Yes."

Dr. Wendt walked over to Gephart Tyler and said, "Excuse me, but the number has changed; we are all going to the CDC in Atlanta with all sixteen books."

Gephart said, "Got it, chief!"

While waiting for their travel plans, Dr. Wendt carefully put all sixteen books in individual plastic bags and all sixteen plastic bags in one big bag. Dr. Wendt then looked at the head of the FBI in Warwick and said, "Would you like to join us, and you, too, Detective McGuiness? You both have been so much help to us here, and I think you should go along and be a part of our group." Dr. Wendt continued, "I like your names to be with ours since you helped us find the corrupt. Come and share in our excitement!"

Both of the men were delighted and, of course, said, "Yes!"

Gephart Tyler said, "Okay, men, we are all off to Atlanta, Georgia. Get your gear together, and let's get to the Province airport. I wasn't aware that our Air Force was at our beck and call; they stayed here waiting for us!"

In thirty minutes, they were all in Warwick police cars being taken to the airport. The sixteen books were put in an air-tight metal container before they left the lab and would be put in the luggage department on their flight. No one was taking any chances.

Dr. Wendt called the CDC in Atlanta to tell them the latest news and to get ready to tear apart the ink on sixteen books. Dr. Wendt was so excited. They all ran to the plane and were in the air in minutes.

SATURDAY MAY 22ND
PRESIDENTIAL ADDRESS
8:00 p.m.

"Good evening, fellow citizens and people everywhere."

"Although we finally found the reason for the undiagnosed deaths in the United States and worldwide, we are still not out of the woods.

The FBI, The CIA, and the CDC are sure what we have just experienced in the world is bio-terrorism. We have had no one claim credit for this devastation, and we may never know who is behind this evil form of terrorism.

"You have been advised not to touch any books. I'm planning on keeping this advisory in effect for a very long time because we don't know how many books or the names of the books that have been printed with the poison ink, so please do not touch any book anywhere, or magazines or newspapers. Do not touch anything with ink print."

"I'm certain you will be happy to hear that you may eat whatever you wish now. We have lifted the curfew, and as of tomorrow at 8:00 a.m., planes will fly in and out of the United States again.

"Starting Monday morning, I hope you all can return to your jobs if they have been looted or damaged; I am sure your employer will welcome your presence. It is about time we get back to our normal routines. As we return to our normal daily lives, let us not forget the people who have suffered the worst: the victims and their families. Please keep them in your prayers and your daily lives. They will need us the most, so please give them your time, energy, and love."

"The loss of so many of our loved ones is horrific, but how our country worked together when we were down and beaten says a lot for the citizens of the United States. I am very proud to be your leader and your friend."

"Our great country made it through the worst time our country has ever seen. Keep the neighborhood street parties going and learn to love each other; we all still need each other very much."

"Please feel free to continue to call our national hotline number: 1-800-555-5555. We are here twenty-four hours a day for every one of our citizens. Please remember that no problem you have is too small to call on your country."

"You'll never know how very happy I am to be able to speak with you tonight."

"God bless you all, and God bless the United States of America."

CHAPTER 56

SATURDAY, MAY 22ND
DR. RUDOLPH WENDT CDC
ATLANTA, GA

For the first time in weeks, Dr. Wendt was smiling. He was the first one who identified a poison in the ink. The third poison he tried was the first winner, and it was plutonium. It was too early to know how much plutonium was used with other poisons poured into the ink at a printing press in Nashville, Tennessee.

Dr. Hertz found the second poison used, and it was selenium. One of the German scientists found the third poison, venom, from several poisonous snakes. After finding the third poison, the scientists started discussing how the bio-terrorist figured this out.

Dr. Wendt said, "Whoever did this has had to practice and practice mixing poisons until they got just the right mix, and I'm sure hundreds, maybe even thousands, died during their experiments."

Dr. Hertz replied, "Just what kind of a person would even think of doing this? Someone got the idea, and away they went, mixing and mixing portions of different poisons until they found the right combination to kill us."

They all worked until midnight when Dr. Wendt said, "I don't know about the rest of you, but I'm going home and sleeping in my bed and seeing my family." Dr. Wendt continued, "Let's call it quits for tonight and start again at 8:00 a.m. when our minds are sharp."

As everyone agreed with Dr. Wendt, one of the scientists yelled, "I just found radon gas!"

Dr. Wendt replied, "That's wonderful; I wonder how many potions of poisons, gases, and acids we will find?"

Dr. Hertz said, "This would make a fabulous movie!"

Dr. Wendt said, "I'm leaving on that comment; let's close up shop for tonight. Sweet dreams, everyone. I'll see you in the morning, and again, thank you all so much for being here when we needed you the most."

Dr. Wendt strutted out of the lab; he was a very proud man. He walked to his car, and as he got in, he thought, I sure do hope this car starts; it hasn't been driven in weeks or maybe a month, and I hope this battery is still alive! His car started on the third try, and he drove toward home with a wonderful feeling flowing within him. He couldn't wait to get home and see his family; he would wake them up and didn't care what time it was. He wanted to celebrate!

Dr. Wendt pulled into his driveway, turned the car off, grabbed his briefcase, and hurried into his home. Once inside, he yelled, "I'm home!" Everyone got up and greeted him!

As he walked upstairs, his wife was walking downstairs. They met on the stairs and hugged and kissed, and Mrs. Wendt said, "Welcome home, Ruddy; you'll never know how much we have missed you."

He entered his daughter's room and said, "Catherine, your dad is finally home."

She sat in bed, hugged her dad, and said, "I love you, Dad."

Dr. Wendt said, "Breakfast at 6:30, sweetie!"

Dr. Wendt entered his son's room and said, "Christopher, I'm home."

Christopher jumped out of bed, hugged his dad, and said, "Good job, Dad, and welcome home."

Dr. Wendt said, "See you for breakfast at 6:30, son."

Dr. Wendt then went into his and his wife's bedroom, took off his clothing, and said to his wife, "Dorothy was certainly correct; there is no place like home!"

The Wendt's fell asleep in each other's arms.

CHAPTER 57

SUNDAY, MAY 23RD
THE CDC
ATLANTA, GA.

Dr. Wendt was smiling as he drove back to the CDC. He and his family had a wonderful breakfast together, talking and catching up on everything. Dr. Wendt told his family, "I almost forgot what a good-looking family I had waiting for me at home."

Dr. Wendt parked his car in his own parking space, grabbed his briefcase, and headed back inside the CDC. He knew it would be another long but exciting day; he could hardly wait until they found all the different ingredients that killed so many people. This was the part of his job he liked the best.

He dropped out his briefcase at his office, put his white lab coat on, and headed for the best-equipped lab in the world. Several men were already hard at work when he arrived at the lab. They greeted each other, and Dr. Wendt said, "Any new poison found?"

His scientist said, "No, not yet, Dr. Wendt."

By 8:00 a.m., the lab was filled, and every scientist was busy at work. By lunchtime, they had found the AIDS virus, carbon monoxide, and sulfuric acid.

As they were walking to the cafeteria, Dr. Wendt said, "They meant to kill us all, and I'm positive that anyone with an underlying illness or pregnant women went fast; it is Sunday, so I'm not going to swear!"

They all ate a quick lunch and got back to the lab. Every scientist felt just like Dr. Wendt; they couldn't wait to find out what else was used to kill their fellow citizens.

They were only back working in the lab for an hour when one of the German scientists found oleander poison. Dr. Wendt asked, "Have you ever seen an oleander plant? They are most beautiful when they bloom but very poisonous!"

They continued to work for hours with no new poison found; they were getting bored and wanted excitement in the lab. Gephart Tyler said, "I'm not a top scientist, but I just found arsenic."

Dr. Wendt replied, "You go, Gephart! What a concoction they have made up!"

Dr. Wadeson said, "Just how in the world are we going to test all of these different ingredients without killing someone or something? How will we ever know the exact amounts they used?"

Dr. Wendt answered, "We'll find out all right, but we may have to test it on lab rats, which I don't like, but I don't think we will have to do it eventually."

They were all busy testing and testing when Dr. Wendt said, "Holy shit, I just found DMSO or Dimethyl Sulfoxide; they must have had top scientists working on this. Dimethyl Sulfoxide is what pushed the chemicals through the skin on the victim's hands."

Uranium, lead, and dimethyl mercury were found within the next two hours.

Dr. Wendt said, "I know we will never know this, but I sure would like to know how long it took them to come up with the proper portions. This is unbelievable; we are up to twelve different ingredients already!"

It was getting late in the day, and soon, it was time to close the lab. Every scientist had been working so long and hard; it was about time to return to normal working hours.

Dr. Wendt said, "It's about time we stop for the day and head home for dinner. As soon as he said that, he thought about the German scientists who couldn't go home for dinner. Dr. Wendt continued, "Would you top German scientists like to join my family for dinner?" They all smiled and accepted Dr. Wendt's invitation. Dr. Wendt said, "Meet me in my office in ten minutes, gentlemen."

Dr. Wendt left the lab and rushed to his office to call his wife to let her know they would be having guests for dinner. He thought, I've only been home one night in the past month, and I'll probably be in trouble with my wife already!

Dr. Wendt entered his office and called his wife; she was delighted to have company and said, "We'll have a picnic in the backyard, good fresh air with hot dogs and hamburgers."

Dr. Wendt answered, "Honey, you are a gem. Thank you, sweetie; we'll be there in thirty minutes."

The German scientists had a great time eating a home-cooked meal, plus Germans loved hot dogs. Dr. Wendt stopped for beer, and they all toasted to their friendship and accomplishments.

Around 9:00 o'clock, Dr. Wendt's son Christopher drove the men back to the CDC and used his dad's security key card to let the men back into the CDC.

CHAPTER 58

MONDAY, MAY 24TH
MORE DEATHS IN THE UNITED STATES

Even though they had found the killer, people in the United States were still dying. These people must have started to read the book right before the press secretary released the killer on TV, or maybe these people didn't have a TV but had one of the books with the poison pages. Either way, it was still very sad for everyone; the damn counter on the TV kept increasing. The total was now over fourteen million people dead due to bioterrorism.

None of the poisons had been mentioned to the talking heads on the news and probably never would be, so all they had to talk about was that the problem was solved, yet people were still dying from undiagnosed deaths. The news media was certainly very good at making the news worse!

Although the country was returning to normal and people were back to work, they were still scared, and the talking heads didn't help. On channel 8, CPC news reported that they might have another form of killing.

"First, our president tells us to stay home and read a good book, and then the news tells us we may have another form of killing, just what the United States citizens needed to hear right now!"

The president's press secretary was pissed and got on the phone and reamed out the CPC news station. They were advised to get that report off their news ASAP, or the government would penalize them immediately. That was all it took, and they immediately pulled that delightful news message off the air.

At least most people were back to work, so they couldn't watch the news all day. Hopefully, this would raise the morale of the United States citizens.

What they had to face at work was bad enough.

At almost every business in the United States, at least one person or friend didn't show up for work because they were dead; that was bad enough to face, let alone another form of killing. The damn news media should all be shot.

CHAPTER 59

MONDAY, MAY 24ᵀᴴ
EMIL
BALI, INDONESIA

Emil was listening to the news when he heard the latest death count. He jumped up and down joyfully, saying, "After fourteen million comes fifteen million!"

Emil danced around his beautiful room, smelling the wonderful salt air while lavishing in the thought that they were about to make their quota.

Emil rang his bell, and his beautiful servant Kastria entered the room, "Yes, Mr. Emil, what can I do for you?"

Email answered, laughing. I'll take a scotch, water, and my favorite snack at the pool."

His servant answered, "Yes, right away, sir."

Emil walked out to the pool desk and sat down. Emil thought, I think I died and went to heaven; the birds are my angels, the blue water is my salvation, and the white puffy clouds are my bed of honor. Emil was never as happy as he was at that moment.

Emil thought, Who would have ever believed that a poor, malnourished boy from the Middle East could live like this? This is a splendid paradise, and it's all mine.

His drink and favorite snacks were delivered to him at his table. His servant said, "Anything else, Mr. Emil?"

Emil answered her, "Yes, I would like you to start preparing for the biggest party Bali has ever seen; I'd like to invite everyone here on Sunday at 5:00 p.m. for the party of their lives."

His servant replied, "Yes, sir, Mr. Emil. I will get the staff working on this immediately."

As she turned to leave, Emil said, "Thank you, my dear."

When Emil was on his third scotch and water, his lady friends started to arrive. He partied with them at the pool and in his bedroom until the sun rose the next morning.

CHAPTER 60

Nelson Whitcomb, Gephart Tyler, and Dr. Wendt briefly met at 8:00 a.m.

Nelson Whitcomb said, "We are listening, but we have heard no chatter about the poison pages; I wish we could catch these sons of a bitches!"

Gephart Tyler agreed, "We at the FBI have no earthly idea who did this to our country; not one of our informants have a thing to tell us, and I would have thought by now we would have a lead, but nothing. This is a huge embarrassment to all the security bureaus in the United States."

Dr. Wendt said, "Well, at least we now know the killer; we just don't know how many different books. We have found twelve poisons, gases, and acids, and we are still testing and testing.

Nelson Whitcomb replied, "The president is on my ass day and night to find out who did this, and I haven't one clue."

Gephart Tyler said, "Nelson, you need to be honest with the president; if no one has claimed this victory yet, we may never know. The president must resolve his passion for the answer; you know we can't do everything."

Before Dr. Wendt left for the lab, he said, "Just think where we would be today if Maggie Ciamlse hadn't started an online women's book club in Warwick, Rhode Island. We are just plain lucky to have found her; we are proud of that. Tell the president to put that in his pipe and smoke it!"

Dr. Wendt left the meeting and went to the lab. When he arrived, he heard some great news: they found another dimethyl cadmium gas. Dr. Wendt said, "Great job, that makes thirteen different ingredients; I wonder how many more?"

Dr. Hertz said, "Isn't thirteen enough?"

Dr. Wendt said, "Yes, of course, it's enough, but we need to know if there are any more, so keep on checking and testing everything you can think of. Get your chemistry books out; maybe that will give us a clue to any more we might find; let's have a review."

The scientists went to the library, got book after book off the shelves, and searched through every page. At 6:00 p.m., they were still researching books, nothing new that they hadn't already found.

CHAPTER 61

Every scientist at the CDC in Atlanta was reading books, just what no one was supposed to do!

Dr. Wendt entered the library and said, "We still have more deaths; we need to get every book printed in the past year for testing."

Dr. Hertz said, "Do you have any earthly idea how many books we will have in the lab?"

Dr. Wendt said, "Yes, I do, but people are still dying; maybe we have overlooked something."

Dr. Hertz got up, went to the phone, and ordered a copy of every book printed anywhere in the past year!

Dr. Wendt said, "I would like some help in the lab; I'd like to figure out how much of each ingredient they put in the ink, which may take us a year!" Dr. Wendt continued, "I think I have already figured out the arsenic. I don't think they could have used more than 2,000th of a gram for five gallons of ink they used when they printed the books."

Dr. Wendt got up and started to walk to the lab; ten scientists followed closely behind.

In an hour, the lab looked like a Presidential Library! You had to step over books to get a book; this was a nightmare for all the scientists, but it had to be done. When they checked a book for arsenic, and there weren't any, the book was thrown out of the lab.

In the next six hours, they found two books with arsenic in them. One book was titled Read It and Weep, and the other title was The Third Chapter. These two books would be tested for all the same ingredients.

It was time to leave for the day. Dr. Wendt said, "Good night, everyone! See you in the morning. Hang in there; we are making progress!"

CHAPTER 62

THURSDAY, MAY 27TH
PRESIDENTIAL ADDRESS
BURN EVERY BOOK

Finally, when real TV was returning, and you could watch a good show instead of the news, another Presidential Address was at 8:00 p.m.

Rose said to her husband, "Another TV night is gone. I'm so sick of this, and my favorite show is on at 8:00 p.m."

President Hamilton R. Bennett stood behind the podium and began his now boring speech.

"Good evening, ladies and gentlemen of our great nation, the United States of America."

"This will be a brief address tonight. We want all United States citizens to take all their books into the center of your streets and burn them. This will be the best way to eliminate all the books since we have so much trash that still needs to be picked up.

"Please watch the fires closely so no one gets burned, and ensure the fire is out before you retire for the evening."

"We appreciate all of your help."

"God bless you all, and God bless the United States of America."

CHAPTER 63

THURSDAY, MAY 27TH
DR. WENDT CALLS PRESIDENT
DO NOT BURN BOOKS!

Dr. Wendt was sitting in his den at home watching TV when the president delivered his message. Dr. Wendt almost had a heart attack. Dr. Wendt ran to the phone and called the president's direct line.

The president answered the phone, "Hello."

Dr. Wendt screamed at the President, "This is Dr. Wendt at the CDC in Atlanta, President Bennett. Who told you it was safe to burn the books?"

The president answered, "My staff thought that would be the best way to dispose of all the books."

Dr. Wendt replied, "President Bennett, the smoke and the fumes from the books could kill; we have not only found poisons, but we have also found gases and smoke from them will kill people, Mr. President, you must get back on TV right away and stop people from burning books, or you are going to have a lot more deaths!"

President Bennett said, "I or we did not realize that burning the books would cause yet another problem. Oh my God, I'll get right back on TV. Thank you, Dr. Wendt." The phone went dead.

Dr. Wendt said to his wife, "What next? The president should have checked with us before making that announcement to the public; just what in the hell are they thinking about in Washington, or maybe I should say, what the hell are they not thinking about in Washington?"

Dr. Wendt and his wife returned to the TV to watch the president of the United States make a fool out of himself!

CHAPTER 64

THURSDAY, MAY 27TH
SECOND PRESIDENTIAL ADDRESS IN ONE DAY
DO NOT BURN BOOKS

Within five minutes, every TV station in the United States had a severe news alert from the president.

There stood the president behind his podium again.

"Ladies and gentlemen, I made a terrible mistake; I advised you to burn your books when it is unsafe for you to burn them. If you have started to burn books, please put the fire out immediately and do not breathe in the smoke or fumes from the burning books. If you hear this message and see your neighbors burning books, PLEASE stop them."

"This message will be continually flashing on your TV until we are sure that everyone knows not to burn your books."

"I apologize for all the inconvenience to my fellow citizens."

"DO NOT BURN BOOKS; DO NOT BREATHE IN SMOKE OR FUMES OF THE FIRE IF YOU HAVE STARTED TO BURN YOUR BOOKS."

The last statement came up on every TV screen in the United States every three minutes; so much for finally being able to get back to normal and watch TV.

CHAPTER 65

THURSDAY MAY 27TH
EMIL
BALI, INDONESIA

Emil was just about beside himself with laughter. Emil just happened to be watching TV when all this took place with the president of the United States. Emil thought to himself, This is better than killing fifteen million people. I hope all my friends have seen this worldwide; if they have, I bet they laugh their asses off. Emil thought That's pretty cool, laughing your asses off because of the asshole, the President of the United States.

Emil took a sip of his drink and then held his drink up and cheered the president, the dick head! Emil said, "That's a great name for him, Dick Head!"

Emil thought to himself, It's a shame someone notified the president that burning the books was dangerous. We may have had a kill count of twenty million people, but we must kill only fifteen million!

"Eat your words, Dick Head: you are not so wonderful after all!"

CHAPTER 66

FRIDAY, MAY 28TH
CDC
FEW PEOPLE STILL DYING FOUND 13 POISONS

Dr. Wendt entered the lab at 8:00 a.m. sharp. He said, "I almost had a heart attack last night when the president said to burn books; I called him and said, 'No sir, no book burning.' Why didn't they check with us first?" Dr. Wendt continued, "I hope the burning stopped before it started; we certainly don't need more deaths. By the way, fewer people died yesterday than any other day this month; now that's great news.

Dr. Wendt then said, "By the end of today, we should know if there are any more poisons, gases, or acids in the poison ink; I'll be glad when this is over. Now we just have to keep checking for other books and the amount of each ingredient used; it sounds easy, but it isn't!"

All the scientists worked until 6:00 p.m.; they only took a quick lunch break all day. They were all tired and weary. They had estimates of some more of the ingredients used in the poison ink, but just estimates. They would have to get an estimate on all thirteen ingredients before testing and killing rats.

Although the worst was over, none of the scientists liked to kill anything; they considered it a necessary evil.

They closed down the lab, and they all headed out of the CDC until 8:00 a.m.

CHAPTER 67

Dr. Wendt met with Dr. Wadeson in the hallway, saying, "Let's hope there are no deaths today. We can't find any more poisons, so this would be a great day for this to end."

Dr. Wadeson replied, "Do you think we will ever be able to find the correct portions of each chemical they used for five gallons of ink?"

Dr. Wendt answered, "If we do, we are just damn lucky. It will take us a very long time to figure this puzzle out, and I am not sure we should ever find the exact portions because if we do, then there is a possibility that someone else may get their hands on the formula and use it again!"

Nelson Whitcomb approached Dr. Wendt and Dr. Wadeson and said, "I guess my job here is over since I am not a scientist. I will leave now with Gephart Tyler rushing to Nashville to the printers who printed the first book, "The Third Chapter," and hoping to find out who worked there and put the poison in the ink." They all shake hands.

Dr. Wendt said, "I'm going to miss you, Nelson; you must stop by and see us. You and everyone working on this epidemic are now my family!" Dr. Wendt continued, "This last month has been the worst month of my life; getting degrees from Harvard was easier than what we have all gone through this month. Good luck, Nelson, and let's hope we never meet again like this."

Gephart Tyler wanted to stay at the CDC because he was also a scientist, but he had no choice; he had to leave with Nelson to find the asshole who killed all of these US citizens. Gephart shook Dr. Wendt's hand and said job well done!

Nelson and Gerhart walked to the front door and left the CDC in Atlanta.

Detective McGuiness and the Warwick crew had left the CDC yesterday and were safely home in Rhode Island.

The German scientists were also staying; after all this, they also wanted to know exactly how much of each poison was used. Besides that, they enjoyed being in the United States, loved the lab at the CDC, and learned so much from this experience.

All was back to normal at the CDC in Atlanta. Every scientist was different; they were happy and smiling now. The work they had to do now was different from what they had just experienced, even though they were still stepping over books in the lab.

Gephart and Nelson left for the airport, where the US Air Force plane was waiting for them to take them to Nashville, TN.

CHAPTER 68

SATURDAY, MAY 29TH
EMIL
BALI, INDONESIA

Emil's beach home was very busy. Decorations hung everywhere, and trucks brought food and beverages into his home. The aroma from the kitchen filled the huge home. The next day at 3:00 p.m., the party of a lifetime would start for those invited to Emil's in Bali.

Every inch of Emil's home was being cleaned and polished. The floors looked like glass. New plants were planted on the pool deck, and the crew cleaned the pool and the huge Jacuzzi. The sauna was ready for those who wanted to use it at the party, and one thousand huge towels were neatly folded in the pool locker room.

They set up fifty cabanas with tables and chairs for those visitors who wished to stay out of the sun. Emil had thought of everything.

Emil was sitting on the pool deck, watching his home become a party home. He watched the men deliver chairs and tables and told them where to place them. When they delivered the champagne fountain, Emil asked them to set it flowing immediately, and he was ready to party. Emil's life was perfect even though the death count hadn't reached 15 million yet; he was smiling and sipping his glass of champagne.

He filled his glass again and sat back down on his pool deck. His cell phone rang; it was the boss, and Emil's boss was upset that they hadn't reached their goal of 15 million deaths. Emil said, "It's not over yet; they are still dying, and I'm sure there are thousands of dead people they haven't found yet. Don't worry, boss; we'll make 15 million!" Emil laid his phone down on the table and rang his bell, and he was hungry. Emil kept saying to himself, "We must reach 15 million, just 15 million, please!"

After Emil ate his lunch, he walked on his beautiful Bali beach. He thought to himself, The weather is beautiful, the perfect temperature, the perfect environment, everything is perfect, and I'll be the king of Bali after tomorrow!

CHAPTER 69

SATURDAY, MAY 29TH
PRESIDENTIAL ADDRESS- 8:00 p.m.
PRESIDENT HAMILTON R. BENNETT

"Good evening, fellow citizens; I hope everyone's mind is at ease tonight. The worst epidemic of our great country can now be considered officially over.

"The CDC in Atlanta has found the poisons mixed with the ink when the killer books were printed.

"It's very difficult for many citizens to get their lives back to normal since so many have lost their loved ones. It will take our country a long time to return completely to normal.

"I share my sadness with all the families who have lost a loved one, and I hope you all know that all your fellow citizens are also feeling your sorrow.

"Almost 15 million people have been lost because of this evil epidemic. No one has taken credit for these killings, and we may never know who inflicted this devastation on our country or why.

"Our country is in a healing stage, and every citizen should be helping others get their lives back to normal. It all depends on us, the American citizens, and how fast we can put this tragedy behind us and continue our lives like we were living just last month."

"The Month of May has tested us more than we could have ever imagined could have happened to us in our country. May will go down in history as the month from hell in the United States of America."

"I am praying for you all. God bless America, and God bless all our citizens of the United States of America."

CHAPTER 70

SATURDAY, MAY 29TH
GEPHART AND NELSON
GO TO NASHVILLE

After the CDC, CIA, FBI, and DEA discovered what was killing people, they started their investigations. They first contacted the book publishers that published The Third Chapter. They gave them the name of the printing company that made the copies of the book, so they were a big help! Their second investigation was underway to talk to the Nashville Printing Company, where they printed The Third Chapter books.

Gephart and Nelson were now in the car on their way to the printers. They finally arrived at Nashville Printing Company and immediately asked to speak with the owner. The secretary told them, "I will go get him!"

A short, chubby man walked into the lobby and said, "Hello, I am Mr. Brown, the owner of the Nashville Printing Company. What can I help you with?"

Nelson Whitcomb said, "My name is Nelson Whitcomb with the CIA, and this is Gephart Tyler with the FBI. We have a critical problem, and we need your help." Nelson continued, "Your company printed the book "The Third Chapter," which caused millions of deaths in the United States!"

Mr. Brown put his hand to his brow and said, "You have got to be kidding! It is horrific to think my operation is responsible for this catastrophe, but how are these books killing people?"

Nelson said, "I wish we were kidding, but we are not and need your help as the books were printed with a poisonous substance added to the ink! The customers who purchased the book "The Third Chapter" seemed to only read through the third chapter, and something would come over them, causing their immediate death. We have determined that the poison from the dried ink was absorbed through the reader's fingertips each time a page was turned. The toxins would flow immediately through their blood system and attack their vital organs."

Mr. Brown said, "What can I do to help you?"

Nelson said, "You will first have to shut down every printing press and allow our forensic team to take samples of the ink being used in every press.

Mr. Brown said, "Every printing press will be shut down," as he got on the warehouse loudspeaker and commanded that all printing presses be shut down immediately! Following the shutdown, the technicians and Mr. Brown were put in a room together to be interrogated.

Gephart asked, "In the past year, were there any shady characters running the printing presses?"

Mr. Brown yelled, "Hell yes!" Mr. Brown continued, "We have had a few that I will never hire again and should be in jail. We have had some who didn't talk at all and one who never came for their last check!"

One of the printing press operators said, "I worked next to a guy who never said a word to me, wouldn't answer me, and I don't think ever took a bath. Get this: the guy drove an ugly old pink Cadillac long before the song came out!"

Gephart said, "What was his name, and what nationality do you think he was?"

Mr. Brown said, "Yeah, I hired him, and I know for a fact that he was from one of those countries like Iran, and all I know is that he is the one who never came and got his last check. I believe his name was Duke or something. I would have to check my files for a last name."

Gephart said, "Would you please do that right now?"

Mr. Brown said, "I am on it!"

One of the other printing press operators said, "Yes, I remember him because he was shacked up with my old girlfriend Cinnamon."

Gephart was getting excited with this news. Gephart asked, "Do you know where he was shacked up and where Cinnamon is today?"

The printing press operator said, "I know exactly where it is," and then gave them the address! "I was just there the other night to see Cinnamon. She told me her boyfriend, Duke, left her alone to pay for the sleazy room, and she was still furious about it!"

Mr. Brown entered the room and said, "The check was made to Duke Mashaduk."

Gephart was thrilled to connect a possible suspect that caused this devastation finally. Gephart said, "I will go to the police department and see if they can find anything about an ugly, old pink Cadillac here in Tennessee and Nelson,

have your driver take you to her address so you can interview Cinnamon."

Nelson answered, "Got it, Gephart; we can meet back here."

Gephart kept telling the driver, "Faster, faster, I must get there ASAP!"

His driver answered, "Yes, sir!"

Finally, they were at the Nashville Police Department, and Nelson ran inside as fast as he could because every second counted toward another life. He went to the front desk, asked for the Chief of Police, and said it was urgent. "I am from the FBI in Washington, DC."

The policewoman said, "I will see if he is available." She made a call, and within five minutes, two policemen came to get Nelson. Nelson thanked them for being so prompt, and within a minute, he was facing the Chief of Police in Nashville. The two men shook hands, and Gephart told him why he was there. It only took him a few minutes to explain the urgency of his visit. The Chief of Police was only happy to help Gephart because he understood the high priority of the situation.

Chief Jacobs told Gephart, "We have no knowledge of an old pink Cadillac, but I will forward this message to every county in Tennessee, and it shouldn't be long before we know if anyone found such a car. In the meantime, can we get you anything: coffee, soda, something to eat?"

Gephart replied, "It's been a very long day, and we now know eating or drinking anything is safe. I want the Chief of Police and your entire squad to know the ink from the published book "The Third Chapter" was tainted with a poisonous substance, causing the death of every reader, and was not associated with anything they ate. I will take anything you have available to eat and drink."

The food and drinks came, and Gephart nervously sat waiting for a response if anyone had located a pink Cadillac. Gephart finished everything he wanted to eat and drink and started to talk about all the deaths and what an atrocity this had been for their country, the United States of America.

About forty-five minutes passed until the department got a hit. The city of Jackson, in Madison County, found an old pink Cadillac without a license plate way off the highway on an isolated dirt road. It was sitting in their yard if they wanted to come and get it! Gephart said, "Yes, we will be there in the morning to get it, and thank you so much for your time!"

Gephart got up to leave and left with a skip in his step. He was so excited. One more step in finding the bastards who did this to our county. His driver returned him to the Nashville Printing Company, where he waited for Nelson to return, hopefully with more good news.

Nelson and Gephart met each other back at the printing company, and they began to talk. Nelson said, "Well, after beating on the door for what seemed like a lifetime, Cinnamon finally answered the door, and boy, was she a sight to be seen!" Nelson continued, "She was dirty, the ugliest bright orange hair I have ever seen, and a smell that smelled like no other. Cinnamon said, 'Come on in, what can I do for you, you good-looking man?' I couldn't get the door to go any further to open, and I couldn't get it close. It was hung up on the dirtiest carpet I have ever seen, so I left it open to air out the room!"

Nelson continued; I told her I was with the CIA in Washington, DC, and I was there to discuss a man she used to live with named Duke. Cinnamon said, 'That lousy bastard, I knew he was up to no good; what do you want to know, and how have you hooked up with my old boyfriend?'" Nelson said, "I met this man at the printing company where Duke worked, and he was nice enough to give us your address." Nelson continued, "Do you know where Duke was originally from, what country? Cinnamon said, 'Hell no, he barely talked to me. He only wanted sex from me and then left me here to pay the rent. I have no idea where he went when he left. Duke was a weird one for sure!' So, I asked Cinnamon, 'What kind of car did he drive?' Cinnamon replied, 'An old ugly pink Cadillac, which I wasn't even allowed to touch ever, and I mean ever! I was never allowed to get in the car, so he would never take me to work, the cheap bastard!' I then asked, 'Did he have a cell phone?' Cinnamon said, 'No, he was too cheap to pay for a cell phone. If he got any calls or made any calls, he used the phone in the room!' I then asked, 'Did he have an accent when he talked?' Cinnamon said, 'Nope, he sounded like us when he spoke, which was hardly at all.'"

Nelson's last question was, "Did he leave any of his belongings behind in the room?"

Cinnamon said, "Hell no, nothing for me to sell to help pay the damn rent!"

Then Nelson told Cinnamon that he was sending the forensic scientist team to the room to dust for fingerprints and look for any items of interest.

Cinnamon said, "Bring them on; it's fine with me. Duke's in big trouble, isn't he? I knew it, that bastard!"

Nelson replied, "Even if I knew, I couldn't tell you. I will call and get the forensic team here ASAP." Then Nelson said, "Thank you for your time. The forensic team will be here in about an hour. Here is my card if you think of anything else to help us find Duke, and I need you to get dressed and leave while the forensic team is here. Again, thank you." Nelson turned and left the room, leaving the door hung on the carpet.

The first thing Nelson did when he got in the car was to call the local Nashville CIA forensic team and tell them the address, get there ASAP, and let him know immediately what they found out.

Nelson told the driver, "Back to the printing company, please." As he returned to the printing company, Nelson found a comfortable chair while waiting for Gephart to return. Nelson only had to wait briefly before he saw Gephart walking toward him with a big smile.

Gephart said, "We are getting close. We found the pink Cadillac and will need the forensic team to get the car and tear it apart; there must be one fingerprint somewhere in the old car!"

Nelson asked Gephart, "Where did they find the old pink Cadillac?"

Gephart replied, "On a dirt road off Highway 40 in Madison County!"

"A dirt road?" Nelson replied. "We must go there and investigate the area. Where would he have gone after ditching the car?"

Gephart said, "Probably a helicopter. We will have to call the air traffic control center to review the flight radar for that period for any helicopter landings in that vicinity." Gephart continued, "We must ask Mr. Brown for the last day Duke worked. You must go back and ask Cinnamon if she knows the date Duke left her!"

Nelson said, "Oh good, I get to see Cinnamon again!" So Nelson got in his car and told his driver to take him back to Cinnamon's apartment. While driving back to Cinnamon's, Nelson got a call from the CIA forensic team, who informed Nelson that the only fingerprints found in the apartment belonged to Cinnamon. There were no other found items of interest.

Nelson got there just as Cinnamon was ready to go to work. He knocked on the door, and Cinnamon answered, "Well, hello, Mr. Nelson.

Are you here for pleasure or business?" Nelson replied, "I need to know if you know the date Duke left you."

Cinnamon said, "Hell yes, I do. The rent would be paid on the first day of May!"

Nelson said, "Duke did stick you for having to pay the rent! Thank you so much, Cinnamon, and have a very nice evening."

Cinnamon closed the door, and Nelson started walking to his car as fast as possible to escape that sleazy hellhole!

Gephart's job was much more pleasant than having to deal with Cinnamon. He knocked on the door of the printing company, and as luck would have it, Mr. Brown unlocked the door for him.

Gephart said, "Thank heavens you are still here. I need to know the last day Duke worked at your printing company."

Mr. Brown said, "I was just looking over Duke's files, and as far as I can tell, his last day of work was May 1st."

Gephart replied, "Thank you so much for your help, and remember, what has happened to the USA is not your fault. Duke just used your company to do his dirty work, and we will never mention your company's name." Gephart then shook Mr. Brown's hand and said, "Thank you. You have been a wonderful US citizen."

As Gephart left, Mr. Brown said, "I am so happy I could help you, and I am very happy that this catastrophe is over."

Nelson made reservations at the Hilton Hotel near where they were. "Nelson then called Gerhart and told him to come to the Hilton near the printing company when he was finished, and they would meet in the lobby."

Nelson only had to wait ten minutes until Gephart showed up! Nelson said, "What did you find out?"

Gephart answered, "Mr. Brown said the last day Duke worked was Friday, May 1st."

Nelson said, "Cinnamon told me the same date; she remembered because that was the day the rent was due!"

Nelson said, "I am starving. Let's hit the dining room."

Gephart replied, "Me too, let's go!

The two men ordered a big dinner with dessert! Nelson and Gephart ate and didn't say a word until they were finished eating. Nelson was the first to talk and said, "I was as hungry for a good meal," Gephart replied, "Me too, I was staring!"

Nelson said, "Dear Lord, I forgot my bag; it's in the car!"

Gephart answered, "That makes two of us. I wonder where we can find our drivers."

Nelson said, "They are both probably sleeping by now. It's been one of those days. Let's not worry about our change of clothes and get a good night's sleep!"

They talked to the girl at the front dest and got their room keys. The two men walked to their rooms and said goodnight to each other. Nelson added, "I bet I will fall asleep before you!"

CHAPTER 71

SUNDAY, MAY 30TH
NELSON AND GEPHART
IN NASHVILLE

Gephart Tyler was up and ready to start the day after a good night's sleep. He kept calling Nelson, but Nelson never answered his phone, so Gephart walked next door to his room and knocked on the door. Nelson answered the door and said, "Good morning!"

Gephart answered, "Good morning to you, and why haven't you been answering your phone?"

Nelson answered, "My phone is dead, and the charger is in the trunk of my driver's car; I guess before breakfast, I should retrieve it so it can charge while we are eating breakfast!"

Gephart replied, "Good idea; my phone must also be charged."

The two men left the room toward the lobby, hoping to find their drivers. Walking into the lobby, they saw their drivers sitting and talking while drinking coffee. Nelson and Gephart said, "Good morning, gentlemen; it looks like you beat us for coffee!"

One of the drivers replied, "Yes, we are all ready to get this day started."

Nelson said, "We are also ready, but first, we need to get our bags out of the cars so we can change clothes, charge our phones, and eat a good breakfast!"

The two drivers stood up, headed for the front door, and walked to where the cars were parked. Nelson and Gephart both got their bags, and Nelson said, "We should be ready to roll in about an hour. We will meet you back in the lobby!"

Nelson and Gephart stopped by the dining room to get a cup of coffee and sprinted to their rooms to shower and get ready for the new day. As they approached their rooms, Nelson said, "It should only take me twenty minutes, and I will be ready to go eat."

Gephart replied, "Come get me when you are ready."

Both men looked professional in their clean clothes. After all, they headed up two of the most important divisions within the CIA and the FBI! They headed to the dining room with their bags for breakfast.

They got breakfast and another cup of coffee and ate when Nelson remembered he had to charge his phone. Since both had to charge their phones, they quickly went to the phone charger center to the right of their table and plugged their charges into the sockets.

Nelson said, "Mine will take a while. I will have to finish charging mine in the car."

Gerhart answered, "How did we ever live without these wonderful phones?"

While eating, Gephart said at their table, "If I take one more bite, I will explode!" The men finished eating, retrieved their phones, and took an extra cup of coffee for the road.

They found their drivers sitting in the lobby, and all four men walked to their cars. Nelson told his driver, "I must charge my phone, and please don't let me forget my bag again!" They all laughed!

Gephart, laughing, also said, "Me too!"

Nelson told the drivers, "We are going to the Nashville Police Department."

Nelson and Gephart were so excited for this day to get started. Gephart oversaw getting the flight radar information about the helicopter. Nelson was in charge of checking the US flight database and contacting the National Customs division to determine if Duke Mashaduk had flown on any flight segment in the US or was processed through immigration and customs abroad.

On the drive to the Nashville Police Department, the driver asked Gephart, "Have you seen the new numbers of suicide deaths in the United States since these unknown deaths started? There are now over 500,000 thousand deaths by suicide in the United States!"

Gephart responded, "No, I haven't seen nor heard the latest numbers. This number makes this catastrophe even worse. Why on earth would anyone want to do this to the citizens of the United States?" The rest of the drive to the police station was in silence.

The drivers for Nelson and Gephart parked next to each other in the police station lot, and all four men got out of the cars.

Nelson said, "I wish you did not have to wait while we are in the police station. There are so many wonderful things to see in Nashville. If you want lunch, feel free to go get something to eat. We will call you when we are ready to leave if you are not here."

The drivers for both Nelson and Gephart said, "Thank you!"

Gephart and Nelson walked into the Nashville police station and asked to see the Chief of Police. Within five minutes, the two men had rooms to use to further their investigations.

Nelson immediately picked up the phone to speak with the Federal Aviation Administration. Nelson introduced himself to the operator, explained his role in the investigation of the national epidemic, and the urgency that he speaks with FAA Administrator John Calhoun. The operator immediately transferred the call to the administrator's office and connected him with Mr. Calhoun.

Mr. Calhoun answered the call with, "How can I assist you today, Mr. Whitcomb?"

Nelson briefed Mr. Calhoun on the significant pieces of the investigation and explained how they had tracked down Duke Mashaduk as the prime suspect in the case. Nelson requested the need to obtain a search of all US flight segments and foreign customs passengers processed for the period between the first day of May until the airlines ceased operations for the name of Duke Mashaduk on any registry.

Mr. Calhoun stated, "Mr. Whitcomb, I will have my team immediately begin working on these searches and have that information back to you within a few hours. What is your contact information?" Nelson provided his cell number and thanked Mr. Calhoun for his urgency in getting this information.

While Nelson was working with the Federal Aviation Administration, Gephart was in contact with the Memphis Aviation Control Tower. Gephart requested to speak with the director of the Aviation Control Center. Nelson spoke with the director, Andrew Simpson, and briefed him on the investigation. Nelson explained to Mr. Simpson that he needed the flight control records for any helicopter maneuvers they recorded on radar on May 1st or 2nd in Madison County, Tennessee. Mr. Simpson was obliged to get this information for Gephart.

Mr. Simpson said, "Mr. Tyler, all the flight control recordings for the month are still here at our operations tower. I will pull my best agent to find you these recordings. I can have them to you within the hour. Is there anything we can further assist you with?"

Gephart was delighted that Mr. Simpson could get these recordings quickly and said, "Just getting these recordings will be all I need now. If anything comes up later, I know who to contact. Thank you so much, Mr. Simpson; here is my phone number."

The call ended, and Gephart sat back and sighed in relief that they were getting the recording confirming their assumption that Duke departed by a helicopter operation.

While they waited for the information, Gephart asked "The Chief of Police for the exact place the Pink Cadillac was found. What exit did they have to take to get to the exact place." The Chief of Police answered, "I will get that information for you right now." Gephart said, "Wonderful, and Thank You!"

Gephart heard back from Mr. Simpson of the Aviation Control Center that they have no flight control recordings for Madison County, Tennessee, on May 1st or May 2nd. Gephart said, "Thank you for your fast response to my question, and have a great day."

While Gephardt was waiting for Nelson, the Chief of Police gave Gephart a piece of paper with the exact exit off of I-40 in Madison County, Tennessee. The Chief of Police told Gerhart, "I am sure that coordinates are a dirt road." Gerhart said, "Thank you so very much."

While Gerhart waited for Nelson, he called Dr. Wendt with all of the latest findings. Dr. Wendt just shook his head back and forth while listening to Gephart! Dr. Wendt replied," I am just shaking my head in disbelief; what kind of person or people do this to others?"

Nelson walked into the room and said, "They couldn't find anyone with the name Duke flying anywhere in the world in the past week!" Gebhart said, "We are batting a big 0; they have no knowledge of any helicopter in the area of Madison County, Tennessee, for that entire week! I have the directions; let's go find out for ourselves." Nelson replied, "Let's go right now!"

Nelson and Gerhart said goodbye to the Chief of Police and thanked him for his help, and out the door they went!

CHAPTER 72

Gephart Tyler and Nelson Whitcomb were standing at the exact coordinates where they found the pink Cadillac. Since they only needed one car, they invited the other driver to go with them. Even their drivers got out of the car to look around. If you didn't know better, you would think this was a regular dirt road. When you think about the epidemic and the lives lost, all four men remarked that they felt very sad about the loss of lives of so many people in our country. One driver said, "I have goosebumps all over me!"

Gephart said, "We know he was flown by helicopter from this place, but where did they go?"

Nelson said, "It had to be another place in the USA because a helicopter wouldn't be going to a foreign airport."

The driver said, "Where to next, as he kicked the dirt?"

Gephart said, "We must see the pink Cadillac; we are going to the Jackson Police Department to find out where they have stored the pink Cadillac, and then the four of us will find a quick place to eat. I know everyone must be hungry."

Once inside the Jackson Police Department, they asked to see the police chief. It didn't take long for the Chief of Police to escort the three of them to the back lot of the police department. Once they were standing next to the ugly pink Cadillac, the Chief of Police said, "It's unbelievable that a car this old didn't have one fingerprint. The forensic team took hours of their time and found nothing! Maybe the driver of this car had his fingerprints removed from his fingers. You know, some people do that!"

Nelson replied, "We searched the room where he was staying, and no fingerprints there either. Maybe you are correct, Chief!"

Gephart cringed and said, "Ouch, that sounds like a very painful procedure!"

Nelson and Gephart started to take pictures of every part of the ugly pink Cadillac.

Nelson said, "At least we have pictures of the old car if nothing else! It's hard for me to believe that our great forensic team found nothing when dismantling the car."

They all walked back to the police station in Madison County, and Nelson and Gephart shook hands with the Chief of Police in Jackson, Tennessee, and thanked him for all his help.

All four men returned to their car, and their driver said, "Where to now?" Nelson replied, "Let's eat!"

While they were looking for a good place to eat, the one driver thanked them for allowing him to come along to see the old pink Cadillac!

They all perked up when they saw the Chic Filet sign, but Nelson said, "It's a shame, guys, we can't eat there. It's Sunday, and they are closed on Sundays!"

They finally found a chain restaurant they all liked, headed toward it and parked. Gephart said, "Good, I am starving again!"

They all got out of the car and enjoyed a good, hot, late lunch!

During lunch, Nelson said, "We have done all we can here, so when we return to Nashville, take us directly to the airport. Our plane is waiting to take us back to Washington, DC."

Nelson and Gephart thanked the drivers at the airport and wished him well. They walked into the airport toward the first policemen they saw. They both showed him their badges and asked for help getting to their US plane waiting for them on the tarmac.

After the plane took off, Gephart called Dr. Wendt at the CDC in Atlanta to tell him what they had discovered. At the same time, Nelson called the President of the United States to brief the President on all the details.

CHAPTER 73

E mil was livid, throwing things at the TV, kicking chairs around, and breaking anything of glass he could get his hands on while using every foul word one could imagine. Emil was pissed because he had not yet killed 15 million US citizens!

Emil exclaimed, "How could these ignorant men figure this out so fast? Damn them to hell, the bastards!"

He was screaming at everyone to leave and not to talk to him. "Stay away; leave me alone! Fuck all you stupid people, especially the people in the United States!"

Emil thought, Without the stupid people who killed themselves, we are only at 14,893,752 deaths! I need 15,000,000 million to die in the United States!

I am sure those men will never find out where I am. No way. I am way too smart for them! I must take a day or two to think and figure out what I can do so they never find me here in paradise.

They don't know my name is Emil. Everyone thinks my name is Duke. I would bet my life that they did not find one fingerprint of mine anywhere! I am going out to the bar to drink! I can think better the more I drink!

When Emil got to the bar, he told the bartender, "Take the day off!" Emil then took a stool and sat on it inside of the bar and said, "Now this is how it should be; I can spin around on this stool and get any alcoholic beverage I want to drink!"

He grabbed a glass, put some ice in it, and filled it to the rim with his favorite drink, bourbon. The more he drank, the less he thought, and the staff found him on the floor inside the bar the next morning, drunk as a skunk! He wouldn't move, so the staff left him there all day until he decided to try to return to his house by himself. The entire staff was laughing at him, but Emil wanted no help and finally got up the stairs and inside his house and fell on the sofa and fell back to sleep!

CHAPTER 74

EMIL SLOWLY opened one eye but was having trouble opening his other one! Emil screamed aloud, "What in the hell happened to me?" He finally sat up and very slowly opened his other eye. His head felt like he was in a boxing match with himself. He needed pills for the pain! Since his staff was either at home or sleeping, he thought, I must get my ass up and get my pain pills before I die of pain.

Emil stood up and, with much difficulty, headed for his bathroom, where he kept painkillers. He was walking slowly and unsteadily, almost falling once, when he grabbed a chair to steady himself and thought, What the hell has happened to me? He finally made it to his bathroom and got the bottle of Vicodin. He grabbed the glass on the counter, filled it with water, and took three pills.

When he looked into the mirror and saw what he looked like, he almost threw up the pills he had just swallowed. Emil screamed, "What the fuck?" Emil started to remember why he was feeling so bad. He walked to his bed, lay on the blankets, and said, "Dear Jesus of mercy, this is much better!" The longer he lay there, the more he remembered what happened, and the thought of bourbon made him sick to his stomach!

After thirty minutes, the pain pills started to kick in. He remembered he was tending a bar and thinking about what to do next because the fucking United States figured out what two books were killing people. His next thought was to turn the TV on to see if the death count had reached fifteen million.

Emil mumbled in a low voice, "Just fifteen million, please!" When he saw the death toll number, he said out loud, "I can't remember what the last number of deaths there was" Then he said, "Have another drink Emil, your stupid ass. I am lucky I am not dead now!"

As Emil went to the kitchen to get a mimosa, he remembered going inside the bar to think about what to do because the Americans found out what was killing them. I should have stayed away from the bar and may have come up with an idea! He sat down at the table and took a sip of mimosa, and he felt better already!

Speaking out loud, Emil said, "I bet I will hear from my big boss today. Hopefully, he will have an answer to what I should do now." Then Emil added, "I am not going to drink much today, so I can think clearly!"

Emil then returned to his bedroom and lay down after finishing his mimosa. He was starting to feel like he was alive again. Emil turned off the TV, got under the blankets, and fell asleep. He slept like a baby until one of his beautiful female staff workers woke him up at 9:00 a.m.

Emil got up out of bed, ordered another mimosa, and said, "Just sit my mimosa here. I am going to take a shower!" Emil then went into the bathroom, brushed his teeth, and took a long shower. He then grabbed an extra big towel, wrapped it around himself, and headed for the mimosa. He got dressed, decided he looked better in the mirror now, and exited the bedroom to a table outside to have brunch. Emil moved to a chair where the sun could hit his face. He closed his eyes and relaxed while taking in every ray of sunshine until they brought him his brunch and another mimosa.

While eating, Emil thought, I think I will call my boss instead of waiting for him to call me.

Emil was finished eating, so he put his napkin on his plate, got up, and walked to his office, where he sat on his 5,000-dollar chair before a beautiful walnut desk. He took out his keys and unlocked the middle drawer on the right side of his desk. When the drawer opened, Emil saw at least forty burner phones. Emil picked up one of the phones, closed the drawer, and locked it. Emil then unlocked the bottom drawer on the left to get his boss's phone number, coded on several pieces of paper, and mixed in the stack of papers within the drawer. Emil found the first paper with the first three digits of his boss's phone number, rooted around a little more, and found another paper with the next digits, and finally, at the bottom of the stack, he found the last digits of the phone number. Emil purposely recorded the phone number with three pieces of paper, making it very difficult for anyone to figure out the phone number for his boss.

Emil used a pointer to put the numbers in his burner phone. He put the phone to his ear and waited, one ring, two, three, four, five, six, and on the seventh ring, Emil only heard, "Yes."

Emil answered, "Hello, boss; this is Emil in Bali, and I just want to know if you have watched the TV?"

Emil's Boss said, "Yes, the show was good, but I had hoped it would be better.

Emil replied, "That is exactly what I was thinking; any ideas?"

Boss replied, "Everyone I talk to says the show would be better for you if you went to see the president of the country. His name is Suttok Biddedo. For a price, you could watch with ease and even help him because he is building a new capital in East Kalimantan. Of course, he could help you with the show for a price!"

Emil replied, "Very good idea, boss; I was thinking about sightseeing in Jakarta, where the capital is now!"

Boss replied, "This would be great for the show because the president of Indonesia is also in charge of the police!

Emil said, "That is great; that will make the show much easier to continue."

Emil's boss replied, "Please tell the president I send my regards, and let me hear from you after you meet with him."

Emil answered, "I will happily tell you what he thinks of our show. Goodbye."

The boss replied, "Sounds good; goodbye for now."

CHAPTER 75

The president of the United States was smiling again! He started his speech by telling the people of the United States of America how proud he was of them.

"Today, a new historic change took place in our country. A special meeting was called for the House of Representatives and the United States Senate. Every member from both parties was present for the special meeting. For the first time in America's history, everyone agreed that we would work together and help our country return to being the wonderful United States of America.

We are no longer a two-party government because everyone agreed to start helping all of the people and businesses get back to where they were financially before this epidemic took place in our wonderful country, The United States of America.

Starting this Friday, there will be a new government building in every city in the United States called "We Are Here To Help!" It will be open from 8:00 a.m. until 8:00 p.m. to help our citizens return to normal. We have allotted Fifteen Million dollars to each state to help you all with things like burials for the families that lost their loved ones, for windows broken at businesses, and for stock that was stolen, to name a few things. Nothing is too small or too large for us to help our American Citizens retain their lifestyle.

At our meeting, we were appalled by the number of homeless in the United States who were helped through this epidemic by being put in every prison in the United States so they had food and shelter. So we are opening a huge building in every large city equipped with beds for the homeless to live in and kitchens where people cook to feed our homeless. We will also have counselors at every facility to help homeless people get back on their feet and live a normal life.

This epidemic has helped us realize how many of our citizens need us, so we are now here to help.

As you can see by the smile on my face, I am happy to be your President and all of Congress is now smiling with me.

Goodnight, and God bless every American citizen! This Message Is from your President and every government official.

WE ARE HERE TO HELP!

CHAPTER 76

Emil was now in his office and preparing to call for an appointment with the president of Indonesia, President Sodukee Bidedo. He unlocked his drawer full of burner phones and picked one up. He had already done his homework and had nine different phone numbers to get an appointment with the president of Indonesia.

Emil thought, I certainly hope someone in the capital speaks English. There are about eighty different languages people speak in Indonesia. Javanese is the most common language in Indonesia, but I can't pronounce that one word. This should be interesting! They say only ten percent of people in Indonesia speak English.

Emil picked up the burner phone and dialed the first number. Someone answered, but Emil had yet to earthly idea what they said. When the person who answered the phone finished, Emil quickly said, "English," and waited and waited. Finally, someone said to Emil, "No English here!"

Emil kept trying different numbers, and by the sixth number, he succeeded. The person who answered the phone spoke English, and Emil immediately became excited! Emil started to tell the person on the other end of the phone why he was calling. He wants to meet with President Sodukee Bidedo to donate money for his new capital building. He said that he lived in Bali and could help the president.

The Englishman said, "Sir, may I please have your phone number so I can call you back after I speak with the president about this matter?"

Emil answered, "Yes," and slowly gave his number to the man.

The man said, "I will speak to the president and get back to you."

Emil said, "I thank you so much, and I look forward to hearing back from you."

Then the man said, "Okay, goodbye."

Emil said, "Thank you so much. Goodbye."

Emil disposed of the phone immediately and said, "I need a drink!" Before Emil left his office, he took special care of the sixth number and put it in several places so he wouldn't lose it.

Within five minutes, Emil sat at the bar sipping his favorite drink, bourbon, and smoking his favorite expensive cigar! Emil thought The only thing in my life that could improve it would be to see fifteen million deaths on the TV screen. Emil held up his glass and said to the bartender, "Cheers, and I'll have another one, please!"

CHAPTER 77

WEDNESDAY, JUNE 2ND
DR. WENDT CDC
ATLANTA

Dr. Wendt had this terrible feeling and needed to speak with the President about it. So he called the President's personal line. The President answered Hello, Dr. Wendt said, "Hello, this is Dr. Wendt from the CDC, and I need to speak with you, Mr. President." The President replied, "I certainly hope nothing is wrong, Dr. Wendt. Dr. Wendt answered, "No sir, nothing is wrong. I just have something important to speak with you about." The President said, "By all means, Dr. Wendt, what is it?"

Dr. Wendt replied, "We have been working in the lab every day trying to figure out how much of what poison they mixed together to kill our citizens, and I think we should quit. If we ever figure it out, then there is always that worry that somehow it will end up in the wrong hands and somewhere there will be another epidemic; I think we should quit and let it be, but I didn't want to do that until I personally spoke with you." The President answered, "I had not thought of that scenario, but you are correct; I agree with you. Quit and move on to something that helps others. You are correct. It could end up in the wrong hands, and we certainly wouldn't want that to happen."

Dr. Wendt said, "Thank you, Mr. President; I feel so much better now. Thank you for your time; we will move on to something that helps others."

The President said, "Goodbye, Dr. Wendt, and thank you so much for your caring attitude; we need more people in our world like you."

Dr. Wendy replied, "Goodbye, Mr. President, and Thank You."

CHAPTER 78

JUNE 3RD, THURSDAY
EMIL MEETS THE PRESIDENT OF INDONESIA

Emil entered the Gulf Stream private plane parked outside at a private fixed base operator's tarmac at the Jakarta airport. The private plane had two pilots and a cabin attendant.

After settling into a plush leather lounge chair, Emil asked the flight attendant for a drink. She replied with a big smile, "Sir, I would be happy to prepare your cocktail. Would you like me to double it, as the pilots have told me to expect a bumpy ride?"

Emil replied, "Well, with that news, make it a double, and hurry it up!" Emil put his head back and closed his eyes as he waited for the cocktail.

As the plane took off, Emil downed his cocktail. Within five minutes of the takeoff, the cabin attendant served him another cocktail and asked Emil, "May I offer you any appetizers? We have a shrimp cocktail, caviar, and an assortment of cheese and crackers.

Emil replied, "Yes, I would like caviar."

When the plane landed, he went to a tiny terminal and walked outside to look for a limo! Emil had to settle for an old red taxi cab that he thought would break down before they got to his hotel. Emil thought to himself, So this is Jakarta. Dear God, why am I doing this? I can hardly wait to see the hotel; it smells bad here!

The old red taxi cab got him to his hotel, which, to Emil, was like the room he shared with Cinnamon in Nashville, Tennessee!

Tomorrow was the day he met with the President of Indonesia; Emil checked in and placed a wake-up call, so he looked like a million dollars when he met the President. When the call came to wake him up, he called room service and ordered lots of coffee, two mimosas, and two eggs over

"

easy with bacon, biscuit, and gravy. Emil thought to himself, I can't wait to see what I get to eat, and I bet the coffee is terrible because this whole place smells bad to me!

Emil was surprised that so many people spoke English, and he was also surprised that his breakfast was good. Emil ate it all, drank three cups of coffee and two mimosas, and then went into the bathroom for a long shower with hot water; he was surprised he had hot water!

It was 10:30, and his appointment with the president of Indonesia was at noon. So, Emil got dressed in his $3,000.00 light blue suit, his $900.00 navy blue shoes, a light blue pin-striped shirt, and some wild tie, all shades of blue and different designs, which probably cost $1,000.00!

Emil thought, Not only do I look rich now—wait until they see my jewelry! He then put on his gold Rolex watch, gold rings, and three gold chains around his neck. He had to work with the gold chains, so they laid perfectly on his suit!

He looked into the little mirror and said, "Damn, why can't they have two stand-up mirrors like I have at home to see the entire me front and back?"

Emil was ready for his appointment, so he got on the old elevator, and when it finally stopped at the lobby, he went to the front desk and asked for a limo to take him to see the President of Indonesia at the capital. The cute little girl at the front desk said, "I am so sorry, but we have no limo; I will be more than happy to get you a taxi!"

Emil answered, "I should have figured; get me a taxi."

Emil arrived at the capital of Indonesia on time. He told the man at the front gate his name and appointment time and another guard walked him into the capital's building. Emil thought immediately. I can see why they are moving the capital; nothing is beautiful here.

The guard and Emil then got on the elevator to the floor that the President's office was on. They walked to the president's office, and the guard knocked on the door and told whoever answered who was there to meet with the president. Emil was then taken immediately to the president's office. When Emil entered the room, the president welcomed Emil, who was then told to sit.

The President, Sodukee Bidedo, said, "So you want to give us money for our new capital? How very generous of you, Emil. So, you live in Bali; what a beautiful place to live. Emil, I am very happy you want to give us money for our new capital, but one million dollars is like a penny for what we need." President Bidedo continued, "Why do you want to give us money? What is your reasoning?"

Emil answered, "I would like to give you the money so you and your country never tell anyone I live in Bali."

The president replied, "Why are you hiding, and if so, why?"

Emil answered, "Unfortunately, I have several ex-wives looking for me for money, and not one deserves a penny after what I have already given them!"

The president replied, "Ah, a woman's problem; so many men have them. Since I need funds for our new capital, I can and will keep you safe in Bali for fifteen million."

Emil said, "That's much more than I offered; I can give you more, but fifteen million is a lot of my money!"

The president quickly said, "It's either fifteen million or none."

Emil was dumbfounded; he never expected this and was mortified. Emil replied, "Are you telling me that the price for helping me will be fifteen million dollars, and you won't negotiate?"

President Bidedo answered, "You are correct, Emil; it's either fifteen million or nothing. It's all up to you, and by the way, how many ex-wives do you have?"

Angry now and sweating, Emil answered, "Way too many, President Bidedo. The women always act like they love me but only love my money!"

President Bidedo said, "I know how you feel, but for me to keep you safe in Bali will cost our county a lot of money; keeping one safe here is a very big chore."

Emil answered, "So you are firm on this. I will be safe from these money-hungry women for fifteen million dollars?"

President answered, "You have my word, and I suggest you change your name if you are using your real name now."

Emil stood up, put his right hand out to shake the president's hand, and said, "We have a deal. When I get home later today, I will send you fifteen million dollars wherever you want me to."

The president stood up, and they had a long handshake. President Bidedo said, "My secretary will give you the information as to where to send the money, and as soon as we receive it, no one in Indonesia will know where you are, Emil!"

Emil said, Thank You, President Bidedo; it has been my pleasure to meet you."

Emil went to the president's secretary, who gave him all the needed information.

Emil could hardly wait to get out of the capital; he thought, I don't need a drink; I need ten of them!

Emil was escorted out of the capital's building, and the guard saw that he got a taxi again; Emil thought, At least this taxi isn't red!

Emil had the taxi driver take him to the closest bar to his hotel. He didn't have much time until his plane would take him back to Bali, but he did have time to drink a few strong alcoholic drinks quickly.

After Emil had a few drinks and his nerves settled down, he returned to his hotel, got his bag from his room checked out, and told them he needed a taxi again. Emil spotted a liquor store down the street and walked fast to get his bottle for his plane trip.

After he got in the taxi, it was no time before he was back at the little terminal at the airport and on the plane back to his beautiful woman, fresh air, and a very calm mind. Emil was now safe from everyone in the world!

Within minutes of Emil leaving his office, the President of Indonesia called the President of the United States to tell him about Emil's visit. The President of Indonesia was aware of the killings in the United States and wanted to make The President of the United States aware of everything Emil said to him.

Within minutes of the call from the President of Indonesia, President Bennett called everyone he could think of with the great news.

The CIA, FBI, Homeland Security, NSA, and Dr. Rudolph Wendt! Shouting joyfully, the President told everyone, we got him, let's get him!

The Air Force and the Navy coordinated the trip to Bali, Indonesia, for everyone who worked on the biggest case in United States history to get Emil. What a party this was going to be! Everyone involved was finally going to meet each other. Admiral Drake of The Land of Liberty called the President with all the information for their trip to Bali, Indonesia.

CHAPTER 79

JUNE 4TH, FRIDAY
EMIL

Emil told his cook he had bumps and asked her what the bumps meant. She answered, "You cold, sir? Does your mouth hurt, sir?" She said, "I have never had bumps; what are they?"

Emil said, "Just look at my arms. I have bumps all over them and have never had this before!"

The cook answered, "Maybe you drink too much, sir. Have you been bad, sir?"

Emil answered, "No, I have never been bad, not even as a child. What made you say that?"

The cook answered, "Well, sometimes, sir, I see you being bad and hear bad coming from your mouth, sir!"

Emil said, "What do you know anyway? I would have been better off finding a fish and talking to the fish instead of you!"

Emil turned and walked away but stopped in front of the huge TV. Emil said, "Damn it, only three people died in an hour; what the hell is going on?"

Emil spits at the TV and walks down to the water's edge. Emil thought, for some reason, that today was a different day. First, I can't find my woman, and second, the bartender ran out of orange juice and had to get some. Nothing is going right today; maybe I will go back to bed until tomorrow morning! I can't even see a fish to talk to; where are they all today?

Emil decided to go for a swim; he thought the salt water might eliminate his bumps! Emil swam like he knew how to swim when a sting ray bit him on the leg. He screamed, "Ouch," and couldn't get out of the water fast enough! He knew about the sting rays and what to do, so he slowly walked back to the house, put medication on his bite and a big bandage, and headed for the bar. That damn bartender better be back by now with my orange juice!

Back at the bar, the bartender had orange juice and said, "Sir, would you like your mimosa now?"

Emil said, "Hell yes! Make me two; this day is terrible for some reason!"

Emil took his two mimosas to his bedroom to prop up his leg from the string ray attack.

I think I will drink my drinks and then take a nap, and when I wake up, this day will be perfect, like all of the other ones have been!

CHAPTER 80

JUNE 4th FRIDAY
5:00 a.m. IN NORFOLK, VIRGINIA
ALL ABOARD FOR BALI, INDONESIA

Everyone was there before 5:00 a.m.—great job coming from the president! All the men were present, but that didn't mean a few weren't just a little afraid of being on this venture! As the admiral suggested, everyone had a little sack with their few needed things.

Gephart told Nelson, "I certainly hope they feed us when we get on the ship!"

Nelson replied, "I am sure they eat better than we do!"

The first plane landed, and Admiral Drake said, "Who are the first lucky four men?"

Gephart for the FBI looked at Nelson from the CIA, and Nelson said, "We are."

James Fieser from the NSA said, "I am ready, sir!"

Vincent Walker from Homeland Security said, "I am ready, sir!"

The four men got in the back of the Navy aircraft, and someone said, "Buckle up," within a few minutes, the aircraft was flying among the beautiful clouds!

The admiral yelled, "Number two, plane ready," and four men climbed in the back and buckled up; the door closed, and the admiral yelled, "Plane ready for takeoff!"

The same happened two more times, and four United States Navy planes were headed for the Navy Ship "Land of Liberty!"

The President of the United States did not go with the rest of the men because the President only flies on Air Force transportation.

It didn't seem very long until Nelson said, "I think I see the Land of Liberty over there to the left!"

Everyone looked at each other and thought, This didn't take long!

The pilot then said to the men, "Get ready for the landing of a lifetime. Have fun, men!"

All four men looked at each other as the plane descended to the end of the ship with brakes screaming stop! And that is exactly what happened; the plane suddenly stopped at the other end of the ship.

Gephart said, "Just how cool was that?"

The door opened, and the four men grabbed their bags and were escorted inside the ship. Within twenty minutes, all four planes landed safely, and all the men were seated together for breakfast; everything one could eat for breakfast was very delicious!

Gephart told Nelson, "I am thinking about joining the Navy!"

As the men were getting up from eating breakfast, a new group appeared in the dining hall: the wonderful Navy band!

Nelson said, "God bless America!"

The men were told to enjoy their adventure, roam the ship, and look at the beautiful ocean. The men talked about how walking on the ship was like walking on your home floor. Not one of them ever got sick!

They were shown to their quarters for rest if needed, but only a few did; the rest of the men were amazed at every part of the ship.

There was way too much to see to waste time sleeping, and they had all day to inspect the entire Land of Liberty!

CHAPTER 81

While President Bennett was having a very relaxing flight to hook up with his helicopter, Emil was having a terrible time. His leg was swollen to twice the size from the string ray bite, and so far, only two people in the US have died that day.

Emil thought to himself, I need a very strong drink. I hope to make it to the bar. He was using an old stick that he found lying around to help him walk.

As he was nearing the bar, he heard thunder. He said, "What the hell! It never rains here, and where there is thunder, there is lighting!" Emil stopped, looked up at the sky, and said, "Yep, we are going to have a thunderstorm here, the first since I arrived."

Emil walked as fast as he could to the bar. He was just about there when the loudest thunder he had ever heard rolled in his ears! Emil thought to himself, Should I be scared? Emil then looked down at the ocean; the waves were high and rolling very fast. He yelled, "I am already having a bad day again today; get out of here, you ugly storm!"

He reached the bar, and the bartender said, "Very bad storm coming, sir. Be very careful; it storms long and hard when it storms here."

Emil replied, "The storm is not after me; it's just here to clean off the beautiful trees. I will take a three-shot bourbon over ice!"

The bartender said, "Yes, sir, and I pray you are right about the storms. I am very scared of the storms. I see what they can do."

Emil answered, "You men here are a bunch of wimps; you are scared of everything. Be a real man, and be brave!" Emil drank the drink in two minutes and ordered another. Emil asked the bartender if he had ever been stung by a sting ray.

The bartender said no. "I know to avoid them; they can greatly hurt you!"

Emil said, "Look at my leg; see how brave men get around?"

The bartender replied, "Very bad, sir; you need a doctor!"

Emil laughed, saying, "A doctor for a little bite; no, not a brave man, only a sissy like you, and where is my drink?"

The bartender replied, "Sir, you are not very nice; everyone here thinks you are a mean man. Your favorite woman left and is in hiding somewhere on this island!"

Emil replied, "You know, you all can be replaced; give me the bottle and a bag of ice. I don't have to listen to a stupid bartender with no balls!"

Emil took the bottle and bag of ice, his walking stick, and started to walk away from the bar when the lighting hit the chair next to him; Emil laughed and said, "See, the lightning is not going to hurt me; it is scared of me just like you are, you sissy!"

Just then, the thunder cried out, and the rain started to fall with each drop the size of an ice cube; Emil walked back to his house for safety as fast as he could! It was a hell of a storm that lasted for hours and hours!

Emil had to order food, another bottle of bourbon, and another bag of ice to his bedroom; he was not about to go back out in the storm! Emil thought, *everything was going so well, and suddenly, this place was getting as bad as the cheap room I had with Cinnamon; what in hell is going on?*

Emil constantly looked at the TV for more deaths, but none were coming or showing up yet! Emil said to himself, "Damn it, where are my deaths? I must make my quota. Die, people! Die! What the hell is wrong here?"

While Emil was having a terrible time in Bali, President Bennett was getting ready to land on the island of New Guinea in Indonesia, where he would get on an Air Force helicopter and then fly to the Land of Liberty, headed for Emil and his tropical paradise!

CHAPTER 82

JUNE 5TH, SATURDAY
DR.WENDT ON THE LAND OF LIBERTY

After what I have seen this past month, this is like a vacation! How could I explain my actions to my family or dearest friends and see and correct them? Last month has been like an entire year; so much has happened. To be on this beautiful ship, the Land of Liberty, is like no other treat I have ever endured.

When we took a trip to Disney, I thought that would be my most memorable trip. This is real; Disney is just fake, made-up things for children to adore. This is the real thing, and I am so happy it only took us a little over one month; someone greater than any of us has helped us through this nightmare.

When I have the time to think about the last month, it overwhelms me. We lost millions of US citizens, and life was at a standstill. We had to eat the same meal for two weeks, which isn't even important considering the lives we lost.

May has been through the month from hell, and to think, if it hadn't been for a woman's online book club in Rhode Island, we would still be going through hell.

How did this all happen in one month? I hope it all happened in one month because we are the United States of America, and when we get Emil, he will be hearing, "God bless America!" I shake my head and say, how did this happen in one month? Then I think it could have taken us years! A greater power than we, the people, helped us, and I am so grateful for whomever it is!

Being a scientist, I have to know who, what, where, when, and how, and it never stops! Well, guess what? It has stopped,

I am going to enjoy the vacation of my life, but I can't wait to see what this man looks like who would do this to us and kill so many wonderful people who loved to read!

CHAPTER 83

President Bennett had no earthly idea where he was; he saw no one, but what he saw was beautiful. He had been told that he was on the the biggest island in Indonesia, New Guinea, in a remote part of the island, so no one saw him or his helicopter.

President Bennett and his Secret Service boarded the helicopter. It would not take long, and he would be on the Land of Liberty with his friends and the Navy band!

President Bennett was excited; this had also been a vacation for him. Thank heavens. He was not going to Russia to talk to the Premier! He was now on the helicopter with as many Secret Service members as could fit in a helicopter.

The Air Force pilot asked the President if he was ready to leave, and the president said, "I am more than ready to leave; let's go!"

The helicopter rose to the sky, and President Bennett was so excited because he was one step closer to getting Emil, THE BALI BASTARD KILLER!

It didn't take long until President Bennett saw the Land of Liberty Navy ship.

President Bennett asked the pilot, "Is that our ship in the Indian Ocean?"

The pilot answered, "Yes, and not far from Bali, Indonesia."

When the helicopter landed on the Land of Liberty, the President's Secret Service exited the helicopter first. President Bennett shook the hand of the pilot and thanked him for a smooth ride.

When the president got off the helicopter, his Secret Service men surrounded him, just in case there was anyone or anything that could harm the leader of the United States of America. The president and his men were escorted inside the ship, but he saluted all the men on deck before the president entered.

The president was taken immediately to the mess hall for a better-than-ever big breakfast! He sat with his Secret Service men to eat; they were all good friends and talked and talked about their trip to the Land of Liberty! They were all smiling and having the time of their lives; they all agreed this was like a vacation!

Admiral Drake came to see the president, and they talked about the plan to capture Emil, the Bali Bastard!

Admiral Drake told the President, "This is our plan of action, everyone. Take the rest of today to relax, and at 3:00 a.m., we will start our journey to the end of Bali, where Emil lives. We should arrive there by or before 5:00 a.m. Mr. President, when do you want the Navy band to start playing 'God Bless America'?"

The president replied, "As soon as we can see where Emil lives."

Admiral Drake answered, "I will alert the Navy band, Sir. Enjoy your day, and you will be escorted to your quarters after eating." Admiral Drake said, "One more thing, sir; all the snipers and NAVY SEALS have already been given their duties."

President Bennett replied, "Great job, Admiral; thank you for your service to the United States of America."

After the president and his men finished eating, they were taken to their quarters and told to have a pleasant day on board the Land of Liberty.

The president and his men agreed to walk around the ship and see everything they could take in for a wonderful memory of this event!

The president shook hands and saluted about one thousand times while walking around the ship. The president said, "I feel so honored, but my hand and arm are getting tired!"

The president and his men agreed that the Indian Ocean was the most beautiful water they had ever seen. They silently stood for at least twenty minutes, enjoying the view.

The president told his men, "I think I am ready for a little nap; I want to be wide awake when we get to Emil's house; I don't want to miss one thing when we capture him!"

They all headed together toward their quarters. The president's private quarters were behind four quarters for the president's protection. The president closed his door, removed his shoes, and entered the bed. It didn't take our president very long to be fast asleep; he was emotionally wiped out! It didn't seem very long when he was awakened at 3:00 a.m. He jumped out of bed, grabbed his toiletry bag, and headed for the bathroom. It didn't take the president very long until he looked like the president, perfect in every way.

He opened the door, and his Secret Service men were ready for

him; they all walked together toward the ship's bridge. Once there, they all had coffee and donuts, the normal gourmet at 3:00 a.m.

While the president sipped his coffee, he and Admiral Drake had a long conversation. Admiral Drake told the president how close they could get to Emil's house without getting the ship stuck in the sand.

The president told Admiral Drake, "By the looks of this bridge, it looks like you are equipped with everything you could ever need."

Admiral Drake replied, "Yes, sir. We have the best of the best on every Navy ship!" Admiral Drake continued, "This will be awesome because no one at Emil's house will be awake this early until they hear our band playing 'God Bless America' through our loudspeakers!"

CHAPTER 84

Emil grabbed his stick and got up out of bed to use the bathroom. While in the bathroom, Emil heard music. He couldn't make out the song, but he heard music.

Emil said out loud, "Just who in the hell at this house is playing music at this hour in the morning? I am going to find out and fire their ass!"

With his stick in hand, Emil opened the bathroom door and left his bedroom, only to hear the music playing louder! He hobbled with his stick as fast as possible to find the music's source! The closer he got to the front of the house, the louder the music was.

Emil said, "What the hell is going on?" He opened the front door, and with the full moon still shining, he could see small boats approaching his house. Emil yelled, "Holy hell, what is going on? Someone, please turn that damn music off; it's the same song repeatedly.

Emil continued, "Fuck, the boats are landing on my beach, and oh my god, men are running toward me with guns drawn; how could this be? I am supposed to be protected by the President of Indonesia; that bastard sold me out, and I believe that song is called 'God Bless America'! Bastards, they all are bastards, and they are getting closer and closer to me. Please, no, I haven't met my quota. These damn fucking Americans! Here I stand, defenseless with a damn stick and no gun!"

Emil then heard, "Drop the stick and put your arms up in the air; you are under arrest by the United States military."

Emil did what he was told, and within seconds, he was in handcuffs and being pushed around.

Emil yelled at the top of his voice, "Take it easy! I have a sore leg, and turn that damn song off!"

One of the snipers said to Emil, "You have killed millions of our United States citizens, and you have the nerve to complain about your sore leg. One of us should just put a bullet in your head so your leg won't hurt anymore, you bastard!"

Two men grabbed Emil's arms and started walking toward the boats while the music played on and on and got louder and louder the closer they got to the boats.

Once all of the men were back on the boats, one sniper took the megaphone and yelled to the ship, "WE GOT HIM; THE BALI BASTARD WAR IS OFFICIALLY OVER!

President Bennett was the first to speak to Emil when the boats returned to the ship. "Emil, welcome to the Land of Liberty, the United States of America. 'God Bless America,' the most beautiful song you have ever heard?" The Navy band was still playing it while the president spoke to Emil. "You are going to have the pleasure of hearing 'God Bless America' every day, all day, and all night until we return to the United States of America." President Bennett said, "Take this worthless bastard to the brig!"

Admiral Drake and the president had Emil's brig all ready for him, with speakers of the United States Navy band playing "God Bless America" taped so it could play over and over again. They would give Emil his quota of hearing God Bless America owe fourteen million times! One time for every American he killed! God made this payback in Heaven!

THE END

9 798990 895805